Praise for *The Sweet Shop Owner*

'A remarkable novel . . . There is a touch of Joyce in Graham Swift's revelation of the hidden poetry of small men's lives'
New York Times

'The themes are already the themes of a mature novelist— the choices (and lack of choice) that determine the shape of men's working lives, the way people struggle to make sense of their personal stories, the criss-crossing of private and public history . . . a quiet but beautifully shaped book'
Maggie Gee, *Literary Review*

'In his moving first novel, *The Sweet Shop Owner*, Graham Swift illuminates the history of one man through flashbacks on the last day of that man's life. Through the succinctly evoked provincial decades one of the engrossing features is the difficulty of love and communication between generations'
Alan Hollinghurst, *London Review of Books*

Graham Swift was born in 1949 and is the author of ten novels, two collections of short stories, including the highly acclaimed *England and Other Stories*, and of *Making an Elephant*, a book of essays, portraits, poetry and reflections on his life in writing. His most recent novel, *Mothering Sunday*, became an international bestseller and won The Hawthornden Prize for best work of imaginative literature. With *Waterland* he won the *Guardian* Fiction Prize, and with *Last Orders* the Booker Prize. Both novels were made into films. His work has appeared in over thirty languages.

The Sweet Shop Owner

GRAHAM SWIFT

SCRIBNER

LONDON NEW YORK SYDNEY TORONTO NEW DELHI

First published in Great Britain by Allen Lane, 1980
This edition published in Great Britain by Scribner,
an imprint of Simon & Schuster UK Ltd, 2019
A CBS COMPANY

SCRIBNER and design are registered trademarks of The Gale Group, Inc.,
used under licence by Simon & Schuster Inc.

1 3 5 7 9 10 8 6 4 2

Simon & Schuster UK Ltd
1st Floor
222 Gray's Inn Road
London WC1X 8HB

Simon & Schuster Australia, Sydney
Simon & Schuster India, New Delhi

www.simonandschuster.co.uk
www.simonandschuster.com.au
www.simonandschuster.co.in

A CIP catalogue record for this book
is available from the British Library

Paperback ISBN: 978-1-4711-8735-3
eBook ISBN: 978-1-4711-8736-0
eAudio ISBN: 978-1-4711-8737-7

Typeset in Garamond by M Rules
Printed and bound by CPI Group (UK) Ltd, Croydon, CR0 4YY

MIX
Paper from
responsible sources
FSC® C020471

For Candice

ONE

1

'In the end.' 'In the end'? What did she mean—in the *end* he would see?

Dear Father,

  I have the £15,000. The bank notified me last week. Thank you for sending it at last. I'm sure this is for the best and how Mother would have wanted it. You will see in the end.

  I think we can call everything settled now. Don't bother about the rest of my things. You said I should come—do you really think that's a good idea? After all that you say I've put you through, I should have thought you'd be glad to be finished with me at last.

  Dorothy

He sat up, in the double bed, holding the letter before him, looking at it fixedly as if it were really a code in need of breaking. It had come four days ago. He'd read it perhaps fifty times, so that he could remember the words without needing to see them.

'—finished with me at last.'

So he had seen her perhaps for the last time. And there was not even, before that final signature, a farewell, a 'take care', a 'with love, your daughter'.

He looked at his wristwatch on the bedside table. Four-thirty. Light spread behind the pale green curtains.

But she would come, surely. Now she had the money. She would come—she hadn't said she *wouldn't*—through the hallway (she still had her key to the front door), past the mirror, the barometer clock, the photographs of Irene and herself on the wall. Her eyes would be moist. She would find him in the armchair in the living room, by the French windows where he always sat—where Irene had sat with her medicine—still, silent, his hands gripping the armrests. She would go down, weep, clasp his knees, as though she were clasping the limbs of a cold, stone statue that stares out and beyond, without seeing.

He would be history.

He folded the letter, smoothed it and switched off the bedside lamp. There was the usual pain in his chest. In the half-light everything stood as if fixed in position for ever. The dressing table with its angled mirrors; the walnut wardrobe; the two green and white regency-striped chairs; her silver-backed hand-mirror; the china figurines, a shepherd and a shepherdess in eighteenth-century costume forever on the point of flying into each other's arms. Nothing had changed (you took nothing that showed, did you, Dorry?). Nothing would change.

He drew back the sheets. His belly pressed clammily against his pyjama cord. You could feel already the beginnings of a hot June day.

There was always the sunshine. It had shone then—June, 1949—through the windows of the nursing home. Trees brushed outside and bees had buzzed in and out of the open windows. Should they have allowed that, with all those babies? He had come, ushered by the nurse, laden with flowers. This might change everything. There was a little thing, wrapped like a gift in a shawl beside her. He had approached the bed with outstretched arms. But she had looked up, immovable, chestnut hair stuck to her forehead, and her eyes had said: There, I have done it, paid you: that is my side of the bargain.

'The flowers, Willy. Give the flowers to the nurse.'

Light seeped through the folds of the eau-de-nil curtains, turning the room into a dappled pool. She had always slept nearest the window. She could never get enough air.

And would you be glad to know, child—would you understand—that you were just one side of the bargain?

No matter. You've got the money now. You're paid.

And today, Dorry, is your birthday.

He could almost smile at the neatness of it.

He sat up, puffing. In the mirror he could see the reflection of his flushed face, the arc of stubble, the bluish lips, the slightly goggling eyes. Someone mimicking himself. He did not sleep. He was used to early rising. Besides, he would pass long stretches of the night awake, his body sprawled, wooden, like a toy in its box, his mind adrift in the dark. Even before, when she'd breathed laboriously beside him—her face in sleep as it was in waking, solemn, long-suffering—he'd lain like that, like a puppet. And only she had known how to make his little wired joints move, to make his body shift and jerk into action.

Do you know where that money really came from?

The dawn was gathering. Outside he could hear it: the rustle of the breeze in the lilac; the chatter of sparrows. He levered himself slowly to get out of bed. First the good leg then the bad. No exertion, no excitement. Doctor Field had said. And don't carry on working seven days a week

6

at that shop; take a holiday. It'll kill you. (Doctor Field—Save my wife.) But there came a time when precautions were irrelevant.

He looked at his watch. Nearly five. No need of alarms. That system hadn't changed. Getting up, getting ready, going off, seven days a week. And when he'd resisted, shirked, kicked against it (but that had seldom happened), she had been there with her command, to prompt and reprove, to goad him into life like a malingering schoolboy. Do it: play your part. Up at five-fifteen. Wash, shave in the rose-pink bathroom—when he didn't get a shave at Smithy's. Breakfast: two eggs, soft-boiled (then Field had said, cut out eggs and butter), tea and toast, at five-thirty. Time enough not to hurry, to dress neatly, to gather his briefcase—the leather had become soft and creased as a glove—to kiss her—her cheek was there to be kissed—to drive to Briar Street in time to collect and mark up the papers, to arrange the shelves, to open at seven-thirty. And Sundays the same, only an hour later.

No, it hadn't changed. But, sooner or later, you do something for the last time. And then it becomes, perhaps, a kind of victory.

He put on his dressing gown. No longer in her watchful presence. Spread the blue-bordered tablecloth, laid the table, placed the blue and pink patterned china—they never ate hurried, makeshift meals ('Let's do it properly')—as if she were looking still and approving (not a piece of that china had ever been broken), and as if, today of all days, there had spread over her face one of those rare, knowing smiles.

'That's right, Willy.'

He took from the wardrobe the dark blue suit, with the maroon braces and the maroon tie and the pale blue shirt with just the thinnest dark stripe. Today of all days he must dress the part. There, on their hangers, were the other suits. The charcoal for formality, the pale grey for sociability, the dark grey for work, the two tweeds, brown and light green, for Saturdays and Sundays.

He straightened his tie. She had chosen all his clothes. Not as gifts, not as little flatteries. She'd seldom given him things in that way. A gold tie-pin once (which she'd advised him to keep at home in a drawer); a silk Paisley scarf. And never, even years ago, had she watched him try on a new jacket before the mirror, button a new waistcoat—tilted her head, put a finger to her cheek, the way women do. She wasn't like that. But she'd seen that what he got was proper. And always the best and most lasting materials and, always, value for money. Her judgement was firm.

'That child. She will do something stupid one day.'

There. He was ready. The last time. Jacket brushed, shoes polished, hair combed. And if she'd been standing there, in the kitchen doorway, or had settled by then (for she couldn't stand for long) with the blanket by the French window, she would have given him that little nod, that flicker of the eyelids, as if she'd pressed a switch inside him: 'Go on now.' And Dorry would be upstairs still, in her cotton nightdress, asleep. He would look in to see her, as he always did. As if she might have fled already. Hair tumbled, one arm raised on the pillow, as though to touch someone.

It wasn't a fight, we might have made peace.

Sunshine gleamed in the hall. He picked up his hat and briefcase. Only then did he remember. The keys. The keys to the house, to Briar Street, to the till, to the safe in the stock room, to Pond Street. They were on the bedside table, by Dorry's letter. He went to fetch them. He paused by the sheet of notepaper, breathed heavily, then folded it into his breast pocket.

She'd come.

2

They pressed round in ragged fashion to take their money. Andy, Dave, Phil, Stephen, Bob. T-shirts, jeans, tennis shoes, uncombed mops of hair. By eight they would have changed into school clothes: uncomfortable figures in uniform. They held out their hands while he jingled money.

They could be slightly in awe of him. But they knew his weaknesses, his fondness for children, for childishness, his enjoyment of their laughter (for he didn't laugh himself, no one ever saw Mr Chapman actually laugh), and his way of winking, or seeming to wink—perhaps it was only with them—at his own solemnity. So they knew he would frown at their pranks—when one of them hid behind the ice-cream fridge and popped up with a shriek—yet wouldn't forbid them. And what of his own pranks? That way he made a coin disappear up his sleeve (you never saw it) or the way he slipped into their newspaper bags, when they weren't looking, a bar of chocolate, a stick of toffee. Yes, he liked his tricks; he had a clown's face, glum and top-heavy. Though that old bag, Mrs Cooper, would have none of it. She called them louts—she called all boys louts. 'Don't excite Mr Chapman, with his heart. Don't upset Mr Chapman, with his poor wife dead.' But who had ever seen Mr Chapman's wife? Though Phil said he had once, passing the house on his round—she was standing at the window, looking as if she were sinking in a pool. Yet what did it matter? If they played their pranks, if he liked it, if it cheered him, if they got out of him just once at least (they knew it was there) that laugh he never actually showed; before his heart stopped ticking right there in the shop.

They watched him as they watched all adults, as if they were life-size models at work, but with a suspicion, in this case, that that was just how Mr Chapman regarded himself.

'One pound. One pound twenty-five. One pound fifty.'

He distributed the notes and coins. His fingers were soiled with newsprint, which made them look as though they were moulded from lead.

'One pound fifty. One pound seventy-five.'

Once they did it for half a crown. Now it was nothing less than a pound. Their hands closed. He wouldn't see them again.

Six-thirty. But already the sun through the plate-glass

window was warm. He switched on the little electric fan over the door into the stock room.

'Which one of you's going to pull down the awning?'

That was something he could no longer do. No exertion. And they vied, when the weather made it likely, for the honour of getting their hands on that long, murderous pole, flexing their muscles on the pavement and pulling at the catch above the name-board.

'Phil, you do it. And don't smash the window in the process.'

They sniggered, shouldering their bags. But he hadn't finished.

'Before you go—' he hesitated, thinking of a suitable pretext. In his left hand was a black tin box labelled 'Paper Boys', with the lid open so they couldn't see in. They thought he had emptied it. 'As it'll soon be the summer holidays—' he fished in the box and drew out a column of fifty pence pieces which he let slip, three at a time, into each palm—'a little bonus. A little surprise.' He looked severe. 'Not a word to your mums and dads' (but they weren't stupid), 'and if you're late once in the next fortnight,' he paused—they wouldn't appreciate this prank—'I'll ask for it back.'

They looked up, duly surprised, thankful, puzzled. A good bunch, a cheerful bunch. They did what he asked and they earned their money. They came every morning by six-thirty, sleepy-eyed, rising before their parents, muffled in the winter in little anoraks and scarves. And there was a sense of constancy and devotion in watching them, through the glass of the shop door, riding off with their sacks, pedalling their bikes to appointed streets; so that he would think, 'Don't swing like that into the main road: there are lorries,' and 'Don't get caught by a policeman, cycling without lights.' But you had to take note of that little glint in their eyes which spied out extra ten-pences; and you heard them mutter under their breath: 'Henderson across the common pays his boys two quid.' They were wise to it already. You had to watch out.

He scanned their faces sternly, like a commander his best men. And they knew perhaps, grinning back at him, that if he didn't laugh it wasn't because he couldn't.

'Right, now you've got your money. Before you go, take something each from the sweet counter. Only one thing, mind you.' He wagged a finger. This was necessary. If you didn't give them things they pinched them anyway.

'Thanks, Mr Chapman.'

Fifteen thousand pounds.

At a clap of his hands, as if they were performing animals, they were off, swinging their bags over their heads, chattering over their new-gained wealth, making off with it, racing each other on their bikes round the corner of Briar Street.

And they were gone, leaving only Phil on the pavement, with his flop of blond hair, locked in battle with the pole and the awning. Would he do it? There, it went. And there he was, standing grinning in his mauve T-shirt with 'YAMAHA' across the front, like a knight-at-arms with that pole under his arm, almost demolishing a display in the window as he bore it back through the door.

'Bye, Mr Chapman. Thanks for the money.'

'Bye, Phil.'

And Mr Chapman laughed—was that really a laugh that crossed his face? Phil would go and tell the others, speeding after them with the news: Mr Chapman laughed. But they wouldn't believe him, Phil was always telling stories they'd say.

'Bye. Take care now.'

They were paid.

The sunshine slanted through the glass over the door on to the counter and the piles of remaining morning papers which lay before him. He never read the papers. Years of marking them up, stacking them, and taking them, flicking them into a fold with the wrist and holding them out between two fingers, palm cupped for the coins, had blunted his curiosity for their contents. But he still glanced each morning, and kept through the day in a little catalogue at the back of his mind so that if it was mentioned he would know, items like 'Plane Crash in Brazil', 'Drama at Embassy', 'Worst Ever Trade Figures'. And there it was, this morning, on the page his eyes scanned:

'PEACE BID FAILS.'

She had always read her papers. He had them delivered (that had been Phil's round, number three, Leigh Drive and Clifford Rise) and he brought home in the evening copies that weren't sold. She'd read them, sitting in her armchair, beneath the tall standard lamp with its twisting wooden stem. Oh not because she liked news. It was only to take stock, to acquaint herself, to hold sway over the array of facts and regard them all with cold passivity. And sometimes, indeed, it was as if she didn't read at all, her head hidden behind the outspread page, but peered through it, as through a veil, at a world which might default or run amok if it once suspected her gaze was not upon it. And he'd wait, stirring his tea, the clock ticking, not daring even to rattle his cup, until at last she would cast aside the paper in a weary gesture, her eyes moving wanly to the French windows. So predictable, these papers.

He didn't read them, but he liked them. Their columns,

captions and neat gradations of print. The world's events were gathered into those patterns.

Dorothy had read them, read them with a will, wanting to discuss and argue over the dinner table, her little brows taut with the desire to make her mark. And Irene had sat on the other side, holding her knife and fork tightly so that they snicked at her plate like scissors, and refused to be drawn. All this excitement, this nonsense. I won't have it. I won't suffer it. You deal with her. And she would look at him: she is *yours*, don't forget; I gave her to you.

The floorboards creaked under the weight of his stool and a faint rustle, like crumpled paper outspreading, came from the lines of shelves behind him. Sometimes, in the early morning, the shop seemed to speak, as if it wouldn't let pass the association of years without a whisper, a breath of friendship.

It was cram full—not one of those shops where there was plenty of space and an air of fluorescent-lit efficiency. Behind him, stacked in columns, rose cigarettes; tipped, plain; above, cigars, below, loose tobacco. To the right, along the polished, uneven shelves towards the Briar Street window, were the jars—drops, lumps, fruits, toffees, jellies, mixtures—and the boxes, milk and plain, hard and soft centres, with on the top shelf, bordered with ribbons and embellished with puppy-dogs, waterfalls, sunset harbours, the luxury two- and three-pound boxes. On the counter in front, and beneath, behind sliding glass doors, were the bars and sticks, chews and tubes, sherbet dabs and banana-splits—the things the kids chose coming home at four—wrapped in sickly colour. And to his right—beyond the till, along the remaining counter towards the ice-cream fridge and the crates of lemonade and Coca-Cola—the magazines and papers, spread, overlapping like roof tiles: tense headlines, pop-stars, orchids in flower, fashion, foot-ballers, naked girls.

It thronged, it bulged.

And none of it—that was the beauty of it—was either useful or permanent.

Beyond the sweet counter, taking up most of the Briar Street window, was his own addition. Toys. Dolls, teddy bears, jigsaw puzzles, model cars, rockets, cowboy hats, plastic soldiers, and, hanging from the framework over his head, three clockwork monkeys each with a fez and a musical instrument which played if you wound it up: a drum, a pipe, a pair of cymbals.

All that was his work. Coming home, twelve years ago, he'd said to her, 'I have a plan.' And her face had pricked up, beside the French window, as at some rumour of rebellion. 'Toys. I will sell toys in the shop.' She had looked, and repeated slowly the word—'Toys'—as if rolling round her mouth a morsel of something whose taste she hadn't fixed. And then—the identification was made—the wry smile touched her lips. He'd known it would please her. Her eyes widened (matchless, grey-blue eyes) and had looked into him, through him, as if they sent out swift, invisible cords to seize and sweep him up. 'Yes. Why not?'

And then she'd added: 'You will make sure, won't you, there's a profit in this?'

He looked at his smudged hands clasped on the counter. He must wash. It was ten past seven. Traffic was building up on the High Street, making the shop windows vibrate gently.

As he twisted himself from the stool he felt the pain grip suddenly his left side and shoulder. It was always there, but sometimes it attacked in earnest. *Angina pectoris*. It sounded like the name of a flower or a rare species of butterfly. Dorry had read Latin. He knew what to do. There were trinitrin tablets in his breast pocket, next to her letter, and there were more in a drawer beneath the till. Mrs Cooper knew and was instructed. Irene had used them too, along with all her other pills. With both of them it was heart trouble.

He paused. No stress, no excitement. No, he wouldn't reach for the tablets—it would mean pulling out her letter.

He hung on. Not now. The body is a machine, Doctor Field had said. And there—it went.

He padded, slowly, through the doorway hung like an oriental arch with coloured strips of plastic, into the stock room to wash his hands and slick his hair with water.

Mrs Cooper was due at any moment—with her basket, her amber horn-rims, her hair permed rigid as wire and her look of steely dedication. Sixteen years his assistant. She had been a plump blonde once. Besides himself, only she had a key. And she said, 'I'll get it,' thrusting out her bosom, when there was something to be fetched: 'You mustn't strain yourself.' And she said, 'I'll manage,' that time when he had to go off and leave the shop, chasms opening beneath him, because *she* was in hospital, stricken but unfrightened, tubes and wires plugged into her. Dorry had come—that time.

'You don't have to begin so early, Mrs Cooper,' he'd said. And she'd said, 'Oh, call me Janet.' But he didn't.

Mrs Cooper would come. She'd put her basket with her handbag against the wall in the stock room; take off her cardigan, pat her hair, put on her blue nylon shop coat, pick up the kettle with one hand while she did up her buttons with the other, and ask, as if every time it were a novel suggestion, 'Tea, Mr Chapman?' She'd make the tea and bring it to him, vigorously stirring in the sugar. He'd sip it as she filled up spaces on the counter with fresh stock, and he'd say, glancing out of the window, 'Warm, Mrs Cooper, warm. Any plans for the weekend?' And she'd say, as she always did, 'Weekend, Mr Chapman? I'm surprised *you* know what a weekend is.'

But, sooner or later, there's a last time.

He dried his hands, drew the comb through his thin hair. Passing back into the shop, he took from a box on one of the shelves a fat, half-corona cigar, undid the cellophane and lit it.

And Mrs Cooper would say, coming in and seeing him puffing smoke, 'Mr Chapman! You know you shouldn't smoke them.' And he would say, laconically enough, 'But I sell 'em.'

He perched himself on his stool and puffed hard. So Mrs Cooper would view him, peering in for a moment through the shop door as she rummaged for her key—behind glass, behind the undergrowth of display stands, wrappers and dangling toys—peering back at her, lastly, from behind blue fumes, his face red, swollen, like an overripe fruit, his eyes wide, impenetrable.

3

'There is a place on the corner of Briar Street. It's a good site. I've already seen Joyce and we have the first option.'

She put down the cup and saucer on the table—the blue cup and saucer with the thin scrolls and the pink moss-roses. A wedding present. Her lips drew inward; they were shrewd, circumspect, even then. And he thought, Yes, of course—seeing it fall into place—I will be a shop owner.

'Do you approve?' And she waited. For she wouldn't overbear, insist—that wasn't her way. She would let him consider and judge and say 'I approve'—that was the man's role and the husband's, and she wouldn't deny it him.

'Why not?' he said, with a cautious grin. 'Well, why not?'

'You will need to look it over,' she nodded, 'and see Joyce yourself. And you will have to know the prospects and get to learn the business. My brothers can help you there.'

'Of course,' he said.

'Good. Then it's settled.'

She smiled. A lovely smile, like a shining seal upon a contract.

And what she really meant, reaching again for her cup, sitting back and crossing her legs, smooth, perfect legs, under her beige skirt, was: I will buy you a shop, I'll get you a shop. I will install you in it and see that you have all you need. Then I'll watch. I'll see what you can do. That will content me. I'll send you out each morning and watch you come home each night and I shall want to know how you are doing. I shall want return for my investment. But I shan't interfere, only watch. You will be free, absolved; for the responsibility—don't you see?—will be mine.

Her lips hovered over the rim of her cup. Her face had this way of seeming to float.

And all I ask in return for this is that there be no question of love.

She fingered the pearls at her neck, drawing in her shoulders. And only for an instant had there flickered in her eyes that other look which he could never reach, never touch, never quite rescue: 'Save me.'

The blue and pink tea service glimmered on the table, and she cut the cake—a Dundee—with the ivory-handled slicer on the cut-glass cake stand. So many presents. You ate off them, sat on them, slept between them. That lavish family of hers. Furniture, china, glass, bed linen; not to mention the house itself, the garden, with the lilac tree and hydrangea bushes, or her furs and jewels, most of which she kept locked in cupboards and drawers and never brought out, as if condemning them. But it was all for her, the only daughter. Not for him. She liked fine, fragile, precious things, things which you couldn't use. And he had the podgy hands of one who would let slip such things and break them. And, besides, (he'd overheard what her brothers had said, at the wedding reception) he was 'only something to occupy her with'.

'Don't worry,' she said, 'don't worry about the nonsense that family talks.'

They posed for photographs. June, 1937. There was a marquee in the garden, smoked salmon, turkey and champagne; and the feeling you get on a journey when some landmark looms into view, soon to be passed by. A scent of cut grass; red and white carnations. The chatter rustled like a breeze through the hats and flowers. Her brothers were there, Paul and Jack, with wing-collars, moving smoothly among the guests, as if their sister made a habit of getting married and they had done it all many, many times before. His parents sat, along the table, looking flushed and attentive. They would be dead soon, one after the other, as if by mutual arrangement, in a space of months. But tonight, when it was all over, they would have the neighbours round and, amid bottles of gin and beer, they would dance, that quiet pair, on the worn carpet in the back room. Yes, better do it now, better rejoice; our son's wedding night, that is something to celebrate. They had scraped every penny, in those stringent times, so as not to be outdone, to give the set of silver cutlery which stood on the damask tablecloth on the trestle table among the other gifts. But what they most gave, silently, generously, was their thanks.

Her parents whispered gravely to each other, as if the event were for them the completion of some shrewd act of diplomacy. And should he cast his eyes a moment their way, they would break off their discussion, in deference to his place of honour, and give him wide, immaculate, approving smiles. They had made their money out of immaculacy; out of little laundries dotted about the streets of southeast London. They had contracts with hotels, shipping lines. And they'd won their custom on the promise of whiteness: white sheets and white shirts, white pillow-slips; as white as the white wedding cake that rose in icy tiers before them. And the brothers, who had partnerships, investments, interests of their own, smiled too, the same smile, approving, not friendly. Yes, he'd do. He'd do for a bridegroom. To have a wedding you needed a bridegroom.

He felt like someone borrowed for the occasion.

But he didn't mind. That condescension. Not when, with his head growing lighter, he'd stood up to make his speech and said simply, gawping: 'Thank you, thank you . . . thank you really, thank you all.' That was all that was expected of him, and they'd clapped and cheered as at masterly oratory. Nor when, after more champagne and words with relatives he didn't know and wouldn't meet again, he had wandered through the house like a stranger, and heard her mother say to another—he caught no more—'a difficult girl', and had glimpsed afterwards, upstairs, through the half-open door, Paul on the bed and Jack in a chair, their waistcoats undone and their grey ties pulled loose from their collars, like weary gamblers, and eavesdropped on those words that passed between them. No, he didn't mind. Landmarks were like that. They slipped by. They did not belong to you. And if you put out your hand to touch them, they parted and dissolved and grew flimsy like the world after champagne. And he didn't care. For in the night now, his body sprawled like a toy's, the world receded, he could reach out and touch her.

'Don't listen to all that nonsense, Willy.'

'Something to occupy her with.'

*

So why then? Why him?

He watched the cigar smoke drifting through the beams of sunlight over the counter.

He had planned nothing. Not for himself. And yet he knew: plans emerged. You stepped into them.

That was why he liked it at Ellis's. The printworks. Setting up the type so that there was correctness of spacing, the letter size graded according to the importance of the words; an overall effect of regularity and order. The content was unimportant. It was the layout that mattered. And just to show it was not a mere exercise, a playing with shapes, you had to roll up your sleeves and get your fingers covered in ink or machine grease. There was always a little mess, if there were patterns. Old Ellis called him 'my lad'. He had a bald head and a thick, drooping, melancholy moustache. They were disappointed, of course, Mother and Father. Had they got him to grammar school just for that? ('Lacks talent and initiative,' his reports had said.) Where was the return for their scrimping and pushing? But he liked the daily routine, the taking of orders, the clattering machine room at the back with the grille-like window overlooking the Surrey canal, and almost jaunted to work, on and off the tram, with a concealed laugh inside him.

He planned nothing, though every day had its pattern and was spent in making patterns. Until she came in that day—Mr Ellis was at lunch and he had temporary charge—to place her order.

'Laundry lists,' she said. 'The laundry lists and other material for our new branch. Mr Ellis was phoned, and I'd hoped . . .'

She looked peeved at not being able to see the proprietor; annoyed at the grubby little printworks and him in his shirtsleeves with inky fingers; and annoyed too at having been sent out like an errand girl on this mission. For that showed. Someone who might have sent an assistant, an office boy, had deliberately sent her and she didn't like it. She was meant to command, not obey.

'You had better attend to it.' And she did command, and he obliged. 'This is what we want.'

He took the typed-out sheets and scanned them through, his pencil poised. It was only the simplest of things, a laundry list, but as if to show, since she was to command, that he was slow, had no initiative, he read aloud the words in front of him:

'. . . Waistcoats, Men's Shirts, Collars (stiff), Collars (semi-stiff), Vests (long-sleeved)—'

But she stopped him. 'That's a fine little rag-doll.' It was meant to be peremptory. Her lips drew inwards. But he grinned as though at a quite good-humoured remark. And no, he wouldn't be bothered by her cuttingness. It wasn't what it seemed.

He took the papers and showed her the samples of lettering and layout, explaining slowly, for that was his way. And she listened, never for one moment losing that air of authority, yet held, perhaps, by his simpleton's manner, by his ungrudging deference. Her hand drew in her collar. 'Yes,' she said curtly. 'Yes, yes.' And through his labouring words, as through a little mesh of visible dull print, he looked at her beauty.

When he saw her a second time, three days later, walking on the common, it was different. Twice. That was pattern, that had the feel about it of something meant to be. She was leaning on the railings overlooking the space where the children played on swings, roundabouts and see-saws, and she had the same look of someone sent unwillingly on an errand, loitering resentfully. So he must stop (a plan would emerge) and say, 'Miss Harrison? How do you do?' and, as she looked up, half in annoyance, half with the look of a girl caught playing truant, continue in his dumb way, 'Passing by ... er, lunchtime ... couldn't help ... laundry lists are ready.' And she, recognising who he was, recovering that old command, must nod, say, 'Ah yes,' and turn her head away to look over the railings.

She would let him linger, if he must, but she wouldn't welcome him.

She wore a straw-coloured outfit; heavy, unnecessary make-up, as if to mask her face.

'Cheerful bunch,' he'd said, eyeing the children, mouthing the words in the blunt, crass way he'd read the items on the laundry list. Her face didn't move. 'Hey, look at that!'—as a boy swung higher and higher till it seemed he would either fly off or turn full circle. And he'd pulled from his pocket, in a greaseproof bag, four cheese sandwiches which he extended to her in a gesture at once bluff and chivalrous, like a knight laying down arms.

'Oh—no thanks,' she said, slightly ruffled—for it was not like her to be lingering in parks, to be watching children on swings, to be speaking with strangers. Yet she was.

They stood in silence, thinking of things to say.

'You like watching children . . . ?' Her tone seemed to say: 'You're a child yourself.'

'Yes. Don't you?' His cheek was full of cheese sandwich.

She didn't answer; only looked at the swings with anxiety.

'I sometimes wish,' he said, trying hard to empty his mouth, 'I could join in myself.'

'But you wouldn't?'

'Why not?'

He saw the sudden challenge in her eyes. And was that a smile somewhere in that held-aloft face?

'Well, if you feel that way . . . ?'

'It's Chapman. Willy Chapman.'

'—why *don't* you?'

'Why don't I?'

Her head seemed to wobble on her neck.

And he hadn't hesitated. He gave back her look (did she think he was stupid?). He knew it was a test. He crushed up the greaseproof bag with the remainder of his sandwiches inside and stuffed it in his pocket. He walked to the end of the railings and across the patch of asphalt. Children stared at him. And looking back at her, very straight, defensive, he knew that was how it would be. She would stay, always, behind the railings, watching his readiness, his simplicity, his taking things at face value. She wouldn't join in. She would watch; he would do. For he did it now, went up and did it, the man from the audience taking the stage. He climbed the steps of the kiddies' slide, hitched up his jacket and slid down. And as he did so he knew he was hers.

Yes, that was pattern. That was not adventuring. She had said, Why don't you? And he did. And afterwards it was precisely the predictable formula that pleased him: meeting in parks, sitting on benches, his being the humble suitor, buffing his shoes, scrubbing his nails before seeing her, being spruced and set-to by obsequious parents who saw the chance of a fortune.

And there it was—a fortune—duly made over to him by the proper forms and ceremonies, in the corner of a railway compartment, bound for Dorset, while the golden light of a late June afternoon flickered through the gaps in passing rooftops. And it was saying, 'Don't worry. Don't worry, Willy, about all that nonsense.'

'They're always passing judgement, making comment. Jack and Paul especially. Forget them, Willy.'

A breeze blew through the open window. There was pink and blue confetti in her hair.

And what she was really saying perhaps was: 'Don't talk of Father and Mother, or my brothers. I don't want to discuss them. Don't you see? I was the only daughter, I was the odd one of the family. I was a beauty. I had no life. That is why I chose you—with no talent, no initiative—for the justice of it, the symmetry. Don't think I will change.'

He had put his arm out to her. 'I'm not thinking of them,' he said. His voice sounded odd and strident. They were in a first-class compartment with no other passengers. His hand was on one of those smooth, perfect legs. He would have slid it up her pale green skirt. But her face had turned towards the sun-brushed window, her fingertips were at her necklace.

'Not now.'

I was the odd one of the family.

Yet her face was exquisite, with its detachment, with its sulky pallor, as she turned back, making him hold his hand as if he were a thief caught in the act of plunder.

Outside, the stations were passing. Woking, Farnborough, Basingstoke. London was left and the munificent house in Sydenham Hill in which they were clearing away the wine glasses, the white napkins, and discussing with satisfaction how the thing had been done. The June sun was sinking over smooth, cooling fields and willowy streams, over reddened, long-shadowed figures caught, nonchalant, by hedgerows and gates, cycling in lanes, grouped at tables outside pubs. The evening air was melting their rigour, their daytime reserve. But she wouldn't relent, and let those features lower their guard. She only took and squeezed his hand now and then and gave him those short, quick smiles that were like small coins thrown without fuss to someone who has done a service. And she let him lead her, when she prompted, along to the dining car, where she sat, ordered a light meal, toyed with her fork, and eyed him warily, circumspectly, as though considering an action of the utmost delicacy which could no longer be postponed, and asking herself, 'What must I do? What must I offer that would suffice? What would be a satisfactory concession in the circumstances?'

Then the sun had sunk, she had put on a little cream scarf and he was carrying cases. And there, suddenly, were the country cottages, and the honeymoon hotel set back from the road, seen already as if in a frame, as if in a photograph in an album opened many years after; the downs of Dorset, pillowy in the dusk, and, beyond, the sea, somewhere murmuring under cliffs. June, 1937. And already landmarks were passing, thick and fast, faster than the passage of the train across the southern counties. Already the church, the bridal dress, and the speeches under the marquee. And she wouldn't relent.

They unpacked clothes in a room which smelt of polished wood and lavender. What had her mother told her, of the dangers of loitering and the wolves that prowl? But how could he be a wolf? He was a pet dog to be led on a lead; he would run when you called. Oh, she did the right things. She walked with him down a lane where the trees bent like arches and rested her head in the crook of his neck, so that if one needed to demonstrate (if ever it should be a case of demonstrating) one could say, Look, sweeping one's palm over the scene, there is the picture. But the picture was incomplete.

33

Later, in their room, with the wooden beams, she undressed deliberately, slowly, as if she were unwrapping a gift, as much as to say: 'There, see the reward you have got. And do you think such a reward will not ask certain things in return?' Moonlight, like some theatrical trick, filtered through the lattice windows and lace curtains.

'Willy,' she said, stopping him. He was poised and trembling, ready to take his gift. 'Willy, I'm sorry. I'm not—all I should be. Do you forgive me?' And what should he have done? Protested, demanded explanations, with her lying blanched in the moonlight? Her face was a mask; sometimes it seemed not to be part of her body. She let him continue, without shrinking, without encouragement, as if it were only done for the form's sake, as one of the terms of the agreement.

Afterwards he felt he had not touched her, not touched that beauty. He sat up to light a cigarette. Her breasts pointed at him. She pulled the sheet up to her chin. Her face, there on the pillow, hair stuck to her brow, was like a victim's; and yet it looked at him, for all the world, with triumph, with majesty, and as he bent to her, it smiled quickly and benignly, like a throwing of coins.

Every night their clothes hung over the chair by the bed, stirred by the breeze through the window. And every day the pieces of the picture fell into place: the boat trips to

Weymouth, the little scenes of themselves arm in arm on the beach or at tables for two, about which the nodding onlookers might whisper, 'honeymooners'; their 'Mr and Mrs' in the hotel register. But if only she would say, 'I love you.' No, not even that, if only she would say—sometimes it seemed she used him like an excuse—'I know that you love me.' But she wouldn't. Not even when the moment was ripe. When the evening sun burnished the sea and they walked back, in the cool, along the cliff tops. Swallows dived. Cow-parsley frothed in the hollows. Her dress was white with diagonal rows of blue flowers. No, that was not included, not part of the bargain. Wasn't the rest enough?

Yes, he would have said, enough, plenty. Were it not for that vision of himself flailing in the current—even in that smooth and molten sea which spread beneath them like a tribute of silk. Unless it was she that he saw—struggling in the gold water, beating her arms to be free of it, though her face was as golden as the waves. He stood there on the cliff top. He couldn't save her. He owed her eternal service, for he couldn't save her . . .

Every morning she read the papers. She bought them at the hotel or at the little general store in the village, where she also bought postcards, stamps, cigarettes for him. It was her holiday, her honeymoon, but she kept up with the papers. But only as a kind of safeguard; to keep abreast of the facts, so she would not be seduced by all that sun and sea air. And one day she said, sitting on the tartan rug on the beach, as if they must get up at once and start digging defences: 'There will be a war, Willy.'

That was only a few days before they left. They would never holiday again till Dorry was a little girl. 'There will be a war.' But even before that, he had noticed, she was predicting, preparing, asking herself what must be done with their future life. So that if, as they sat there on the beach, he should put his arm about her neck or nestle his head in the lap of that blue-flowered dress, she would have to humour him, mask her annoyance at the inter-ruption of her thoughts, like a father, deep in work he has brought home from the office, having to indulge the whim of a child.

'In a few years. You see.'

'Yes,' he said. He did not dispute her predictions. History came to meet you. 'Stop reading the paper, Reny.'

He lowered his head onto her skirt. Her lap smelt of salt and sunshine. But her face turned, out and away, unsmil-ing, to the horizon, as if warships might loom.

So what must he do? He never planned. He could only play tricks for her, obedient tricks, as he had when he climbed that children's slide. He would make her smile at last, with the right trick, like the sad princess in the

36

story. She stroked his hair. He was like a cat in her lap. He would show her as he showed no one else his little stock of laughter. So he'd take the pebble from the sand and make it vanish up his sleeve; and then, twisting his wrist, return again. And he'd flip forwards and stand on his hands and walk ten yards down the beach. No one thought he could do that. Yet no one knew him. He'd been an athlete of sorts once. But she wouldn't laugh; though he kicked his bare white heels in the sunlight and gulls took off in alarm. Her face watching him (while the blood rushed to his head and his fingers clawed the sand) was tensed and urgent. And he only knew he mustn't topple, not for his life, topple from that fool's posture, snapping the little wires that ran between them.

Was it that same evening, as they clambered up the cliff path, through a little dell with elder trees which the sun filled like a pool, that it happened? Her blue and white dress was taut as she climbed in front of him. Little marks of sweat appeared on it. She panted with the heat. They stopped to rest on the grass bank, behind the elder trees. And he meant, if nothing more, to pick a stem of grass and tickle her chin with it, for that would make her laugh. But when he turned she was gasping, her chest was heaving, long jagged breaths came from her throat, and she tore at the stem he held out to her, in panic, as if she were really drowning, clutching the straw, as if it were closing in to suffocate her, that golden summer-time.

It was asthma, she said, stretched on the bed in the hotel. 'I've had attacks before ... The heat ... It runs in my family.' She had recovered her composure; her breath was quiet, her face was calm. But he knew now the picture would never be complete. Those hands flailing in the sunlight.

4

'Weekend, Mr Chapman?' She said it, right on cue, plonking the tea down before him, her face the colour of the milky liquid in the mug. 'As if *you* would know what a weekend is.'

'But that doesn't answer my question, Mrs Cooper.'

'Well, no plans actually.' The horn rims glinted. 'But then if you were to have something in mind—I'd be glad—you know—to look after things.'

He lowered his face to his mug. How many times had she tried that one?

She smiled.

'Go on. Give yourself a treat for once. I'll manage. Look at that sunshine.' Her eyes darted to the window. Across the road the lime trees quivered. 'Take a trip to the coast. Get some air.'

And what she really meant was: 'We could both have a

39

treat, you and I. We could get the train together. Stroll arm in arm on the pier. You will put the question at last. I will no longer have to work.'

'When did you last have a holiday? You're not chained to this place, you know.'

'I last had a holiday, Mrs Cooper, in sixty-three. Teignmouth. Do you know Teignmouth? Devon. There are associations with the poet Keats. Know Keats, Mrs Cooper? My daughter Dorothy was fourteen.'

She blinked and tightened her lips; though her tongue smarted of course to have its say about that good-for-nothing of a girl. All that nonsense about literature, poetry, Shakespeare (guess how *he* knew about the poet Keats) and underneath it was only the money. But she saw, all the same, how it hurt him, how when you said the name there was a sort of wince in his eyes; as though he pulled down a shutter: Don't trouble me any more.

She avoided his eyes now. She allowed a slightly wounded expression to cross her face. She'd never deserted him, in sixteen years. When Mrs Chapman died; when he phoned up that time and began, 'Mrs Cooper, I'm afraid you must manage without me for a few days . . .'—hadn't she offered to do all she could, to come round in the evenings to cook, to tend ('No, Dorry's at home,' he'd said); and hadn't she even wept a tear herself all alone in the shop, at this very same hour, when normally she would make his tea and say, 'How's Mrs Chapman, Mr Chapman?' Not that you hadn't seen it coming. She'd been ill for years. But to see him return to the shop again for the first time, with his face empty, a dummy going through the motions. You knew then what made him tick.

'Is there nothing, Mr Chapman, nothing at all?' She would have comforted him. A fortnight after the funeral she had her hair done; bought a new corset. But it was all Dorothy then. Dorothy, Dorothy. She might have had her chance, with time, if it hadn't been for Dorothy. So she was almost glad when the little bitch ran off like that, taking the things, demanding the money (if only he'd said just *how much* money). 'Oh I'm sorry, Mr Chapman, truly sorry. See how they turn out in the end. Better off without her. Is there nothing? Nothing at all?' And he'd relent at last and see, surely, how she'd been his comfort all along.

She ran her palms down over her hips.

'Sixty-three, Mr Chapman? That's eleven years ago.'

'Yes. Eleven years.'

She snorted, as if the stretch of time made its own comment. Her throat trembled slightly. Her horn-rimmed glasses and large, curved nose gave her the look of an ageing bird of prey. Her features were all strained and compressed with effort on the end of that loose neck. Perhaps it was her corsets.

'She's grown up since, hasn't she? More's the pity.'

'Yes, Mrs Cooper.' She'd never been beautiful, with that bird's face. 'She's grown up. She takes her own holidays now.'

He finished his tea. She picked up the mug and held it next to her bosom. She would pour him another.

'Well, don't you fret over that. She's not worth it.' And she could have almost reached out and touched his hand there, resting on the copy of the *Daily Express*. She knew what he was thinking, with those little glances of inspection. She wasn't much to look at. She knew that. And perhaps that was what kept him there behind his shutters. For Mrs Chapman must have been beautiful, that must have been the trick of it. Though she'd no way of being sure. She'd never seen her, incredible though it was. In sixteen years Mrs Chapman had never come into the shop. But it must have been beauty—what else?—that kept him running to heel like that. And if *she* could do it, in an invalid chair, why not herself?

'Another cup?' She gripped his mug tightly in her fingers.

'Please.' He offered a brief, consoled expression. He knew what she was thinking (did she think he was stupid?).

She would get her reward.

The clock over the door showed twenty past seven. 'Almost time, eh?' he said. Traffic was accumulating outside. Figures bobbed along the pavement. Every day you watched them, the same faces, through the cluttered window, and you got to know. *They* were office cleaners coming home; they were from the vinegar factory; they were the night staff from the telephone exchange. Across, on the opposite corner of Briar Street, was the hairdresser's. Sullivan's: Styling for Men. They'd taken down the red-and-white barber's pole which used to twirl endlessly upwards, so that it seemed like a rod of infinite length, forever passing, disappearing into the bracket that held it. Smithy wouldn't have allowed that. Smithy had shaved him in the mornings, when Dorry was young. He had sat him in the chair beside the window so he could look across and keep an eye on the shop; and Mrs Cooper, if she looked carefully, could make out his round face, rising from white sheets like a coconut at a fair, swathed in lather. It was a bargain: he got his shave, Smithy got a pinch of tobacco and free magazines for his customers. Then one day young Keith came over, with his tight trousers and a pale face: 'Please, Mr Chapman, it's Mr Smithy ...'

Across the High Street only the café was open. The Diana. Dirty cream paint and wide windows on which the condensation trickled in winter. Who was Diana? A goddess, of something—Dorry would know. They opened every morning at seven, half an hour before him. One saw the regulars going in for their beans on toast or sausage and egg and their hot, treacly tea. Patterns. Most of the old shops over there had gone. The electrician's had once been a baker's, the off-licence a coal office, the do-it-yourself shop an ironmonger's. But the estate agent's—next to Simpson's the chemist's—had always been there. Hancock, Joyce and Jones. At a quarter to nine a grey-haired secretary, prim (all his secretaries were prim, proper things now), with a white handbag, would come to open up, stooping with one hand still on the key as she picked up the mail. At nine-fifteen, Hancock, in his dark blue Rover. On odd days, Joyce. And what of Jones? There were the little rows of notices in the window, all with photographs, some with prices. 'For Sale, Freehold.' Yes, Leigh Drive might be there, with the hydrangea bushes under the bay window. Dorry might see to that. Hancock would rub his hands and cast a meaning eye through his window to the shop and then to her. But Jones would never know. Yes, most of the shops were gone. But the Prince William still loomed up, with all that new red fancy-work, over Allandale Road; and the chemist's shop (though it used to be Lane's before Simpson's). And old Powell's was still there, with the great gold letters, painted to give the illusion of depth, on deep green, over the window. He hadn't appeared yet. Round the back, stacking boxes. But at eight o'clock he would emerge, pull down his awning and start to put out his display, taking the roundest, firmest oranges, the ripest tomatoes to place outside. They were not the ones you got if you asked; you got the second best from inside. That was the trick of it. Every day in his grey, greasy cardigan; polishing the apples, setting them one by one on the blue tissue paper. A little water on the watercress, a sprinkle on the lettuces, to make them tempt. Unsubtle old shark.

Mrs Cooper reappeared through the plastic strips with his second mug of tea. She glanced at the clock as she approached and caught his eye. Her throat strained. No, he hadn't forgotten—today of all days. At half-past seven on Friday mornings the shop opened; at twenty-five past he paid her. That was the system.

'Our usual little business,' he would say. He would clear his throat; and she would look up, as if she'd forgotten, and instinctively rub the palms of her hands on her nylon shop coat. For this matter of money required clean, immaculate hands.

He opened the drawer of the till. It was already there, made up, in a little brown envelope with a rubber band. And beside it another brown envelope.

'There.' She took the envelope and, as always, in one

movement, without looking at it, slipped it quickly into the pocket of her shop coat. As if to show it meant nothing to her.

And then, taking her empty hand from her pocket and clasping it with the other, she would give that little disappointed glance.

She turned to lift up the counter-flap and move to the door. But he stopped her.

'Something else, Mrs Cooper.'

'Something else, Mr Chapman?'

He had the second envelope in his hand.

'A little—well, call it—a bonus. As it's summer. As—' he couldn't help lending his eye a sharp twinkle—'as it's the time for taking holidays. There's twenty-five.'

The eyebrows lifted. Mrs Cooper's smile never worked.

'Really, Mr Chapman. I—'

'Now don't say you shouldn't.' He planted the cigar once more between his lips. 'Sixteen years my assistant. Sixteen. You deserve something now and then.'

Little spasms rose and fell in her throat.

'My holidays?' She paused. '*My* holidays. It's too kind of you, Mr Chapman.'

But she didn't look gratitude. Behind her smile her face pleaded, as if she'd expected something else, something more.

But that was all, Mrs Cooper. Take it. The things you want you never get. You only get the money.

'Keep it. Keep it for me till later.'

He nodded, blowing out smoke. 'Very well.' He cocked his head towards the clock. She gave him back the second envelope, lifted the flap in the counter and passed out, as every morning, to unlock the door, unslip the chain and turn round the little plastic Senior Service sign from 'Closed' to 'Open'. Later, when the shop would be closed again, when she would have left and returned to her flat, she would take out the envelopes from her handbag, having spurned them in his presence, and count their contents, running the notes through her fingers; and she would find in the second envelope not twenty-five but five hundred pounds. That would stop her, that would surprise her. She would not know what to do—to phone up, to say, to do nothing. But by that time, by that time, it would be too late.

She was paid.

She returned from the door, straightening the hang of her shop coat, and stood beside him at the counter, awaiting the first customers. He passed his eyes over her vexed, hawkish face, seeing, beyond it, arms lifted in a golden sea. And she, not attempting to return the gaze, stared at the sun, the shaft of sunlight slanting through the shop, falling on the smoke from Mr Chapman's cigar, on his knotted, tarnished hands which rested on the counter, on the words on the front page of the uppermost paper in the pile between them. 'PEACE BID FAILS.'

5

'A gem of a site.'

It was old Jones who spoke, in his black greatcoat, with his florid cheeks and stoop, and his bunch of dangling keys like a jailer's. And they were standing, Jones, himself, and his brother-in-law Paul, in that shop that would one day bear the name Chapman.

Jones sniffed the damp air. He was nearly seventy, they said; had made his pile, but he wouldn't retire. And young Joyce and Hancock, over in his wood-panelled office, were waiting for him to die so that they could take his place and move the name on the letter head from first to last. 'Needs going over. But a gem of a site. Corner. Station close by. Good will of previous proprietor. And how many other newsagents along this stretch?' He ran a finger through the dust on the counter and flicked it away. 'You'll be all right here.' The face, sucking its own lips, was almost apologetic. He was old, tired of business, he no longer cared to encourage or discourage; yet he wouldn't stop working. Perhaps he knew already (one *did* know): two weeks after his retirement, the fatal stroke. A further week, speechless as a dummy, then he died. And that was a month after he'd wheezed to him, coming in to buy chocolates for his wife, 'If you sell, watch Hancock.'

They shivered and their voices echoed in the bare interior. It was November, 1937. Drizzle fell in the High Street. The sea and the cliffs were gone, and he didn't feel much at all, neither encouragement nor discouragement, standing there in that empty place—there were only some old sweet jars and a faint smell of coconut—that would be his. Brother Paul, with his long, clean fingers, took from his inside pocket a silver cigarette case, tapped a cigarette on the initialled lid, and said to Jones, 'You understand of course it will be in my sister's name. In the name of Mr Chapman's wife?'

They trooped through the rain across the road to Jones's office—it was just Jones and Partners in those days—while Jones held the umbrella so that Paul wouldn't get wet. They mustn't get wet, the Harrisons; they had little white laundries all over the suburbs: Jones had secured them all. A dust cart was grinding down Briar Street. In the office, sombre as an undertaker's, with the gas fire fizzing in the corner, were Hancock, lean and suave (without his moustache then), and Joyce, chubby and pert, as though to complement him. They looked up, obliging to Paul, suspicious of him. And already, no doubt, they were spreading the word: 'That is what's-his-name, married to the Harrison girl—the laundry Harrisons—God knows how. House in Leigh Drive. Shop in the High Street. Sheer fluke. None of it his.' And already he could see his legend being shaped. 'You'll act then for Mrs Chapman, Mr Chapman?' said Jones drily, as if he knew a secret. 'Of course, she will have to sign when the time comes.' And as they departed—Paul was ahead at the door, raising his coat collar, anxious to report to brother Jack—the estate agent caught his arm and said, 'A lovely woman, your wife.'

Jones let slip nothing. His face was full of dour discretion. But later when he told her (it was dark by then, the fire was bright and her face was mirrored in the dripping window) that it was done, and she must sign, she said promptly, turning, as if she'd only been waiting for the moment: 'No, you must sign. The solicitors know, Jones knows. Only Paul and Jack don't know. The shop will be yours.' And over her lips had passed—was it? You couldn't tell in the firelight—for the first time without its seeming like an act of charity, a smile.

'You mean—?'

'Yes.'

He had wanted to laugh. So she could play a trick, after all, for all that coolness. She might say next, 'See, I was only pretending,' and melt completely. On the table was a vase, empty of flowers, which they'd bought in Dorset. Was she laughing too, behind the shadows from the fire? Her skin was flickering. He bent forward to find out, lifting his hands. And then he'd seen, through the flames, a blankness, like the blankness in old Jones's face: No, that doesn't mean there is any question. He'd dropped his hands; they were still cold from walking home in the rain. It was as if he'd mistaken the reward and so appeared ungrateful. He had had to look—for it seemed he couldn't look at *her*—at that reflection, thin and inaccessible, in the dark. And she'd repeated, unsmiling, as if offering a bribe: 'The shop will be yours.'

She got up, smoothing her skirt, to make tea.

'Don't say you don't want it.'

She stood looking down at him as if she'd found her balance. He must obey, perform while she watched, or she'd fall.

'They'll find out in time—the family I mean—but so what?'

She seemed to wobble again.

'You'll manage, Willy. Won't you?'

But he had no fears for the shop. To do what was fixed for you, that was easy. The shelves were empty, the counter was laden with dust. But he would clean them, and he would buy the stock (she would give him the money) to fill them. Sweets, newspapers, cigarettes. And though he'd stood there like a dummy with Paul and old Jones, though he knew nothing of shopkeeping, he would get a shopkeeper's coat and adopt a shopkeeper's manner. And in time it would be wholly plausible.

'Yes, I'll manage.'

'W. Chapman, Newsagent, Confectioner, Licensed to sell Tobacco.' A sign would go up like an official stamp. He'd leave every day at six-fifteen, she'd watch him, hand at throat, from the doorway, and he'd return at seven-thirty, bearing in a briefcase the little red and black books which recorded the progress of trade and which now and then she'd open and inspect to make sure there was a healthy margin between outlay and takings. And if he should ever feel, what sham, what play-acting, she would say—how neatly she set out the table, bringing in the tea tray, the china cups, the glass sugar bowl—Let me bear that. Let me absolve you of that. The responsibility is mine.

She put down the teapot. She looked relieved. Perhaps they were both safe.

So nothing would happen? She poured milk, spooned

sugar. That is what it meant, perhaps. The shop is yours: let nothing happen. The dancing foliage of the firelight dappled her face. For one moment he wanted to sweep aside the tea cups, to catch her like some wild thing glimpsed in a forest. But her eyes sharpened, held him, as though to save him from stumbling headlong. She balanced her plate on her knee. Let nothing happen.

Though something did happen. He was fixing the name-board over the shop door; the sign-painter had finished it and he had only to fit it in its brackets. That was two weeks before he was due to open. But he wasn't thinking of what he was doing. He was thinking of the creature disappearing into the forest. He reached out; 'W. Chapman, Newsagent'; he toppled from the stepladder, the name-board clutched still in his hands; broke a bone in his leg and displaced another in his back. And there he was, when the shop should have been open, lying in St Helen's, unable to move, his leg in plaster, having tests done on his back. She came in with detective novels, grapes or bananas, first eyeing him reproachfully, as if he'd let her down perhaps, done it deliberately. Then, as she sat by the bed, her look would soften, as if in some way his accident consoled her and she meant to say: 'See, you too are helpless. When you fall your bones break. How easily you forget how fragile you are.'

Did she foresee then, how intimately she would know that hospital?

'Do what the doctors tell you.' She patted his wrist. How commanding she looked, there at the bedside. And if only she would say, not that she loved him, but . . .

All through the visiting hours the man in the next bed, a hernia case who had no visitors, kept his eyes on her.

How auspicious. To fall and half break your back, when the shop was almost ready to open. He had to sit at home, still trussed and plastered, while she nursed and attended. She never complained. She was the soul of patience. And did her attentiveness then spring from a sense of another bargain struck? (It would be her turn, later, to be the invalid, his the nurse.) Or did it spring perhaps from her having proved her point? There was that knowing look as she helped him manoeuvre his crutches. That is what you get for adventuring, that is what you get for wanting things to happen.

So he would play his part. With a permanent limp. In six or seven years' time people would inquire about it: Was it in the war? And he would say: What war?—I fell off a ladder.

It was summer again, summer 1938. Powell was sprinkling his watercress and lettuce. Smithy's barber's pole was twirling, endlessly, upwards. And the shop was open. Its coloured frontage adorned the High Street. And, sure enough, the customers came, without needing to be asked, for their cigarettes and dailies. He sold out, for the sun shone hot and bright, of lemonade and ice cream. And not one of them doubted that he was the sweet shop owner, that he was in his rightful place, behind the counter. He would play his part. What was easier? To step inside it like a bubble, to feel it buoy you up over the passing days, so that though you moved and gestured and the grime of loose change came off on your hands, you were really intact. Nothing touches you, you touch nothing.

That was what he'd believed at Ellis's, before she'd walked in that lunchtime. And what he'd believed, that far-off afternoon, seated by the window in the history lesson. His head was pressed against the dusty glass. He was a shopkeeper in a schoolboy's outfit. The history master was speaking as if his words were turning into print. Henry VIII and his wives were like characters in costume. They weren't real, but they didn't know it. History fitted them into patterns. He was looking out at the still rows of chestnuts, the asphalt, the footballers on their marked-out pitches. You touch nothing, nothing touches you. All the rest is wild adventure. See how the football players turn their game into grim earnest. Their shouts sound like the screams of fighters. And see them still, unappeased by their fervour, trailing home down the path by the iron railings, restless, greedy for something to happen, for the real thing ...

'Chapman! Are you with us?'

He had laughed then, unheard. And at Ellis's. He'd carried round inside him a little hidden laugh. So that he didn't mind about his school reports (he was only good at woodwork and distance running) or that his parents were disappointed, or that those others around him in that chalky classroom would get on better than him. Let them go to meet history. History would come anyway. Nothing touches you, you touch nothing.

Sunshine slanted through the striped awning. Over the road, outside Powell's, the shadows of the lime trees were black and small. Summer, 1938. Sold out, in only a few days, of lemonade and ices. But he'd learn. He'd make something of it: there, in the night, as he lay sprawled beside her, he pictured it, glimmering in the dark, stuffed with ices, with lemonade, with things with no use.

Trams were passing in the High Street, full again in the late afternoon. People were going home, faces hot, collars loosened, calling in for their papers and evening cigarettes. 'No, sorry—sold out of ices.' But Powell too had sold out of watercress. Trains were unloading. Homegoers were dispersing down the pavements, past the open doors of the Prince William which sent out a cool, inviting waft of beer, and up over the common. The evening sun was making them come alive, and there—was it in the breeze, in the scent of the grass over the common, in the swing perhaps of a summer dress?—a glimpse of something, slipping away, as in the depths of a forest.

He turned round the sign from 'Open' to 'Closed'. Checked the windows, checked the till, checked the locks. How many times, how many times? He was young then. He carried his jacket over his shoulder. He didn't need braces to hoist his trousers and his cheeks were not mottled with red. Only the limp to show that he was no longer all that he was. For once he'd been good at running. Over the common, up the Rise, into Leigh Drive. And there she was, opening the front door, ready to take his jacket and case and the evening paper and to give him a smile, like the scattering of coins.

'Good day?'

This was a sort of code.

'Four pounds. And I sold out of lemonade.'

Clomp, clomp. Who was that banging into the shop as if he owned it? It was Hancock, ducking his six feet under the door, raising one of his long, elastic arms to fish for his wallet, and leaning forward in a sinuous, confidential way as he asked for cigarettes. 'Thought you should know. Old Jones died last night. We all knew, didn't we? Funeral Saturday, already fixed. Shame.' He pocketed the cigarettes and patted the wallet on his palm. 'Mrs Chapman all right?' He looked round the shop. There was a gleam in his eye. 'Great friend of the Harrisons, old Jones. Poor feller didn't want to stop work.' He patted the wallet a second time, turning to go. 'Thought you ought to know.'

Clomp, clomp. What was that? Another death? Yes. The noise of the earth falling on his father's coffin. August, 1938. And again, clomp, a month later, on Mother's. As if they'd said, All right, that's enough—you first, I'll follow. As if they'd done it all in time: lived to see their son come into money and marry a beautiful woman; to dance on his wedding night round the living room. What rejoicing. She did nothing, Mother, in that final month. Only dug out the will which left it all to her—for a month—and made up her own—which left it all to him. You touch nothing. The sun shone at both their funerals, making the white graves in the cemetery sparkle like wedding cakes. Irene stood beside him with her black gloves and black handbag and a black hat with a veil. She took his arm to steady him. And did she see, behind her veil, standing there so firm, that he was no longer all he was?

Clomp. What was that? Only the piles of morning

papers, tied with string, being dumped at the door by the lad from the van. He lifted the bundles onto the counter, cut the string, and there, on the appropriate page, were the notices: Jones, Arthur Russell, August 2nd; Chapman, George William, August 16th; Chapman, Edith, September 24th. The neatness of the columns. Deaths, marriages. The black and whiteness of memorials. He hadn't wanted it in the papers. What sham. But she'd said, it was the thing to do: do it.

Sunlight fell on the piles of papers, on his hands smudged by that same neat print. And what were the headlines then? In September, 1938?

'WILL GERMANY MARCH?'

6

'Ah! The ice cream, Mrs Cooper.' He looked out through the window. 'Wouldn't do to run out on a day like this.'

The blue and cream company's van had pulled up at the kerb outside and the driver was emerging with his pad of pink receipts and invoices and his blue carbon paper.

'Let me,' she said, turning on her heel. But, 'No, I'll do it,' he said. 'You manage here' (for it was not quite nine and they were coming in thick and fast on their way to work).

'Lovely weather.'

'Gorgeous.'

And there he went, in his grey nylon jacket, dodging an incoming customer, out onto the pavement to help the man with his smoking, hoary cartons of ice cream. Sprightly enough, with his limp, and his heart, and his dumb expression. But he shouldn't do it (she thumped at the till); what would she do if something happened? Couldn't she help?

He re-entered bearing three cartons, followed by the delivery man bearing five.

What a fool he was, bringing in the stuff himself, as if it were some sort of precious treasure, and not ice cream to sell on a hot summer's day; opening the black lid of the fridge, making room for the new cartons, taking out two loose choc-ices and juggling them—there, up and down— in his hands. Him and his tricks. He turned to go out for more boxes. And she gave him a stare, with the full vulture-like force of her amber spectacles. You shouldn't: it'll kill you. But what was he doing, staring back at her, blindly, wiping the cold moisture from the fridge off his hands? Smiling, was it? Though his face never moved. Smiling though he wasn't smiling, so that she was obliged to offer back a great, snarling flash of her teeth (which were not her own) and to feel stupid for it afterwards.

He returned and went out again. What a fool he was, prancing about on the pavement, climbing up into the back of the delivery van and hopping down again, as if he were only a kid.

And what was he doing out there? Signing the delivery man's pink pad and slipping him—what was that for?—a pound tip?

He entered again, puffing, carrying the last of the treasure chests. His face was like a red balloon.

Yes, she thought, seeking the source of that invisible smile. It must have been beauty.

7

Sit back, Willy; drink your tea, rest your head, if you like, on my lap (he did not hear, there in the autumn evening by the French windows, but what did he ever hear of those inward commands, spoken to soothe her own nerves?). You're tired. Think of nothing, listen to the clock ticking on the mantelpiece. All day at the shop; and two visits, twice in two months, to the graveside. Rest your head. Sometimes I see in your face that little hidden smile, far behind it all, as if you don't mind, as if you'll play your part, laugh at the joke. How that pleases me. And yet sometimes, like now, when you're tired, it goes out, that tiny flicker of laughter, as if you'd said, no, it's not a joke, things must happen; I'll have what is mine. How stern you look then, how earnest. How frightened you make me. There, be still. Listen to the clock. Relight the flame.

How little you know me, Willy. How little you know

of that young girl (I wasn't yet fourteen) who looked at herself once in the bedroom mirror—the spring night was warm and I'd slipped off my cotton nightdress—and knew that she was beautiful. You think that's what every young girl wants? Something to rejoice over? I had eyes like blue embers and little breasts that pointed at me. But it's not like that. It's like being chosen. It's like being told (that other figure, in the mirror, seemed to tell me): You're special. You must cherish your gift.

That was in '27. I was young. All I knew was that Father had a business and my elder brothers were going to go into it; and that my mother's brothers (how Mother egged Father on in that business of his) had all been killed, one, two, three of them, in a war I was too young to recall. I pictured them like skittles, those would-be uncles of mine. Uncle Mark, Uncle Philip, Uncle Edward. Bright painted skittles, all suddenly knocked down (it said in the Book of Remembrance they were 'fallen'). And later I learnt—it was a common fact so nobody mentioned it—that everywhere there had been knocking down, great gaps and holes everywhere, families with only one or two skittles left standing.

But that was in the past. They talked of Trade and Opportunity, Recovery, the Fruits of Peace. They wanted to forget history. They wanted new life. And when in the school holidays I returned from little educational outings with my girlfriends, to Greenwich, to the Crystal Palace, I felt the eyes of men in the High Street, still standing skittles, waiting at tram queues and outside pubs, turn to look at me. Life, their eyes said, and I felt their message lap around me like waves.

Drink your tea. Be still, think of nothing. It was like something allocated in error, that image in the mirror. When I walked down the High Street with my girlfriends, Joan Proctor, Betty Marshall, Carol Smith, all of whom had thankful little marks of plainness, little blemishes and flaws which relieved them of responsibility, I knew I couldn't laugh out loud, giggle and squeal like them. I held my head and shoulders stiffly like a puppet. They called me 'beautiful and proud', sulky, hard to please, and they blamed me all the more because, having beauty, I should also have grace. But they didn't see how I cowered inside my looks like a captive, how my looks didn't belong to me, and how, when they thought me haughty and peevish (what else could they think, seeing only what I saw in the mirror?) I was really helpless and afraid.

My family nursed my beauty like a rare plant. For it had its uses after all. They set me up into a little emblem, carried me before them like a banner, so they could say, Look, even beauty is on our side. And I knew I was responsible. Father would come home, tired and indignant-looking, in the evening. He was indignant because there was going to be a Labour government. He wore heavy coats, and a scarf wrapped tightly round his neck as if he were always cold or ill (though it was Mother who had the chest trouble) and his face was set and lined as if nothing was more weighty, more pressing than the burdens he bore. Yet he would look at me as if the sight restored him. Mother would say, 'Look your best for Father,' and when I became a certain age she bought me new underclothes, a little white shapeless brassière like a pair of ribbons, and spoke to me earnestly and sharply, yet never quite plainly, of girls needing to be pure, of the duty of keeping one's purity. I never quite knew what it meant: purity. Perhaps it had something to do with the clean white sheets my family laundered—'Pure' it said on the handouts given to customers and stuck in windows, 'All your laundry fresh and pure.' Perhaps it had something to do with those dead brothers of my mother, engraved on the white war memorial. 'Their deaths have purified them,' somebody said of all those skittles. I only knew it was another of those things they looked to me for—pure, beautiful—and which I couldn't provide.

A second cup? Let me pour you a second cup—I'll put it near. Lean back. I'll stroke your brow—no, don't look at me. Lightly, lightly. There. That's better. You are already beginning to look again as you did on the common when I said, 'Why don't you?'—and straight away, you did.

How different you are from my family, Willy, from Jack and Paul. Their bodies are agile and eager, their faces keen and lifted, and yet they are stiffer, stiffer and hollower than you, with your woodenness and your glum expression. They have the looks of statues, trapped in immovable poses, and they already show signs of Father's indignation. They think a lot of purity. On the wall in the office, over the laundry, someone has pinned the motto 'Cleanliness is next to Godliness' and they do not see it as a joke.

There are wicked types, said my mother. Her face was always harsh. Wicked things; better you should never know. But that didn't stop her, or the rest of them, when the time came, from giving their encouragement to Hancock. He was a good sort, they said. He drank with Paul and Jack at the Sports Club. He was good at squash and tennis and drove a green Riley Lynx. And, what was more important, old Jones had taken him in; old Jones who'd served us well and had a sound business and couldn't work on much longer. No, they didn't discourage Frank Hancock. He was tall, springy-stepped, with the air of a participant in some competition. He took me out like a boy on his best behaviour, as if I should reward him in some way. And when he pulled me into the hedge on the way back from a drive to Brighton (how sickly the grass smelt and the stems of cow-parsley) I did not assume it was wickedness at first. He looked at me as if I should have expected this. He pulled up my clothes like a man unwrapping a parcel. 'All right,' he said, 'all right, now,' as if we had both been anticipating. I struggled. The sun was in my face. This was like a performance in which people were really stabbed and wounded. He needed his victory. And afterwards, in the green Riley—it was a careless evening in June with sunlight through trees—his face, watching the road, terrified me. I only knew I wasn't prepared. Life, life.

Lie still, Willy. Don't look up. Think of nothing.

I spoke to Mother. I used the coy evasions she would have used. 'He was not good to me.' 'What nonsense,' she said, 'a nice young man like Frank' (for old Jones had just been visited by the doctor). And I knew I'd failed them. And not only them, but myself. For I couldn't go near the grass or lounge in the sunlight without suffering. I had my first asthma that summer. I was scared I was pregnant, but I wasn't. My eyes were red, my breath strained. Father looked displeased; how it spoilt my looks. And down at the Sports Club Paul and Jack played squash with Hancock and stood him beers (because he always won) and said what a fine fellow he was. I went out with him again in his green Riley, with preparatory handkerchiefs tucked in my sleeves.

I knew what he wanted, with his lean sportsman's body and his prize-seeker's eyes: the figure in my bedroom mirror. But it wasn't mine to give. I even felt sorry for him, that fine fellow who couldn't get the thing he wanted. How innocent maybe he was. Oh, I restrained him. I learnt there is a sort of command in beauty even though inside you wobble like a skittle. Lie still, Willy. Though it only perhaps encouraged him all the more, that disdain. How you pay, Willy, even for the things you never own.

'What nonsense.' I had refused to see Hancock again. I lay in my room struggling for breath. 'Ungrateful!' they said. 'Pull yourself together! What will Frank do? What nonsense!' There in my bedroom mirror I saw almost with relief the red blotches on my skin, and watched my face contort as I gasped for air. I locked the door. Their voices insisted outside. Then one day I smashed the mirror.

Don't move. Think of nothing.

They called in the doctor. Lie still, he said. And they sent me to a Home in Surrey where they talked to me and nodded gravely over me and finally left me sitting by myself in a chair.

They didn't visit me at the Home. They came there once to admit me (Jack drove, in the black Humber, and they gave me discreet, do-as-you're-told kisses) and once to discharge me. I sat in a grey easy chair by the window with my feet on a floor that was polished twice daily. I lifted my legs for the orderly to wield his mop and he swept on around me, so that I was marooned. But I didn't move. Outside there were lawns, a gravel drive, two rows of clipped yews, rose beds, a red brick wall with wrought-iron gates. So neat, so symmetrical. It didn't belong to me, none of it. But I watched the gardener, with the mower, and the rake, and then with the shears and ladder for the yew trees. He had baggy trousers, braces, a red face, and as he worked (I couldn't hear, but I saw his lips draw in and his cheeks expand) he whistled. Patients in striped bath-robes and ill-fitting jackets, for whom his garden meant nothing, for whom there was fire in the rose beds, havoc in the crunching gravel, mooched by, but he worked on, asking no questions. First one yew tree then the next. Was I really ill, Willy? I was concentrating hard so that the orderly wouldn't sink through his shiny floor and the gardener wouldn't slip from his ladder. I was responsible. How still but determined I sat, marooned in my easy chair. The gardener had almost finished the yew trees and the orderly had swept the floor for perhaps the twentieth time when they said I could go. I had found my balance, struck my bargain. 'You are better,' they said. 'Better?' I said. My things were packed in a brown suitcase and I put on my hat, tucking my hair under the rim like a woman who means to get her way. The orderly smiled (he was fond of me), 'Nice to see you well again, miss'; but I didn't smile. I looked at him coldly: for there could be no question, not now. And beyond the lawns, beyond the brick wall, they were coming—I was ready for them—in the black, shiny Humber, Jack at the wheel, Paul by his side, Mother and Father in the back, with their heads erect and their hands, clean as marble, protruding from their cuffs. Down the Surrey lane, eyes watching the flashing trees. They would be coming soon. I was a skittle, Willy, but I wouldn't fall. The gleaming car would turn through the wrought-iron gates. Its tyres would crunch on the gravel.

There, be still. You must rest your back. I'll put on the light; no, don't stir. How little you know how you've kept my balance.

They brought me home. There were little shows of reconciliation. Father bought me a dress, my brothers perfume. They said, 'Are you better?' as to a child that has ceased its tantrums, and I said, 'Yes,' without smiling. But their verdict was firm and businesslike. She has let us down once, she may let us down again; we cannot afford that embarrassment. So when you appeared, Willy, you were the perfect solution. What justice, what neatness. Let her have that little man. He's as simple as she's cracked and she'll wish soon enough she'd settled for Hancock. And if *he* thinks he's walking into money, he'll regret it when he learns how cracked she is. They even bought me the house and gave me a settlement, half in cash, half in shares. For their own guilt in disposing of me had to be paid for, and the greater the payment the more stainless their conscience. What justice. The perfect solution. But they didn't see how *you* would be my solution and how it was they who would lose.

How peaceful the evening is. Your head in my lap. There, look up now: see what you'll always see if you never claim it. Only an image in a mirror, remember? What poise, what balance, Willy, this room, this moment. Nothing must be touched, nothing must be changed.

Had he slept? He woke out of a dream in which the objects in the room seemed to loom triumphantly—the chintz chairs, the clock on the mantelpiece, the pink and blue bordered cups in one of which there was tea he had forgotten to drink, the standard lamp with its spiralled stem. As if time had passed, years, and it was long after, and they seemed to be saying, those familiar objects, 'See, we endured; things remain.' But there she was; her face was above his, lit by the standard lamp and turned to one side. What loveliness. It was her lap in which his head rested, her hand which lay on his hair, and she was reading the newspaper, folded on the armrest of the sofa. She had noticed his eyes opening and her own had turned, widened, enjoined (what jewels!), as if they did the work of a finger to her lips—Don't stir, don't spoil the trick. 'You slept,' she said, moving her gaze at once away from his, back to the paper, as though ignoring something, some mystery perhaps too delicate to probe. And later she said, her eyes still on the paper: 'There will be a war, Willy.'

Mrs Cooper watched him, standing like a sentry, at his counter. She'd worked once before in a shop. It was a book shop. Saturdays only, before the war. She was only seventeen. She'd wanted the bookseller to make a pass at her. She'd climbed up the steps in her new silk stockings to the top shelves. But nothing had happened.

8

War? What war?

He had lost his balance on a pair of ladders, fallen off and damaged his back. They wouldn't take him for a soldier. He wouldn't have the opportunity, as they put it, to 'see action'. Such a strange phrase and such an odd notion—as if there were no action besides wars. Strange as that other phrase which would be repeated, now, over and over again, like the little deft stroke with which a seal is stamped: fallen, fallen in action.

Left, right. They were marching over the crunching gravel, past the rows of black Nissen huts, past the wire fencing, the white flagpole, making patterns for the sergeant, left, right. There was grass beyond the wire fencing, the tussocked downs of Hampshire, twittering skylarks, scudding spring clouds. April, 1940. And some of those khaki figures out on the gravel fitted uneasily into the pattern making. Left, right. What did it have to do with 'action', this drill, this answering by numbers and naming of parts? What was the connection? And, see, one of them in the front rank as they halted, waiting to move off again, teetered forward on his toes, almost toppled, so that the sergeant could bawl—his favourite line—'Dohn anticipate the ordaah!'

He watched from the side window, amid the smells of webbing, waterproofing and polish. For though they hadn't taken him for a soldier they'd given him a uniform: sent him his papers, examined him, made sly quips—'How did you get your back, soldier?'—'Fell off some stepladders'—asked curt questions—'Civilian occupation?'—'Shopkeeper'—and by some unerring logic (they too didn't doubt he was the shop owner, the trader of wares) assigned him to: Royal Engineers, Carbury Camp, Stores. The others would see action—those there through the window were being prepared for action—but his duty would be Issue of Equipment—packs, blankets, pouches, helmets, all numbered, allocated, entered up in the record sheet, stamped, checked. What was the connection?

'Squad Halt! Squad Shun! Squaaad!' Patterns over the gravel. 'That man! Dohn anticipate the ordaah!'

And now they must do their bit.

'Sergeant! Have your men assemble with kit bags.'

'Squaad!'

Right! One at a time, keep the line moving, look sharp. Blanket, ground sheet, move along, waterproof cape, back-pack, side-packs, two, steel helmet—make it fit or change yer 'ed—with netting, move along, webbing straps, bayonet sheath, water bottle, keep it moving—that man, pick up that bleedin' 'elmeht!

'Thank you, Sergeant, carry on.'

'Sh-holdah kit bags! Lehf! . . . Lehf . . .' Over the crunching gravel.

He didn't mind the orders, the regimentation. He was a performer, wasn't he? Give him the uniform, tell him what to do, he'd do it. And it was easy to pretend to be a soldier. To salute, to obey, to clomp one's black heels, even with a limp, over the wooden barrack-hut floor. And see, he dealt as before (how consistent fate was) with items, with things stacked and piled and arranged in long rows under the curved roof of the store block; with lists, inventories (the carbon from the duplicated Army forms came off on your hands along with the blanco from old webbing), stock lists, issue lists, delivery lists. There was a counter, wooden and scoured by continual use (but the Quartermaster made them polish it every day), from behind which you watched the faces entering and passing, passing, keeping the line moving. They never seemed to stop, and you remembered them only by the numbers you recorded on the forms: 120 capes, 120 helmets, 240 side-packs.

'There,' said Private Rees, from Swansea, sallow-faced and listless, removing his gold-rimmed glasses and squinting at them (for that was his reason for not seeing action), 'There's another lot done.'

And up the road they were coming already, the next lot, in the canvas-topped lorries, past the flashing leaves, past the striped pole by the guard house, waiting to be made into soldiers.

'Right!' snapped the sergeant. 'Now lissen-a-me. Look after your kit. Remember: what you 'ave don't belong to you. When the war's over the army'll want it bloody back!'

They badgered him and Rees, and the other stores clerks, because they were safe. And the rest would go and fight. They slept in their own quarters for those permanently on camp but they mixed in the mess hall with the passers-through for Issue of Kit and Basic Training. Private Rees would not be drawn. 'Bugger off,' he said. 'Tell them to bugger off, Willy boy.' But he said (did they think he was stupid?): 'Someone has to mind the store.'

The long barrack huts with their tiers of bunks, the mess hall and the echoing bath-house reminded him of school: the sweaty blasphemy of changing rooms, flaunted manhoods, the belligerence of the football pitch and the running track. They'd wanted 'action' then, in '30 and '31, trailing home, tingling with exercise, out of the school gates. A restlessness plagued them which turned their games into something more than games. The real thing, the thing itself: let us have that. And for a moment their eyes were blind to the rows of still chestnuts, the black lines of railings. They'd sat in the history lesson and chafed at its dryness—would nothing happen?—but here suddenly was 'History'. So Private Rees said, smacking his lips over a newspaper bearing the news of the occupation of Paris: 'History, that's what it is.' As if the statement would save him, immune as a rock, from an invasion of Germans and all the outrages of war. And here suddenly was the real thing. And yet how did it express itself? In barrack huts and wire fencing, in numbers, inventories, lists? 360 capes, 360 helmets, 720 side-packs. What was the connection?

They badgered him in the mess hall. His limp became the target for mocking jokes, and they looked in his face with the shifting looks of schoolboys for signs of injured pride, for signs that their enforced code of 'action' had proved its worth by delivering a sting. But he gave no sign. For over the dinner table, over the white cloth with the blue border, on the evening his final papers and his rail warrant had come, she'd looked at him, looking for the same signs, looking for 'deeds' and 'action', but she'd not found them.

'Count your blessings,' she'd said. 'Why should you go and get yourself killed?'

What firmness. She sat in the chintz chair listening to the wireless bulletins, scanning the papers which spoke of the war in Finland, the threat of air raids, taking note of the facts, as if the course of things was predictable and she had only to observe its fulfilment. Let bombs drop: she wouldn't jump. And when the note-taking was done she would throw down the paper, switch off the wireless (before it burst into morale-boosting song), and, getting up, stare momentarily at the window—though not through it, for it was covered by the dark blackout curtain, and beyond it, anyway, the garden was dank and dead, under that first bleak winter of the war. But she stared. No, it wasn't war, destruction that she feared. It almost protected her, that great ominous blackness, as if she knew where she stood with it—shielded her from sunlight; and she was saved perhaps, so long as there were bulletins and blackness (her body was like a lamp, there at the window) from bright moments which urged: No, there is beauty, we do not belong to history.

But that was before he left for his camp in Hampshire and before she went with her mother to her Aunt

Madeleine's in Aylesbury (for her family had stepped in nobly in the hour of peril to pluck her from the rain of bombs that would fall on London). Leigh Drive stood empty. Her plates and glass were wrapped in packing cases; the pictures taken down from the wall, the wedding photos locked in a drawer. How many landmarks had passed already, swept suddenly far behind by the advent of war? Was it only in '37 he'd been the printer's assistant, coming home in the evening to Mother and Father, who'd never heard of Irene Harrison? And how many new landmarks had replaced them? Leigh Drive, the shop; housing his identity, but not for ever; and perhaps never really; for see, they stood empty, and, look again—the bombs were falling. Two fell in Briar Street, one stripped the lime trees outside Powell's; and one, crashing down near the Surrey canal, flattened old Ellis's printworks.

What would become of the shop? What would become of the sweet jars, the ice cream, the magazines? He pinned up one of those comic notices: Closed for the Hostilities. 'It will keep,' she said. 'It must keep.' Wars pass but sweet shops remain.

'Dear Willy,' she wrote from Aylesbury, 'We are doing our bit. Aunt Madeleine is digging the back garden. I am collecting coat-hangers. Mother writes to Jack and

Paul. Mother especially does her bit. Father is staying at Sydenham. Sticking to his post. He demands the keys to Leigh Drive. He won't get them. Mr Smithy is keeping an eye on the shop. He says he'll get someone to board up the windows and he'll send on any mail.'

He replied: 'Am doing my bit too,' and wrote, '1,980 helmets.' For that was how they told off the war, in tin helmets and letters.

'Mother worries about Father in London. You must have read about last week's raids. He sleeps alone at Sydenham, in the cellar. Misses Jack and Paul. He's by himself now at the laundry. Mother suggests I go to give him some "support", but I think it's really Father's idea. He says he'll protect me from bombs. But I'd be more scared of staying at Sydenham.'

There was this tone about her letters as if she were writing from the thick of the fighting.

He dropped the wallet just as the sergeant came in the door and called attention. He was folding her letter inside it and then it slipped from his hand. The sergeant loured, flexed his shoulders and stooped to pick it up. 'Your wife, Chapman?' he said, looking at the photograph. A beach photographer had taken it in Swanage. The sun was in her face. ''Oo's a lucky man then?' He spoke loudly so everyone in the hut should hear. Then he tossed the wallet back and sauntered out through the far door, flicking with his baton at a pile of blankets, looking for another reason to shout.

'Sod him,' said Rees. But he glanced too at the photograph and smacked his lips.

He wrote: 'The sergeant passes by each day to make sure we are being good soldiers.'

And then her next letter came from London.

'They finally cajoled me down here. Bombs and all. Strange, when they were so keen to pull me out in April. Father very anxious now about the business. He's short staffed and will have to work out quotas. He behaves oddly. It's as if the war is something I shouldn't have to be troubled with—really *his* responsibility—and he apologises to me for it. He says the country should do this and that, we must all do our bit, but it's all a different story when it comes to the laundry.

'I've had a look at Leigh Drive and the shop. They are still standing.'

*

He tucked each letter in his wallet behind the photograph and then when a new one arrived put the old one in an Oxo tin inside his locker. Things must be kept. On still nights you could hear the noise of anti-aircraft fire. He wrote: 'Take care.' But he didn't add—perhaps that was only for the heroes, writing from the field of action—'I love you.'

Should they rent out the shop, he wrote (for she wouldn't run it herself—she'd made that quite clear). Someone might take it. Perhaps Smithy knew of someone. It was only gathering dust there, wasn't it, with its shelves cleared and its windows shuttered up? Besides there was the question of income. You got two shillings a day as a soldier. But she wrote—it was if he'd slighted her—No, that wouldn't be a good plan at all. So that he found himself asking—guessing how many years the war would last—How much money did she really have?

He picked up the grey-green helmets for the Quartermaster and stacked them in piles like dishes.

And yet she'd been to the shop; she wrote so. She'd been to Smithy opposite to thank him for his help and sending on the mail. So she must have gone over to look inside the shop.

*

Yes; though he would never learn (she had paused over her letter wondering how much to mention) how she'd stood alone by the empty counter—Father was waiting, drumming his fingers, at the office and at any moment the sirens might go—how she had run her hand over the rows of empty jars and the bare shelves and sniffed the air. It smelt of coconut.

'3,640 helmets.'

'Back to Aylesbury, for the weekend, with Father—and it looks as though I shan't be returning to London with him. Mother says I shouldn't vex him. He has responsibilities and misses Jack and Paul. For the business, I wonder, or because they'll soon be fighting for their country? Mother waits for letters from them. She prays. I have actually seen her, with her hands clasped in the bedroom. And Jack and Paul haven't even left England. I don't give her your news and she doesn't ask for it. I haven't told you, but Mother had three brothers in the army in the last war and they were all killed. I think that's why Jack and Paul volunteered for the Navy.'

The trucks with the canvas tops lumbered in past the guard house, wheeled round and stopped beside the gravel, and then the new conscripts got out. Some of them tried to vault over the tail-board and sometimes they fell.

He wrote: 'I never knew about your uncles.'

'Letter from Paul. Mother glows. He and Jack are still at Portsmouth though they leave soon for the Mediterranean. Father up for the weekend again. He says to me, "I'm proud of those boys." I think he might have meant this as a dig at you, because he made some sort of apology afterwards. But don't you mind him. Be a good soldier.'

The blond-haired recruit made a soft thrust at Rees, which, perhaps unintendedly, flipped his glasses into his plate. 'You'll need them,' the recruit said, pointing, 'so you can see to frig yourself in the stores.' Rees clenched his fork and held it vertically against the table. 'Bugger off,' he said. 'Willy, tell them to bugger off.' The sergeant entered with two corporals and the men in the mess hall stood up. Rees had a splash of gravy on his cheek and was without his glasses. He was slow to find his feet. 'Getting jealous of the new boys again, Rees?' said the sergeant, stepping close. The blond lad smirked. 'Don't you laugh, sonny,' the sergeant snapped, 'you'll be stopping bullets soon.'

*

'We are planting the vegetables for this winter. Four rows of cabbages and four of sprouts. One of the laundries has been bombed. No casualties, just machinery. Considering there are three all within five miles of the docks this was likely to have happened sooner or later. But Father's mad. It'll mean re-organising and he'll have to send some things at the shops back to customers. I don't want to be roped in. I'm thinking of getting a job here. They want women as insurance collectors. Mother, Father and Aunt Mad disapprove, naturally, but I say to Father, "One must do one's bit".'

Rees, in the top bunk, leaned over to watch him fold up the notepaper. 'Missis?' he asked, knowing the answer, then slumped back, putting his nose to his magazine. He read endless magazines, propped on his elbow, turning the centre-page spread—'This Month's Babe-in-Arms', a girl in stockings and a tin helmet—through every angle. What did he do (he never said), this man who'd expressed one moment of awe at History and then slumped back to spend the war issuing kit and reading magazines?

And on the bunk below he read the letters, looking for signs—'With Love, with All my Love.' And he wondered should he write 'I love you' (for perhaps in this time of war—); though he knew, if he did, it would alarm her, more than war, more than bombs and blackness.

No, she would say, that wouldn't be a good plan.

He wrote, '5,520 helmets,' meaning, 'I love you.'

Up above, the white curves in the sky had grown more complex, then dwindled. On the grass behind the barrack huts some conscripts, off duty, stripped to the waist, played football.

'It seems as if your leave will coincide with Jack and Paul's. They will be here briefly before they go to the Clyde. Have asthma.'

9

She sat opposite the window in the shadows of the living room, and Mr Harrison, in the garden, peering in and holding a camera, was saying, first sternly then beseechingly, 'Come out, Irene. Come out. Don't you want to be in it?'

She held a hand to her throat and shook her head.

She'd met him at the station. Her eyes had been watery and her speech quick and breathy. And there was that other look about her, of someone sent on errands they resent.

'Won't you come out? Don't you want to be in it?'

Up on the lawn, where the October sun fell over the house, in front of the rockery, the Michaelmas daisies and the apple trees, they were taking photographs. Figures grouped, regrouped; fussed and posed, as if it were a function or prize-giving, and they were not dressed for war, those brothers in their dark naval uniforms, but for some 'special occasion'. Mr Harrison bore the camera like a master of ceremonies. Jack and Paul, with caps on, with caps off and held proudly over the breast, jutting their chins and giving self-conscious grins, so that the moment might be captured, manhood vindicated. This deserves a picture, this is something to be kept. And someone leafing through the pages, the school photos, the holiday snaps, would say, '—and there, at Aunt Mad's in their uniforms: what fine boys.'

Click went the camera. The figures broke up, brushed lapels, recomposed. Jack alone; Paul alone. The two with Mrs Harrison, with Mr Harrison, with Aunt Mad, with Mr and Mrs Harrison together.

But the one they most wanted, the one they most needed to complete the picture, sat in the living room and wouldn't take part.

'Come out, Irene, come on out.'

'The sun will go in.'

As they left the station for the taxi someone eyed his uniform and his limp. Perhaps they were thinking, 'Dunkirk?' Her face looked excited, but it was only the illness. In the taxi he said, 'What can be done?' 'I have some new pills.

They help. But there's no cure really. It's not like that.' And, taking his hand, she said, 'Look,' and pointed out of the window to an orchard where a man on a ladder was picking apples.

He sat in the deck chair near the back porch, holding Aunt Madeleine's ginger cat, glad to be out of his uniform. They didn't want him in their photographs. He could sit in peace. The garden looked neat, the far end dug for vegetables. Mr Harrison stood close to the window. The lines in his face were reflected in the glass.

'Come out.'

'It'll bring it on again,' she said, her voice muffled, from within.

Though they both knew, it wasn't the asthma.

'Just for a moment. That surely won't do any harm.'

Mr Harrison moved aside from the window. His hair was combed and smoothed down for the photographs but his face, unseen by the rest of the family, seemed crumpled, and it glared momentarily at him in his deck chair, accusing. 'Won't she come out?'

The cat purred in his hands.

Up the garden the brothers conferred, shifted legs and lit each other's cigarettes, like guests when there has been a hitch in the programme which someone else must correct.

But they looked uneasy, as if deprived of something they'd bargained for.

'The sun will go in.'

At the end of the table Mr Harrison spoke about Churchill, about invasion, about the weakness of the French, while Aunt Madeleine, holding a cake-slice, served up 'Patriot Pie', an economy recipe from a magazine. Mrs Harrison sat with her fingers on her necklace. Each time Mr Harrison declaimed upon a subject he turned to him and said, 'What do you think?' Then, 'Well, Jack and Paul should be here tomorrow,' and 'I dare say you envy them.'

'Irene!' Mr Harrison suddenly barked aloud, turning to the window, as if giving an order. Then he said in the voice of someone at a public meeting, 'Don't let your brothers down!'

His cheeks quivered. The camera he held in his hand might have been a weapon, a missile he would have hurled through the window. Up the garden the figures stiffened, rallying. What was happening? They wanted her to come out but their gaze seemed to shut her in.

'Irene!'

Mr Harrison turned, accusing once more, the camera in his hand. 'What's the matter with her? You should know.'

He seemed to be really craving for information. 'You don't help much, do you?'—looking with contempt at the cat.

He leant forward in his chair. He would have said, putting down the cat: 'Now just a minute, Mr Harrison.' But he saw her eyes, through the window, bright and precarious in the gloom, suddenly fix and hold his, sending little threads between them, taut with warning: Don't fall. Don't fall.

No, he wouldn't enter this particular action.

'She isn't well, Mr Harrison, you know that.'

The older man stood before him, flexing his shoulders, like a man waiting for his opponent to make the first move so as to crush him blamelessly. He drew breath. Sweat oozed in the crevices of his face, strands of hair fell over his forehead. The war wouldn't be for him, as it would for many, a temporary curtain lowered over the past. It would be dropped for him for ever.

'Damn you,' he said softly.

Paul and Jack raised their cigarettes. Mrs Harrison strode towards the house. 'If she won't come out,' said Aunt Madeleine, taking off her wide straw hat, 'then that's the last of the photographs.'

The sun went in. A breeze fanned out over the garden, ruffling the Michaelmas daisies, flipping the black tie from Paul's jacket, shaking the trees beyond the patch which Mrs

Harrison and Aunt Mad, soiling their hands, had diligently dug. For an instant they all stood awkwardly, looking in different directions, actors waiting for a prompt.

'Irene—' began Mrs Harrison, approaching the window. But she paused. For there she was, emerging from the side of the house, tucking a handkerchief in her sleeve, and coming up to place one hand behind him on the frame of the deckchair.

'All right. Where do you want me?'

'You can't blame the French,' he'd said, meeting Mr Harrison's armed scrutiny, but first swallowing his mouthful of Aunt Mad's uninspiring pie. 'After all, they've been invaded many times before.' He remembered his history lessons.

Click. The shutter flicked, drawing its curtain over the past. Paul and Jack, with Irene between. The fair flanked by the strong. Click. 'Smile, Irene.' But she didn't smile. She had come out. She stood where they told her to stand. She took her place in the picture, but she didn't smile. She breathed heavily.

'Just one, please.' Mr Harrison was no longer angry. He was apologetic. Standing looking down at the viewfinder, his head bent, he had an air of penitence.

'Ready?' The brothers leaned in towards the sister. The developed photograph would show her like some captive between two vigilant sentinels.

'Just once for your brothers.'

She looked towards the camera, and beyond it, past Mr Harrison's shoulder, to where he sat in his deckchair. 'You see, you see what I am doing.' Her eyes spoke as she looked at him. She steadied her face like a performer. And she smiled.

Click.

Mr Harrison raised his head with a gesture of relief. As if he'd been forgiven.

'There.'

The shadow of the house had edged up the lawn. Someone suggested tea but Aunt Madeleine thought the sun might go in.

'How many left?' said Mrs Harrison.

'Another two.'

'One of us all,' said Aunt Mad putting her straw hat back on her head.

'Yes, yes.'

'William will take it.'

They all looked at him as if they'd forgotten he was there.

'Would you mind, old chap?' said Mr Harrison. He was buoyant again, once more the master of ceremonies.

'No.' He got up, putting down the cat. Mr Harrison eyed his limp which was always more noticeable after he raised himself from sitting.

'Know how to work it?'

Apples had fallen from the tree and were lying at the edge of the lawn. 'You shouldn't waste those,' Irene said as they drank beer before lunch. Over by the rockery the bottles and glasses were still on the tray on the lawn and wasps were licking them. 'Not with a war. You must keep them.' 'What war?' Jack said, grinning, lying back on the grass, raising his beer glass so as to catch the sunlight in it. But Mrs Harrison looked away, at the fallen apples.

The figures grouped, composed. Mr Harrison wanted to stand between Irene and the brothers with Aunt Madeleine next to Irene and Mrs Harrison beside Jack and Paul. Irene blew into her handkerchief and sat down on the low wall next to the rockery. She watched the wasps at the beer bottles. 'Come on,' said Mr Harrison, afraid perhaps she might succumb to asthma before the picture could be taken. He linked his arm in hers and raised her, as if shouldering a shield. It didn't matter; it didn't matter she was ill, that he was forcing her, that the laundry had been bombed and under the composure there was discomposure. So long as the picture was good, so long as the moment was vindicated.

Already, perhaps, he was preparing his memorial.

'Have you got us?'

'You'll have to move further in.'

The figures shuffled. Mr Harrison, erect and pleased, casting a marshal's eye down the line to his left, the brothers jutting their chins. Irene looked wedged in the centre.

'All right? Got us?'

In the little glass viewfinder they looked as anonymous as the ranks of conscripts drawn up on the gravel.

'Yes, that's better. Don't move.'

'Wait for it,' said Mr Harrison.

'Dohn anticipate the ordaah!' said the sergeant.

'Now.'

The shutter flicked.

Up in the bedroom Aunt Madeleine had prepared for them she was kept awake by asthma. This was the night of his arrival, but they didn't make love. He felt as if he still wore his army boots. Between Aunt Mad's sheets he lay, his body sprawled, dispossessed, like a toy. As if it made no difference whether one touched skins or exchanged letters.

'What's the matter with your father?'

'I think he wants to be forgiven.'

Her body might dissolve if he touched her.

'Forgiven? What for?'

'That's hard to say.'

The figures broke up. Irene stepped back and supported herself with one arm against the wall. 'I'm going in,' she said and coughed. 'There's one more,' said Mr Harrison; but he turned and extended an arm to his daughter. It seemed to convey at one and the same time, 'I'm sorry' and 'Why must you spoil things?' 'I'm going in,' she repeated hoarsely but firmly, disengaging herself.

Perhaps it was time he acted.

He walked towards her, holding the camera. As he approached, Mr Harrison wheeled round and stepped between them, as though to say, 'She's mine, she's ours.' Mrs Harrison glanced towards her husband but didn't move from where she stood with her sons. The black peaks of their caps flashed in the sun. He shouldered the camera on its strap and made to take Irene back into the house. Mr Harrison stepped closer and changed his manner. He became solicitous. 'Yes, Irene, you're not well.' He gripped her arm. 'You should go in and rest, shouldn't you?' 'I'll manage,' Irene said, wrenching free her arm. Her father stepped back unbalanced, and glanced round, appealing, to his family. They looked on as if they were watching a competition.

Mr Harrison turned to face him again; he might have been about to raise a fist. But *her* face was there too, commanding, assuring: Don't move, keep still. So he said only, in a low voice, 'What is it, Mr Harrison?'

'There's another picture to take,' Aunt Madeleine said. As if that might bring order, another pose, another grouping, over the threatened strife.

'One more of Jack and Paul,' said Aunt Mad. Then Mrs Harrison said, 'Yes.'

Mr Harrison looked at the two figures in uniform. He seemed to recall something. He pulled the white cuffs of his shirt down over his wrists.

'In with you then,' he said to Irene. 'Give me the camera.'

'Let Willy take it as he's got it,' Irene said. She walked into the house. The figures in the garden drew themselves up, collected themselves, as if it were better perhaps, simpler, without her. But they all looked diminished.

'What war?' Jack said, raising his beer glass, and Mrs Harrison looked away. She could never have had Irene's looks. But there, as she turned, he saw the resemblance. The slender neck, the head just balanced on it. Then Mr

Harrison said, looking at his wife, 'Photographs! We must take photographs.'

She was behind him, behind the window. He felt her eyes on his back. And he was looking, in the viewfinder, at Jack and Paul in front of the apple tree. They were ready now. As they'd started to pose, Paul's cap had caught in a branch of the apple tree and fallen off. Jack had laughed and, as Paul bent to pick it up, made to kick it from his hands. Paul snatched the cap and feinted at Jack. It seemed a tussle might follow. They both laughed. The commotion sent two pigeons, pecking unnoticed up the garden, clattering into the air—which caused Aunt Mad to chase after them up the path. 'Shoo! Go on! You mustn't eat the vegetables, there's a war on!' The brothers laughed. But Mrs Harrison and Mr Harrison didn't laugh.

And now they'd recovered. Paul had replaced his cap and their faces contrived to erase mirth. As if they remembered the gravity of their situation; or recalled who it was who eyed them through the camera—their brother-in-law, the storekeeper.

'All right?'

They straightened their backs. The sun fell on the apple tree. Jack looked at him as though he wished to stare aloofly through him, but only succeeded in looking narrowly at him. Paul blinked. The moment captured: gallant figures locked in the viewfinder.

Why did he wince holding the camera?

'All right. Now!'

10

'Move along, look sharp.' Along the counter they shuffled—you didn't remember faces, only lists, numbers—past Rees who checked them, yawning, licking the tip of his pencil, out through the door to where they filled their kit bags on the grass worn threadbare now by the trampling of boots.

Helmet, pack, ammunition pouches. Move along. Where to, where to? Where did they go, those carefully listed items? To Maktila, to Mersa Matruh? You read the names in the headlines—gains, losses, landmarks of war that loomed and receded into the sanctified distance in which perhaps flags bearing the same names would hang in cathedral aisles. Private Rees checked the list and, supine on his bunk, read magazines; and he put the letters (fresh envelopes were becoming scarce) one by one into the tin in the locker. Tobruk, Gazala. 'Don't forget,' said the sergeant, 'what you have don't belong to you.'

She went back to London. The bombs ceased to fall, after nine months, and she was released (that was how she put it) from Aunt Madeleine's and the family.

'The asthma is improving. I am going to get a job at the Food Office. They'll make it compulsory for women to work soon. Father says in that case I could assist at the laundry, but I absolutely refuse.'

So she wrote, in her forthright way. But he wondered, what did she do all alone in that blacked-out house? Unless that was what she wanted—to sit still, alone.

On Aunt Madeleine's mat the letters arrived, from Alexandria, long after the deeds of which they spoke. They had seen action, those brothers, the real thing at last, in the sunlit waters round Crete.

'Don't get down,' Rees said, 'that's a long face you've got.' But Rees's own face was hardly bright, propped on his arms on the back of a chair in the NAAFI, pinched round a cigarette, while the endless commands—'By the right!' 'Presehnt!'—drifted in from the parade ground.

'Going to that dance Saturday?'

He patted his leg. 'You should know I don't dance.'

'41, '42, '43. How monotonously, how anonymously those years passed whose events would fill the chronicles. Like the lorries, passing in and out by the guard house, loaded with pale faces. Like the trains which bore him up to London to see her (how many times did he make that journey?), click-clacking over the points, slowly over the sections of bomb-damaged embankment, past the stations whose signboards had been removed to confuse a non-appearing enemy, so that you sometimes forgot where you were. And yet the places hadn't changed. Basingstoke, Farnborough, Woking. The same line had borne them, in '37, to the white cliffs and the seagulls. And out there, beyond the window (if you could see for the bodies, kit bags and cases that crammed the corridor), the same countryside, green, threaded with streams, peaceful under the evening sunshine. 'What war? What war?' said the steam chunting from the engine. Nothing was changed. Save that the drinkers, there outside the pub, were uniformed and were perhaps drowning the thought of comrades killed over Germany; and that gap in the hedgerow which might perhaps have been for a gate or a hayrick was where the Dornier had crashed and the children from the village had scrambled, before the wreckage was cleared, seeking trophies and the smell of an enemy's burnt flesh. So that it was not the same as it seemed, and he found himself, as the train window eclipsed scene after scene, count-ing—counting, as he counted helmets and nameless stations—captured moments, pictures over which curtains had dropped, shutters flicked, counting, where to, where to, till he slept, and someone said, awakening him (had nothing changed?), 'Waterloo,' and they slid into the grey platforms, under the iron girders named after a victory.

'What do I do?' she said (for she'd welcomed him, given him that quick kiss and that touch of the arm that was never really an embrace, and now she was telling him about the job she'd got at the Food Office). 'Count ration books, coupons.'

'Exciting,' he said flatly. He was tired. His head still ached from sleeping in that crowded train.

'There's a war. Who wants excitement?' She was bringing in the things from the kitchen for supper. Her body in the doorway was brisk and slender. But he didn't appreciate her joke. He wanted to say: 'I want excitement.'

She wore an old, out-of-date dress he'd never seen. He was an imitation of a soldier on leave.

'And when all this—excitement—is over,' he said

bleakly, looking to the window where the blackout curtain was now fixed permanently and you could sense the dust gathering behind it, only to be revealed when the war ended, 'what's left then?'

She didn't acknowledge his irony.

'Then? Peace.'

'Peace?'

He watched her laying the table, taking care over the placing of the knives and forks, the mats, the water tumblers, even for this frugal war-time meal. What peace? To Mr Harrison and his two gallant sons peace meant beating the Germans. To old Jones, to Mother, to Father, it meant the grave. But he didn't know what it meant to her or him. Save perhaps a kind of not acting.

What peace? he would have said, but her face, turning, as if at a signal, checked him.

'There. Now I'll dish up.'

Heroes come home from the fighting; they meet wives, lovers. He sat restlessly on the sofa.

'While I'm doing that,' she added, taking a little packet from the sideboard, 'look at these.'

They were copies of the photographs taken at Aunt Madeleine's. He sat at the table and looked at them uneagerly, placing them back in a pile. The one of all the Harrisons in a row was on the top, and as she re-entered bearing the dinner plates she eyed it over his shoulder and said with a little twist in her voice: 'Skittles.'

She continued, the meal finished, her chin resting on her knuckles, on the same meagre theme.

'They will ration sweets sooner or later. You hear things at the Food Office. It's already bad enough with the sugar shortage. It would have been hard work if we'd kept the shop open. They say it's tough for the housewife; it's tougher still for the shopkeeper.'

He nodded, glassy-eyed. The room was bare—with the blank curtaining and the things removed for safety. It seemed to get barer as the war progressed.

Her breasts had grown smaller. Was that the war too?

'Other things will be rationed,' she went on. 'But the war won't last for ever. Three, four more years.' She seemed to regard that prospect with complete equanimity. 'We'll win, yes—but of course at a cost. There'll be rationing long after the war, higher prices. But don't you worry, we'll manage with that shop.'

She spoke as if she'd already arranged for what she said to happen. He couldn't connect her voice with her face. He wanted to say, 'Let's talk about something else. Let's go to bed.' But he said:

'How much money will we have?'

'Money?'

She looked relieved, as if this were the sort of question she could readily cope with.

'Money?' She glanced away as if she didn't have to speak. Her mouth was sly and shrewd. Between them was the photo; the Harrison family all in a row. And he half realised—so that he would ask later, How could she have known? And she saw that he realized and looked quickly, testingly at him, as though to say: 'Be calm, the responsibility is mine.'

'You're tired.' She leant towards him, taking his plate to put on top of hers. 'Let's go to bed.' And then she added, as a kind of condition: 'Tomorrow, go and look over the shop.'

Left, right. The patterns shifted, the figures grouped, regrouped over the gravel. '42, '43, '44: while the headlines spoke (what was the connection?) of faraway action. Messina, Salerno, Monte Cassino. 'Lord grant us victory,' said the round-voiced chaplain as the recruits stood, lined up for prayers, bare-headed, looking at their feet. Corporal Rees (for they'd made him and Rees corporals now) wiped his glasses, replaced them and hummed monotonously through his nose 'Amapola', 'Don't Get Around Much Any More'. The quartermaster yawned. The sergeant prowled from the guard-room to the stores, from the stores to the mess. He was getting fat. His belly bulged over his belt, his neck over his collar. They wanted to know how he did it, with a war on. But he still barked at the conscripts, like an overweight, distempered watchdog.

12,840 helmets, 25,700 packs. When she wrote now from London she added at the foot of her letters numbers of her own. 4,000, 5,000 ration books. Was it the same code? '43, '44. History was drawing up its inventory. And out there, beyond the wire fencing, beyond the outspread downs, overseas, actions were being fought which would claim a special place in that inventory. Could you believe it? It was the same placid scene—chalk downs, May trees, dappled English fields—over which the bombers flew, yet it was not the same; like the ravaged, bomb-scarred streets of London—the same London yet not the same. What was the connection? What war? What action?

Yet here, in April '44, was proof at last of action, here was official evidence.

He held in his hands a simple letter. He held it before him looking at it as if it were a code.

'Dear Willy, Mother and Father have had a telegram from the Admiralty. Jack's ship was sunk on the homeward convoy. There were no survivors.'

*

Click. What you have doesn't belong to you.

'Hey, what's up?' said Rees.

Why did he weep? Why did he put his head in his hands and feel tears smear his palms, coming back in the car from St Stephen's church? Ahead of them (he could see if he looked through his fingers) drove Mr and Mrs Harrison in the black, shining Humber. Why had he trembled as they stood lined in the pew? Mr Harrison had shed no tears. His face was grey and dumb and held in suspense as if he couldn't make some connection. Even the memorial tablet—a plain slab with black lettering which they'd hurriedly had made—seemed to confound him. No flags, no marble muskets, no white tomb where the knight might lie, pure in his armour, his sword blessed and at rest. Twice he leant on Irene's arm during the service, while she looked before her, her features demure yet griefless, like some pale heroine's; and Mrs Harrison, on the other side, coughed and muttered once, 'Poor Paul.'

Why did he weep? Why did he sob into his hands? And why did she look at him as she took off her black hat, her black gloves, eyeing him warily, circumspectly, as if there were something she hadn't done for him?

11

'Where's that child?' demanded Mrs Cooper, looking at the clock and then at Mr Chapman, though he didn't return her urgency.

It was half-past ten. She always called Sandra, the girl Mr Chapman had taken on since the start of his heart trouble, 'that child'; out of contempt for her seventeen years, her free looks, the way she flaunted her little body, even to customers in the shop, and out of a sneaking suspicion, perhaps, that Mr Chapman had hired her for just those things. Where was she? She was supposed to start at nine. Out all night, no doubt, with one of her hot-fingered boy-friends. Always late the next morning as if to advertise it. Up in the cinema carpark, in a back seat, long after the performance had finished, or in that place—now the weather was hot—near the sports ground, by the old allotments, where the orchard had been before the war. You could hear the couples, they said, in the grass, behind the fence, if you walked late along that footpath. Yes, she knew what Sandra Pearce got up to. Coming in the next day, bold as brass, two hours late, and just daring you to say: 'And where have you been?'

She rubbed her nose and straightened a crooked stack of magazines. She glanced at Mr Chapman, pressing her point, but he merely shrugged. He wasn't bothered, oh no. He should have sacked the girl weeks ago. No wonder he couldn't manage his own daughter.

She huffed. That child. But she remembered—taking out some new *Reveilles* from below the counter and counting them—how he had touched her, Terry Cooper, in the dark, that night. It was in the air-raid shelter. First on the arm and then on the knee. Bombs were falling outside, slithering through the sky like tiles; and a man was touching her in the dark. Mum and Grandpa feet away. His fingers were inside her blouse. That was action, that was excitement; something was happening in her life. And later he had married her, fathered two louts on her, then upped and gone. And now, the years had passed—she lifted the magazines onto the counter—and she didn't want action any more, only peace.

12

Irene wrote: 'Dear Willy, Father went again to the doctor's today. Mother made him. His heart's no better. He's been told to stop work completely and rest, but of course he won't. The laundry is losing money. I think he believes nothing will be salvaged out of it after the war unless he stays on personally. He talks of "saving the business". Then again, he says it isn't the money—"Money won't bring Jack back". It's a matter of principle. I don't know what he means by principle. I've never known him distinguish principle from money before. Anyway, he won't stop work. He upsets Mother. He wants to make her responsible for everything. And he makes demands of me, wants me by him. Well he's ill, it's not like earlier in the war. I try to be patient. But I won't have any part in the laundry—that's his affair. I'll stick to the Food Office. He's not going to be penniless anyway, even if the business folds. And most of that money was never his in the first place. Perhaps this is the time to tell you. It came from Mother, and she would never have had it herself if it wasn't for her three brothers being killed. That's how the laundry was started. It can't have all gone. You don't make money in a war, but there's not so much to spend it on either. I know for a fact he put a large sum into Government stock when the war started, in order to do his bit, and he swears he'll never touch it again now Jack's dead. Perhaps that's "principle". Well, we'll see. It's hard to know what his reasons are, the way he behaves. You should have seen him shout at Mother for insisting he went to the doctor's, and later, apparently, he had a long row with the doctor himself. Then afterwards he says to me, "I'm not ill, am I, Reny, my heart's all right, isn't it?"—as if he'd quite believe me if I agreed. I try to put up with him. He swears there's nothing wrong with him, he won't give up the laundry. And all the time he gets more fanatical about the war. We must win soon, he says. Jack's killed, we must win and wipe all the Germans off the map.'

18,000 ration books.

The roads up over the downs were thick with traffic. Lorries, tanks, bulldozers. Troops were being moved to sealed-off training areas. Outside the American camps

MPs in white helmets drove up and down in jeeps blowing whistles and waving arms at the convoys of Shermans. The skies buzzed. Something was happening.

Then, one day in June, it was still.

13

What was that? Had he slept? He woke up. Only the rain falling, heavy and thunderous, on the window ledges, gurgling in the gutters, pattering on the flowers, on the lilac bush in the back garden. Nothing had changed. Light spreading behind the pale green curtains—the blackout curtains had been lifted in April; and on the dressing table the things she'd packed away at the beginning of the war—the Derby figurines, the silver hand-mirror—all replaced unharmed. See, we endure.

Only rain. 'Go back to sleep,' she whispered. Her hair was matted over her forehead. And then he remembered what day it was, the day allotted for victory, and that he ought to be glad (though something stopped him rejoicing) to be there to share it with her.

Victory, victory. The word was uttered and re-uttered on the wireless—how slow they were to make the final announcement—until it sounded brittle and dry: Victory. Yet, outside, rain was falling, drenching the spring leaves. Already flags had been hung from windows, and in the streets on the far side of the common bunting was stretched from rooftop to rooftop, bonfires stood prepared. Would they burn with all this rain? And he too had hung a Union Jack over the front porch (it would be sodden now, wet and drooping), for one must do one's bit; and she had watched him from the front path—momentarily alarmed when he leant too far from the upstairs window—arms folded, unsmiling.

'Go back to sleep,' she said, as if he'd woken in needless agitation. But he wanted to lie and listen to the rain hissing and sluicing beyond the window.

Soon history would be honoured. With cheers, with hymns, with jubilation. Yet how still it seemed. As the day broke, the rain eased, sparrows started under the guttering . . .

He had got a special leave, on compassionate grounds. Her telegram had arrived at the camp: 'Father very ill. Please come.' And so he'd journeyed up to London, on the eve of victory.

'There's hope,' said the sister with a practised smile, 'he's a strong man.' But how weak he looked, lying in the ward (there were no more private beds) among flying-bomb victims in the last stages of recovery or decline—jaw dropped, lips blue, the expression, as at Jack's memorial service, frozen, utterly taken aback. As if there were some trick; this couldn't happen like this. Mrs Harrison sat on his left, Irene on his right. Other patients were listening to wirelesses and he wanted to know—it was the one thing for which he still seemed to rally—'Is there any news? Have we won?' He might have been asking the result of a race. 'No, not yet'—it was Irene who spoke—'soon.'

White sheets, white rows of beds; the white apron of a nurse saying, 'I think it better if you went now.' May 8th, 1945. An orderly was mopping the floor. She walked down the corridor, leading her mother, her lips pressed tight.

There was a fancy-dress parade on the common, planned for after Churchill's speech. Little children dressed in costumes made from cardboard and old blackout material would be exhibited as 'Freedom' and 'Hope and Glory'. Then the parties would follow (already they were queueing in the High Street for food and beer): bonfires, dancing. 'Let's go,' he said. They sat in the garden listening to the exultant wirelesses; the sun shone after the rain. But she looked up: 'What about Father?' 'The hospital said there's no change. And Aunt Madeleine's with Mother.' But he knew that her question was only a kind of excuse.

Sparks flew upwards into the blue evening sky. Along the house-fronts coloured lights were arranged in Vs, candles in jam jars perched on front walls. They were spilling in and out of the Prince William, singing 'Shine on, Victory Moon'. Pianos in the street; kisses for anyone in uniform; children banging dustbin lids; and out on the flattened ground of a bomb site, tables set up, drinks, tinned meat sandwiches, a Victory Pudding (bread, milk and saccharine—the feast of victors) and the bonfire ('bomb-fire' the children insisted), sparks flying upwards, upwards. Speech! Speech! Someone wanted to make a speech. A stout patriarch whose sons even then, perhaps, were encamped beyond the Rhine, stood up, swayed, but only got as far as 'Three cheers for Victory!' Victory! Victory! echoed the cry. But no one used the other word that had hissed gently in the falling rain: Peace.

Figures danced, silhouetted by flame. Composing, recomposing, round and round the fire. Yes, better dance, better rejoice. The war is won: that is something to rejoice over. But he had a lame leg (No, no, not a wound, he explained) and that was his excuse, and hers, for not dancing.

More fuel for the fire: don't let it die. More fuel to make the sparks leap and the dancers whirl. Bring anything. Those old duck-boards from the shelter, those old out-of-date coupons, those letters stamped with the military franking from Cairo and Rome. Burn it all. Burn away the memories of five years, the 'sacrifice' and 'endeavour', the headlines, the photographs, the odour of barrack huts, the names of foreign battlefields, the 39,000 helmets, the 81,000 packs. But it wouldn't burn. For, look, behind the flames, objects immune to fire, heroes of bronze and stone, too rigid and fixed ever to dance, and black names on marble, gold names on bronze, 'undying memory', 'their name liveth'; and one of the names under the chestnut trees by the railings, on the white school memorial, where boys born after the war would be herded on Remembrance Day, was Harrison. No, it doesn't burn, it doesn't perish. Undying memories.

'Irene!'

Who was that? It was Hancock. Stepping out of the shadows, in an Air Force uniform, with a beaker of beer in his hand, and a darkish, slightly curled moustache, grown since the war had started, to give the impression he was a pilot, not a ground officer.

'Well I never. Come for the fun? Hello, Willy old man.'

'Hello, Frank.'

'Hello, helloh. Wangled some leave too?'

He rocked to and fro. Only his feet seemed to hold him to the ground, as if they were clamped with weights. One hand held his beer and the other was extended, palm forward, behind Irene's back.

'Fancy—' He stood, open-mouthed, for a moment, as though embarrassed for something to say. 'Well—there goes the war.' He looked at the fire. He raised his beaker and brought his mouth to it by leaning his whole body.

'Look—' Irene said. She shifted forward.

'Soon be out of this, eh, Willy?' Hancock tugged at his uniform. 'Back to the shop?' He winked, bobbed his head sideways, then stood, swaying, looking at the fire. Burning planks shifted in the blaze. He looked like a man in a train corridor watching scenes go by. 'There it goes, there it goes. All over. Forgive and forget, eh?' When the train lurched his hand touched Irene's waist.

'Willy, let's go.'

Dancers jostled by so they were hemmed in.

'Hey, come on, Irene!'

Hancock spread his arms and went springy like a tennis player.

'Give us a dance.' He held out a hand. 'Don't mind, do you, old man? Don't dance—with that leg of yours—do you?'

Irene stepped back. For a moment Hancock waltzed gaily with the air.

'You've got a nerve,' Irene said.

'Come on now, don't be like that.'

'You've had too much of that beer.'

Hancock looked at him. Strands of his moustache were wet and frothy. Irene seemed to look at something between them. She bit her lip. He didn't understand any of this. They were standing in a row with people dancing round them, as in some game.

'What's the matter with you two?' Hancock said. 'The bloody war's over you know.'

Better rejoice.

He said to Hancock: 'It's Irene's father, he's—'

'No, that's all right, Willy.' Why was she scared?

'One dance.'

Hancock looked spruce and forlorn in his uniform. He swung on his feet. Irene stood still. Her face was lit up like a statue's. The piano played 'Yours'.

'All right,' Hancock said. He shrugged ruefully, then looked swiftly at him as if he'd proved a point. Over the rooftops searchlights were projecting great swaying Vs. 'Just as you like.'

He finished the rest of his beer.

'Be seeing you then.'

He made off through the swirl of dancers, palms extended, smiling now and then at other couples, his tall, agile body moving to the music, seeming to melt into the scene.

'Let's go, Willy.'

*

Across the common, figures were flitting in and out of the light of yet more fires. The searchlights weaved in the sky like diagrams. Why did they walk that way? Past the paddling pool, the children's playground—the slide and swings had been salvaged in '41, but it was the same playground—and up, not by the quickest route but by the path by the allotments, by the houses facing the sports ground. Because they'd walked that way before? When he worked at Ellis's, in those lunchtimes, when it was all yet to come. The same but not the same. There was an orchard of apple trees adjoining the back gardens. She had said once: 'Did you know, that belongs to one of Father's friends?' But the fence was broken now, the rows of trees had not been pruned since the beginning of the war.

Victory, victory. But not for her. Along the path by the privet hedges and blossoming trees her face had tensed, as if to a vigil still to be maintained. Hancock? Was it Hancock? With his false fighter pilot's moustache. 'Watch him,' old Jones had said. But when he asked, 'What was all that about?' she only said, 'That nonsense? Some day I'll tell you.'

Later, up in the bedroom, she said suddenly, spreading her legs: 'All right.'

Victory. But not for Mr Harrison, sinking slowly, surely in his coma, till he died in the small hours the following morning. 'Peacefully,' said the hospital. 'Peace', said the gravestone in St Stephen's churchyard. That was Irene's word: Peace. And had he found it, old Harrison, while his daughter stood, on the eve of victory, by his deathbed? For he'd leave the house to Mrs Harrison (she wouldn't want it—a month after the funeral she'd go to live with Aunt Mad) and the flagging laundry to Paul (far away, in the Far East, where victory was yet to come); but the money, most of the money would be hers.

The searchlight Vs waved over the apple boughs. And what was that, from behind the fence? Voices in the grass.

TWO

14

As the clock showed half-past ten she opened the shop door. She stood for a moment in her white T-shirt, with buttons at the front, and blue skirt that barely hid her bottom, flipping back her brown hair, glancing at them with that look that said (in answer to everything): 'So what?'

Well now we would see, thought Mrs Cooper, looking along the counter, whether he'd give her what she deserved or not.

Though she knew, of course, he wouldn't. He indulged her, this brazen little seventeen-year-old. Pretended not to notice her idleness and impudence; treated her cheek almost with kindness, while her own long devotion he met merely with civility. 'Thank you, Mrs Cooper. That's kind, Mrs Cooper.' 'Mrs Cooper' indeed! And he'd called that child 'Sandra' after only a week.

She watched him. He was counting out change but he had one eye on the girl.

'Sorry I'm late.' The girl grinned, unapologetically, and spoke in that slack, rubbery way which seemed to go with the chewing gum she continually worked and tugged around her mouth, making little sticky noises. 'Got held up.'

She lifted the flap in the counter and passed through the gap, holding her stomach in and making small, sideways movements with her feet—an unnecessary performance, only designed to demonstrate her slimness.

'You'll get held up one of these days,' Mrs Cooper said.

'Yeh?'

Then she went into the stock room, slipping off her shoulder bag, to fetch her shop coat. Which she hardly needed, of course. Hers was pink, in contrast to Mrs Cooper's dark blue. When she'd first got it she'd taken it home and raised the hem six inches. And once—it was a hot day, three weeks ago, just like today—she'd stripped to her underwear to wear only the shop coat on top. Mrs Cooper had gone into the stock room and there she was in her knickers. It might have been Mr Chapman who'd walked in.

Held up indeed.

And still he said nothing. Soft as they come. Only now,

with the girl out of sight, pretending to busy himself at the counter, did he say, in the most unsevere way: 'You're getting held up rather too often, Sandra.' Mrs Cooper caught his eye, pursing her lips. Sack the girl, tell her to beat it. But he looked back with that dim, imperturbable gaze. What was up with him today? She blinked. It ought to be easy to tell a man like him what to do. But it wasn't.

Sandra emerged from the stock room fastening the buttons of her shop coat.

'Morning, Mrs Cooper.' She overcame a yawn.

Mrs Cooper stiffened (Mr Chapman, looking on, anticipated the reply):

'I suppose it *is* still morning.'

The girl hoisted herself onto a stool. She crossed her legs, baring her thighs, and slouched carelessly forward. One shoe dangled under the counter from the tip of her toe. It was a slack mid-morning period, which extenuated her lateness. She leant against the counter, unconcerned with explanations, resting on her elbow and propping her chin on her red fingernails.

'Well don't just sit there,' Mrs Cooper said. 'Tidy up those shelves.'

'Get out some new birthday cards, Sandra, would you, and put them on the racks.' Mr Chapman spoke at last.

'Yeh.'

The girl got up slowly.

Yes, without her own little prompts, Mrs Cooper thought, he wouldn't get her to do anything. Let her lollop like that all day next to him. You could tell why, too. You could tell why he never sent her packing like he should, never had a harsh word. At his age. And with a heart condition. Mrs Cooper's thoughts grew wild and tried to check themselves, as they always did when she was forced to consider Mr Chapman capable of lust. She straightened her shop coat and turned to a customer.

'Would that be tipped or plain, sir?'

The girl moved across the shop to a low, deep drawer beneath the racks of birthday cards and began rummaging unsuccessfully. Mr Chapman got up to join her.

Well, wouldn't you know it?

But she didn't have to pit herself against that girl's foolishness. When had she ever been late for Mr Chapman, or needed to be shown where things were? And yet—she saw how when Sandra leant she leant towards Mr Chapman, and when she lolled on the counter she lolled towards Mr Chapman. And she saw how Sandra had seen (it hadn't taken her long, for all her being a slip of seventeen) that she, Mrs Cooper, had leanings of her own (though they were leanings of a different kind, sixteen years had gone into them) towards Mr Chapman. All of which led her to little panics and to the need to hoist on her armour and trim her nails to the fight. Little bitch. What a struggle it all was. And she knew she couldn't win; she had no answer to that girl's 'So what?' But you had to soldier on, if you wanted your reward.

'Matches, sir? Change a five-pound note? No trouble.'

That voice spoilt it of course.

'This one 'ere, Mr C.?'

There it went, like a rusty hinge.

'No, the other box, at the back.'

Mr Chapman bent down and reached inside the drawer. His face was plum-coloured. Sandra sat back on her heels. The box was jammed so Mr Chapman had to bend closer. Sandra held out two slender, dithering arms, one with a blue plastic bracelet round the wrist, as though to grasp Mr Chapman.

She watched them, feeling spurned. Suddenly, the box came out. Mr Chapman straightened, rose, then abruptly reached to grasp the display rack, breathing hard. Ah there! She swelled again with a sense of her own significance. The poor man. What he needed was looking after.

'All right, Mr Chapman? Look what you've done, you stupid girl! Making him bend down like that!'

She opened the flap in the counter to step forward. 'All right?'

He recovered.

'Yes, yes, all right.'

But his voice didn't seem grateful for her concern. For he bent down again—the obstinate fool—towards Sandra, who said, ''Ere, you wanna watch it.' And, just for a moment, he put his hand, for support, on the girl's shoulder. So even there, where she had the advantage, she couldn't win. She shut the flap. Couldn't he just have another little spasm, so she could take charge quite firmly; make him sit down, fetch him some tea, tell that girl to clear off out of it; take one of his pills from the bottle and scold him with her eyes: See, that's what you get, not being your age. It was a nurse he needed, not some bit of fluff who showed her legs. But she felt herself grasping the counter as if it were really she who needed support.

Sixteen years.

Light flooded in at the window. Over the road the sun had begun to touch, on the corner site, Powell's trestles of tomatoes and watercress; but it would be several hours before its rays probed the Diana café or lit the 'For Sale' notices in Hancock, Joyce and Jones. In the Prince William they would be laying out beer mats, placing ashtrays, cutting the cheese and ham sandwiches. Before opening the door, at eleven, with a cool gust of beer.

He breathed, rather hard, and looked, with just a hint of

anxiety, at Mrs Cooper. That was what she expected. 'How about more tea, Mrs Cooper? I'll take one of my pills.' You had to humour the woman. Loyalty replaced the reproachfulness in her eyes, and she disappeared obediently through the plastic strips.

He returned to his stool at the counter and watched the girl, standing in the sunlight from the window, arrange the cards. Did she tempt and console, as Mrs Cooper imagined? Did her little provocations work on him? No. So why had he hired her?—it was after Dorry had come that last time. As a sort of cheap replacement? But there was no comparison. Dorry, at seventeen, had not known what to do with her beauty—she'd buried herself in books, as though to disown it. This girl traded so much on her attractions (no, you couldn't call them beauty) that they sometimes seemed to him not to belong to her at all. So perhaps it amounted to the same?

He watched the girl finish her task, run her hands over her hips and, now that Mrs Cooper was out of sight, turn to him with a pleased, half conspiratorial smile.

The kettle whistled in the stock room. Sandra returned to the counter. He motioned quickly to her. 'Here, before you have your tea,' (and before Mrs Cooper could see). His hand moved, holding the ring of keys from his pocket, to the drawer under the till.

He took the brown envelope with Sandra's pay and handed it to her.

'Expect you're waiting for this.'

The girl's face came close to his. Her sticky, spearmint-scented mouth moved up and down.

'Going dancing tonight, Sandra?' he asked. (For Sandra had told him once, she went dancing every Friday night, at a disco called Vibes. It was an excitement that had become a routine.)

'P'raps.' She gave a little frown. 'What about it?'

He had taken out the second envelope.

'Here—don't ask any questions. Buy yourself a new dress.'

He indicated the edges of five five-pound notes protruding from the envelope. She widened her eyes, stopped, for once, her endless chewing. Then actually blushed. As if Mr Chapman really did have some old man's fancy for her.

'Oo—'ere—ta, Mr Chapman. But—?'

But his face showed nothing. He looked at her coolly (Sandra thought he had never looked so distant).

'There. A dress, mind you. Nothing else. Don't ask any questions.'

Mrs Cooper appeared with two mugs. The light reflected crisply off her glasses. She passed the girl as if she wasn't there and gave him one of the mugs. 'There. And here's your pills. Now you take it easy awhile. Don't argue.' She put her own mug on the counter. Then she turned to Sandra, with another flash of her spectacles, taking in her slim picture of health. 'Yours is in there,' she said. And added with venom, 'I've sugared it!'

15

'It will keep,' she said. 'It must keep.'

And so it had. Though along the High Street there were the little pits in walls where the fragments had struck, and here and there a window missing, and in Briar Street, not far from the infants' school, sudden gaps of flattened rubble; so that you seemed to walk (but perhaps you always had) through a world in which holes might open, surfaces prove unsolid—like the paving stones over which the children picked their way, returning to re-opened classrooms, dodging the fatal cracks. Yet it had kept. Intact. He had only to remove the boarding from the windows, retouch the paintwork, clear away the dust, and then—that was the most difficult part in that time of scarcity—refill the shelves with stock. And yet *she* knew all about that (it was almost as if she'd planned it), having worked all those months in the Food Office.

It must keep. Though things were scarce. Fewer coupons for clothes; units for bread; and those who said the ration books would go after a year or two were wrong. Prices rose. Half a crown for the cigarettes that in '39 cost a shilling. And trailing round the streets of London in grey demob suits, trailing with them, like their former kit bags, the bundled stock of what they called their 'experiences', were thousands, looking for jobs and homes. There was much trading in 'experiences' but very little in homes. Little to buy, little to spend. And yet they'd said, Victory was ours, ours the reward, and some had spoken cheerily of the Fruits of Peace. And now they'd invented a new term to cloak the facts with an air of virtue: Austerity. But at least those children there, treading gingerly over the paving stones, were assured of schooling, and of milk and orange juice. They were all numbered in a new system so they shouldn't want. Smithy, who was childless, said that was a good thing. And you could count your blessings, with the news the servicemen brought home on Christmas leave from Germany: 'They're starving over there.'

He took down the 'Closed' notice, which five years had faded, from the door; sent off his forms to the Ministry and renewed his tobacco licence. Old Smithy, crossing the road, his barber's jacket frayed and stained (you needed coupons for new ones), greeted his return. 'So, come to mind your own store.' There was a fondness in his eyes. His red-and-white barber's pole twisted upward again, like a twirl of seaside rock. And, see, along the damaged High Street they were returning again, like birds to their roosts, resuming their old ploys as if history could be circumvented and the war (what war?) veiled by the allurements of their windows: the thin assistant in Simpson's replacing the tall flasks of coloured water high on their shelf; Hancock, in his office, scratching with a pencil that fraudulent moustache; and Powell—but they whispered, respectfully, about Powell. There were burn marks all down his back and his left arm—which is why he wore that grey, greasy cardigan and had acquired an ogreish expression. Yet he put out the vivid fruit, such as you could get then, doggedly enough.

Someone had to mind the store. Thrift was what victory cast up, after the cheering ebbed. And he saw what things would be needed, in this time of peace and parsimony. Sweets, cigarettes. Useless things.

Half-forgotten customers from before the war would shut the noise of the street behind them and linger, pick up old threads. The stories would be told—the bombs, the deeds of neighbours, the good or ill luck of husbands and sons—moments captured, sifted out of the actual long privations which did not seem to have ended with the war—stories which grew more unreal, more pensive, the nearer the teller got to the end of them, till he or she would stop, slip onto the counter the coupons and ask, as six years before, for a quarter of mints, a bag of rum and butters. 'And you, Mr Chapman? What about your experiences?'

Experiences? But he had no experiences. Only the 81,000 packs and the 39,000 helmets.

In the evenings they counted the fiddly sweet coupons, threading them on strings at the dining table. And, more than once, he was tempted to sweep aside the carefully collected squares, like some card game that has proved inane.

'We don't have to make money,' he said, losing count. 'We *have* money—now—don't we? So the shop—'

He eyed her over the green baize tablecloth.

'Exactly,' she said in a lucid tone. 'Exactly. Don't you see?'

She held her gaze on him. Her face, fretted already by her illnesses, was as frail as paper. It might crumble away completely.

And he knew: the shop was useless; its contents as flimsy as these interminable coupons they were counting. He was the shopkeeper.

The laughter leapt suddenly from her throat and skipped round the room. Then stopped, like something flung away and lost.

*

Would he hear her laugh again? Never so freely, or so wildly. But she didn't break her bargain. She finished work at the Food Office. She went out on little necessary errands with shopping bag and ration book, or on more secret, private excursions, to bankers, brokers, dealers—though never (what were the traps awaiting her there?) to the High Street. But mostly she lurked, like some shy animal hidden in undergrowth, at Leigh Drive. At night he parted the leaves. Her body glimmered, received but did not yield. In the morning it was only a bedroom with pale green curtains. And yet she was preparing something. Down at the shop where she wouldn't venture, he twisted up the little bags of sweets, rang the till, counted change, folded the newspapers (they spoke of the air lift to Berlin), and presented more expertly to his customers his shopkeeper's camouflage. They didn't realise (they only took their purchases and gave their money) how he'd perfected it; how it was only a disguise that faced them over the counter. Nor how she too sheltered behind that same disguise. For he saw how her preparations exposed her. She was less hidden, perhaps, by that undergrowth, than threatened by its rampancy, its sticky scents of growth; and only his own daily performance reassured her. He waited. In the evening he tended the garden while she watched from the window. Once, when he came home he found her

140

unpacking cases of china. Pastel bowls and vases with white scrolls and tendrils and scenes from mythology on the side. 'Wedgwood,' she explained, without saying where she'd bought them. 'Things like this will go up in value.' And after examining them she packed them away again. 'It wouldn't do to break them.'

He felt afraid when she said, 'I am going to have a child.' Her own voice trembled slightly, though her eyes were bright with the knowledge of a promise fulfilled. As if she had proved a point, and now could be left alone.

That was November, 1948. The blue-rimmed tea cups had rattled on the kitchen table, the kettle hissed. For it was at breakfast she announced the news. So as to give no time, perhaps, for excessive reactions. She eyed the clock. She even led him, in her usual way, into the hall, taking his hat from the peg, ignoring his protest that for such a reason the shop might open late. Those unvarying habits had already formed—the keys, the briefcase by the umbrella stand, the dark grey suit for working—and that day was no exception. 'Your hat, Willy.' Yet she let him kiss her and clasp her tight—was he afraid now she might slip away?—before she opened the front door.

A child. Something to rejoice over. Yet was it pure joy that made his steps seem light on that crisp November morning? Along Leigh Drive, down Brooke Close, over the common, past the swings and the paddling pool with its flotsam of dead leaves. As if the world slid heedlessly under his feet rather than submitted to his tread.

Smithy would be the first to know. Smithy who had neither wife nor child. When the barber came in for his tobacco, he said, tilting his head confidentially: 'I am going to be a father.' Solemn, monumental words which didn't hide the quiver in his voice. Smithy's doughy face had creased. 'Boy or girl?' And he said—only realising then he'd never assumed it would be otherwise—'Girl.'

November 10th, 1948. There was a red poppy in Smithy's barber's jacket and red poppies on the lapels of customers. Hancock would be wearing his Air Force tie and would comb with extra care his tawny moustache. And round the white memorial by the school railings, solemn, pink faces would reverently assemble. He bought a poppy from the seller outside the post office, but kept it in his pocket. Better rejoice. While there is time. Real flowers, not paper poppies. Red roses which he bought at the florist's and carried home as a token.

But she didn't seem glad. Her face showed only the pinched looks of someone labouring to pay a debt. So that he felt, through that lean winter of '48, while her womb swelled, that he'd inflicted some penalty upon her for which he, in turn, must make amends by never showing gladness; taking her hint, leaving the house at six, standing obediently behind his counter: counting, counting the endless change so as to pay his own debt.

She took the roses and placed them, meticulously, in a vase, kissing him coolly on the forehead.

Yet her womb did swell. He put his hand on it and felt it, alive, inside. How palpable, how undeniable. But none of his pride suffused her. As if she were saying, as he laid his podgy, shop-stained fingers on her bigness, 'Enough, don't touch, don't touch any more.' 'I can manage,' she insisted, forcing a grin, as he rushed, playing to perfection his own part of anxious father-to-be, to take the shopping bag, the coal scuttle; 'I'm not an invalid.' But she carried around that weight inside her like something crippling, longing for but dreading the moment of release. March, April, May 1949. Visits to the doctor. With every month she seemed more the victim. So that when the moment came, precipitately—pink on the sheets, and him sitting on the edge of the bed, summoning the nerve to call a car—not even the words which he was forbidden to speak, which broke the terms of the bargain, could stop that drowning expression or the silent cry on her lips—Save me, save me.

'I love you—keep still—I love you.'

*

143

It was her he looked at first; her and not the baby. Though he knew, as he stood there holding the flowers, that that little thing in a shawl in what looked like a wicker basket on a trolley beside the bed was their child. But he barely took in the fact, to look first at her. Expecting, perhaps, to see her changed, irrecoverable—or else restored completely. For this surely would be the moment: her or the child. But she was neither lost nor, it seemed, redeemed. She lay sleepily in the bed. Her face was soft, tired, but the lips firm. And there was that look, as she became aware of his presence: See, I have done it. See, I am a woman after all. That is my side of the bargain.

How warm it was. But should that window be open? A bee had flown in and was buzzing and tapping on the glass. With all those babies. Had nobody noticed? Sunlight was streaming in between the half-drawn curtains. There were pools of it on the parquet floor and on the white sheets of unoccupied beds. And, in between, wobbling with little unseen movements, these wicker baskets, like the fruits of some bizarre shopping trip.

'The flowers. Give the flowers to the nurse.'

He stooped to kiss her but her eyes directed him to the baby. Before his lips could touch hers she had turned herself to where the rim of the wicker basket lay level with the bed, moved her mouth into a smile—it seemed she'd rehearsed with care that melting, motherly expression—and blown a kiss towards the little head in the shawl.

'There. Look.' She sank back.

A squashed-up, wrinkled face. Strands of dark, wet-looking hair. A mouth and tiny hands that seemed to protest feebly at some unpardonable imposition. But the eyes, when they opened, clear, grey-blue, were *her* eyes.

How simple to be the delirious father. To tickle the little body through the shawl, to chortle unlearnt baby-talk: 'Hello. Goo, goo. Yes, yes.' He didn't look up at her—hadn't her eyes said 'The baby, not me'—but he was aware of her, as she watched his antics, settling more firmly on the pillow, relieved, perhaps, by his simple glee, his compliancy, so that she could turn at last, having acquitted herself, to her old pose. She gripped the bedclothes. Was she counting the violations of that pose? June, 1949, in a delivery ward. June, '37, in a honeymoon hotel. Captured moments. And did she know to what she turned, there, in the hospital bed, steeling herself to the way the world looked from in there? Yes, I have made my forfeit, paid my price. But I will take the responsibility. And you will see, you will see it is for the best in the end.

Dorothy, you thought she didn't have a heart. You never loved her. You merely suffered each other. And you thought

I was her slave; she made a fool of me. But you never saw that look she gave me. How could you? And you never knew how I understood, then, how much she'd done for me. You were a little pink thing in a shawl. I was clicking my tongue at you and making absurd faces, and the nurse was smiling by the window, holding the flowers. There was a board clipped to your basket and a piece of paper with entries which read: Mother's Name, Sex, Weight at Birth. Five pounds, twelve ounces. Premature; but numbered, listed. When you grew up you wouldn't go without milk and orange juice. The sun was shining outside on sycamore trees and railings, and a bee was buzzing at a window. You couldn't have seen how she lay on that bed looking through both you and me as though she could see further than the two of us. But you will see.

They let me pick you up in your shawl. See, you can touch, take hold, after all. But the nurse looked mindful. 'Your wife should rest now.'

Four days later they let you both come home. And that same month her asthma began again.

16

Sandra counted out change and shut the till.

'Thirty, forty, fifty—one pound.'

It was approaching lunchtime and customers were multiplying. Outside, the shadows were heavy. Car-drivers leant against open windows in the slowly moving traffic. The pedestrians walking the hot pavement, jackets slung over shoulders, looked parched, in search of relief.

What absurdity. This endless succession of customers each after his little titbit. Papers, chocolates, cigarettes. You could remember faces by the things they bought. He was Gold Leaf; he was *Hi-Fi News*; she was Brazil Nut. Mr Chapman was better at it than she, but then he had had more practice.

'Two, three, four and one makes five pounds.'

What fools! Sometimes she felt like denying them what they asked and making them beg. Every day at the same time the same faces. And every day the same cravings. Morning papers, evening papers, early, late editions, weeklies, cigarettes, chocolates.

Sandra chewed gum and tapped her red nails against the side of the till. If it was Sunday she could be at the open-air swimming pool. The Lido. In her new orange bikini.

Sunbathing and being ogled, on the tickly grass. Or at the coast with Dave Mitchell. Dave had a car, and he'd promised. But then—she let out an audible sigh which made Mrs Cooper, along the counter, turn her head—Dave didn't have much else in his favour apart from his car. It would all lead up to the necessary routine of parking out of sight by some field on the way home. Service rendered; reward given. Things were all rather predictable with Dave Mitchell. Besides—the sea. All those rusty railings and pebbles.

She was bored. She'd give anything for something new. She'd go to the disco tonight, as she went every Friday, with Judy Bates and Linda Steele, looking for something new. But you could predict it all. Someone would start pawing her. Yes, because (unlike Judy Bates and Linda Steele) she had something to offer. And she'd calculate in return *his* assets and give, or not give (though, usually, she gave), the appropriate favour. But all this had become a kind of business. All predictable; nothing new. She'd try anything (even tempting an old man like Mr Chapman). But it seemed she'd already tried everything. Begun early. Behind the fence, near the allotments, at fifteen. Walking home with the blood between her legs.

She looked along the counter and caught Mrs Cooper's sour gaze. Now *there* was something predictable. Still fuming with jealousy because Mr Chapman hadn't been angry, had spoken softly when she was late, then helped her with the birthday cards. Mrs Cooper's little game was obvious. 'Yes, Mr Chapman, let me, Mr Chapman, I'll do it.' But Mr Chapman wasn't interested. That was hardly surprising, was it? One day she'd have it out with that old bag. She'd say: 'You'll never have him!' That would provide some excitement.

She served a man with cigarettes, who called her 'darling' and eyed her unbuttoned T-shirt as she leant forward with the change.

How hot it was getting! Across the road, up the street, they were sitting outside the Prince William, on the little wall by the pavement, glasses of beer in their hands, shirts off. The little half naked plastic dolls which hung in the Briar Street window looked as if they'd stripped for the heat. If only Mr Chapman would let her do the ice cream. That was the best job in the hot weather. Lifting the black lid and putting your arm down into the cold, vapoury box. And you served mostly kids. Kids were best. They never seemed absurd, like these men and their eternal cigarettes.

But Mr Chapman was at the fridge. Relishing it. A small girl had come in asking for two cones, and she watched him plant the wafer cups in his left hand, push up the sleeve from his right, plunge down the metal scoop and with a stylish gesture top each cone and present them to the girl. The girl held out her money, smiling. Mr Chapman didn't smile. He seldom did. Not actually. And yet somehow you felt he did. That's why she liked him. He wasn't obvious. How she'd hated at first that changeless expression, that everlasting blue or dark grey suit, and how important it had become suddenly for her to change it, challenge it. Why not? An old man—it was something different. But he hadn't reacted, no. He'd noticed, but his face had remained unmoved. She'd gone on trying to ruffle him; and it was only after a fortnight that she'd realised she did so because she wanted Mr Chapman to *like* her. She wanted to be liked by this unobvious, red-faced man of sixty.

And perhaps he did like her; for he'd given her, just now, twenty-five pounds, as a gift.

She watched him stooping, rearranging the contents of the fridge. His wife had died, not long before she'd started at the shop. What must she have been like?

'Here!' he suddenly said, producing two choc-ices from

the fridge, tossing one, without further warning, to her and making to toss the other, like a juggler, across the full length of the shop to Mrs Cooper. 'Cool off with these!'

'Oh no, Mr Chapman,' Mrs Cooper protested, staying the throw. 'Not while I'm busy at the counter.' And she looked with virtue at Mr Chapman, and with malice at Sandra.

Sandra returned the stare. She'd never have him. One day she'd tell her.

Mr Chapman leant back on his stool by the fridge so that he looked along the counter. His face was heavy and weary. He was watching her eat her ice cream. She bit off a mouthful. Twenty-five pounds, as a gift. Then he turned, suddenly, away. The thin coating of the choc-ice broke up beneath her fingers and slipped awkwardly. A piece fell on her skirt. She didn't enjoy it.

'Twenty Seniors, darling.'

She licked her fingers and dabbed at her skirt.

A new dress, he'd said. Yes, she'd buy a new dress. She knew the very one. Deep red, with a black pattern. She'd seen it in Slik Chiks. Yes, she'd go at lunchtime. It would suit her perfectly. Sexy, they'd say. She'd wear it to the disco tonight, get all the looks, and pretend all the time it was giving her pleasure.

She'd give anything for something new.

17

The stained-glass window in St Stephen's church was bright with afternoon light. John the Baptist, in brown furs, and Christ, by a blue river Jordan. It shed little quivering patches of colour on the stone floor and the backs of the pews.

'. . . except he be regenerate and born anew of water . . .'

He wore a pale grey suit with a white rose in the buttonhole, and beside him he heard, in the silences of the service, her long, husky breaths. How accustomed would he get to that labouring sound?

Mrs Harrison was not there. Too ill, she said, replying to their dutiful invitation, to make the journey. But Aunt Madeleine was there, in a brown hat with black sequins, a conciliatory ambassador visiting under truce. 'Will Paul be here?' she said inquisitively. 'I'd hoped Paul would be here.' But no one heard from Paul. He didn't write or phone. Aunt Madeleine said he was living in the North. Smithy stood beside Aunt Madeleine, in a sagging coat. For who else could he ask? Hancock? 'Good God, no,' she said, as they discussed arrangements. But it was difficult to deter him. 'Hear you're christening the little one,' he'd said, casting his quick eye round the shop. And how could one say, 'Don't come'? So Smithy was there—he gave little looks of concern for Irene's ragged breathing, and he was the one who opened doors for her, hastened to assist, as if the occasion were one of bereavement—and Hancock was there, sucking his teeth as the vicar spoke. Smithy brought his sister, Grace, thin, delicate and quiet; and Hancock brought—they'd never seen her before—the future Mrs Hancock.

'Irene, Willy, meet my fiancée Helen.'

He gave Irene a little quick glance.

She was young, that Helen. No more than twenty-two. And Hancock, then, was thirty-six. She had blonde hair, waved like Lana Turner's, and prominent breasts.

'Let us pray,' said the vicar.

Why St Stephen's? 'It's the local church,' she'd answered. 'But they'll never come,' (and he meant, without saying, the marble plaque which glimmered, even now, on the far wall, beyond the pulpit; that, and the grave outside). 'They'll never come there.' 'It's the best place—we will have it there.' As if there were some logic. 'We'd better put flowers on Father's grave.' 'No,' she said.

And so they stood, around the carved font, while the colours quivered on the floor, and the vicar spoke, who had spoken over Mr Harrison's coffin.

'I baptise thee in the name of the Father . . .'

(You didn't cry, Dorry, or flail your arms when I dipped you quickly in the water.)

'Congratulations, Mrs Chapman.' The vicar's large and black-haired hand was extended. 'And a very obliging little girl.' Smithy stepped forward from the church porch holding his hat in one hand and dabbled a plump finger, as in a bowl, over the face wrapped in its white wool, then kissed Irene warily on the cheek. Hancock edged in, stood for a moment looking squarely at Irene, not regarding the baby between them, then laughed suddenly as if at his own joke, bent down and kissed the child. That rough moustache against that soft cheek.

There had been rain, but the sun gleamed on the pavement and on the wet laurels in the churchyard. The gravel made sucking noises as they walked over it. Helen giggled, holding her hat, picking her way round the puddles. Little orange spots of mud flecked her stockings. The wind was fresh, through the thin laburnums, making the sunlight clean and chill.

New life. How the past shifted into the background that day, and how the present seemed sharp and clear. New life: held in my hands. 'Don't let her catch cold,' said Aunt Mad. But you were warm, warm to touch, and I held you close in your white shawl while Irene adjusted her hat and straightened the flower in her buttonhole. She held a hand over her eyes against the glare of the wet road and frowned. Then I gave you back to her. The car was waiting at the kerb, glistening with drops. We strode over the gravel. Helen was sitting already in Hancock's new Sunbeam, holding up the mirror of her powder compact to her face, while Hancock stood by the driver's door. The rest of us were passing through the gateway when he reached inside, produced a camera and said: 'Hold it there! Out you get, Helen.' And Helen got out, dabbing her cheeks. Later you saw the picture, in the old album: Uncle Smithy, Auntie Grace, Auntie Mad, Mrs Hancock (though she wasn't Mrs Hancock then), I, with my trousers flapping, and she holding you with that look (yes, you noticed it, sitting with the album on your knees) as if someone had passed you to her and she didn't know where to put you.

'Hold it,' said Hancock. He grinned as the camera clicked.

Sweet sherry, christening cake, tea in the best cups; little bridge rolls with spreads and sprigs of cress on white doilies on the cake stand ... 'Thank you so much, Mrs Chapman.'

Helen's glassy voice tinkled in the hallway by the barometer clock. 'Lovely party. And I'm so glad'—she paused, as if to lay some special emphasis—'to have had the chance to meet you.' There was a crumb of christening cake in the corner of her lips and her face was flushed from the sherry. 'Bye, Mr Chapman.' Hancock hovered in the doorway and, behind him, the other guests to whom he was offering lifts. 'Bye!' How grotesque they looked, bobbing on the door-step. How awkward Smithy seemed, in his best coat and his Homburg (he worked hard at his social graces), out of his crumpled barber's jacket. But *you* had no pretensions, you were wholly yourself, and you didn't struggle or cry (you'll never remember it) as they passed you round from one to the other, rocked you and dandled you. 'What a lovely thing,' said Helen longingly. 'Isn't she gorgeous?', turning to Hancock; while Auntie Mad cornered Smithy and whispered, 'Tell me, did you know William before he, er, met Irene?'; and Smithy's sister sipped her sherry deli-cately; and Helen, patting her hair, giving quick glances to Hancock, kept letting her eyes drift over the laden sideboard, the silver, the Derby and Worcester in the china cabinet: 'I'll come and see you, Mr Chapman—if I may—in your shop'; 'And tell me,' said Aunt Mad, 'what do you do?' 'Oh—modelling actually—er, photographic work. But I'll stop when me and Frank . . .'; and the cake was cut—white icing with pink scrolls—and handed round on the white and blue patterned plates; and Aunt Mad said to Hancock, 'Well, and how's business, Frank?': Hancock said, 'Can't go wrong, property market's got to expand': and Aunt Mad began again, 'Pity Paul isn't here'; and Smithy said, at last, helping me with some things to the kitchen, 'We'd best be off, old pal—Irene's looking, er, rather tired.' 'You look after that baby now.' He winked. Though it wasn't clear from his voice which baby he meant.

'What nonsense,' she said as the door shut. 'What a performance! Thank God they've gone.' Her breath heaved. 'Take the baby, will you?' She held her forehead as I took you from her. 'Can you put her to bed? I'm going to get one of my migraines.' And she sat in the chair by the French window, leaning forward, her head in her hands, breathing heavily, fingers tightening over her brow, but resolutely, uncomplainingly, as if she'd long been prepared to suffer like that.

It was only when I held you out so that she could say goodnight and as she lifted her face you started to cry, that she winced, as if it were you who made her feel her pains.

'Ssshh. Don't cry. Mummy's got a headache.'

I whisked you upstairs, soothed you ('There, be quiet for Mummy'), undressed you, bathed you, laid you in your cot, waited till your eyes closed, while she sat below.

When I came down her head was still in her hands.

'Is she asleep?'

'Yes.'

'Good.' She looked through her fingers. 'Now I'll go up and lie down.' She got up, gingerly, from the armchair. 'I'm sorry, Willy. You've been good. Thank you.' She put her hand on my shoulder. But it wasn't a leaning for support so much as a gesture of command.

'All right. I'll be up later.'

And still the things needed clearing from the table—the plates, the tea service, the glasses, the remnants of the christening cake, the damask tablecloth.

You thought I slaved for her, didn't you, Dorry, ran to her beck and call?

I carried the piled-up tray into the kitchen. Washed and dried. Brushed the crumbs from the chairs. Put away the silver. New life. Your eyes were hers (they all agreed) and the nose; only something in the mouth was mine. 'Dorothy': we called you 'Dorothy'. There it was in the church register, on the iced cake, on the silver napkin ring Aunt Madeleine gave you. But it was only years later that you yourself, coming home from school (how quick you were to learn things), explained what it meant. Dorothea: God's gift.

*

'Like it wrapped?' Mrs Cooper took down the large box of chocolates for the customer and busied herself (a speciality of hers) with the fancy string and the shiny paper.

'Present, is it, for someone?'

She looked aloofly at Sandra wiping ice cream off her skirt.

'50, '51, '52. How quickly the years pass when you watch the growth of your child. Fourteen years since I first opened the shop and fixed my name, hazardously, over the door; twelve years since the war closed it. Its place was established now. Grey-overcoated City workers on their way to the station spoke of 'popping into Chapman's', and no one remembered the name of the previous owner. And along the façade of the High Street it was other changes that bore witness to novelty. Across the road the ironmonger's had gone and the home decorators (Hobbes' Home Supplies) had moved in. Determined young couples, wheeling prams, would frequent it on Saturday mornings, earnestly choosing linoleum and paint and emerging with rolls of wallpaper (muted shades, tiny raised fleurs-de-lis on pale grounds and heavy braided strips for below the picture rail). Beyond the post office, the electrical shop was stocking televisions, heavy and wooden, ready to bring a Coronation into living rooms. The bomb site had been cleared in Briar Street; and behind the Prince William, where the brewers had sold the little walled beer garden, they were levelling the ground for a garage and a showroom. For petrol rationing had ended and the private car, they said, would boom.

A café had opened next to the baker's. It was the Tudor then—high-backed chairs, gingham tablecloths—and it would become the Calypso Espresso Bar before it became the simple Diana. And, two shops along, behind the wooden partitions of their office, sat Hancock and Joyce. The Sunbeam was parked outside, and now and then, in dry weather, Hancock would pull back the hood and drive up in the leather flying jacket he'd procured from his Air Force days. 'Well, didn't *you* nab anything,' he'd explain, 'working in the stores?' They'd tried to run that business, he and Joyce, with the panache of young bachelors, relying for dignity and esteem on the memory of old Jones. But now they'd have no need to prove their probity, for the houses would begin to be built (hadn't he said to Aunt Madeleine, munching his piece of christening cake, 'Can't lose, selling houses after a war'?); the market would revive, the little 'For Sale' notices would be exchanged ever more rapidly in the window. He was married too (we never went to the wedding because of Irene's asthma), with a house in Sydenham Hill. The blonde Helen would sit, while Hancock worked, in wifely ease, thumbing the fashion pages and the catalogues, listing the furniture, the carpets, the kitchen appliances she would need to have. Did she know how long all that would suffice her? '53, '54. See, the ration books are being withdrawn. Prices have risen, but we are free to spend. And Hancock, coming in with that quick glance round and that competitive twinkle in his eye, said, 'Not doing so badly yourself, are you? Shall we make it cigars?'

And what do you first remember, Dorry? When do the dates begin and the shapes first emerge? When did you first see—was it from the classroom at St Stephen's Primary where you learnt what your name meant, in Miss Hale's lesson or Miss Shepherd's—the patterns forming, beyond the window?

Was it the yellow wallpaper in the room where we put your cot, or the dappled curtains—leaves and flowers round which butterflies flew? Or the cot itself, the wooden bars, the blue rattle shaped like a rabbit and the floppy doll made of knitted wool? That room became your own bedroom, the bedroom of a young lady, a single bed with a white bedspread and shelves for your books—and it's still just as you left it. Was it those things, Dorry? Or was it the smell of soap and powder, the touch of the warm water in the little enamel bath? I always thought you would scream and struggle when I put you in. I'd dry you, dust you with talc and carry you in your flannel nightdress to your cot. The room would be warm from the electric fire. I'd say 'Sshh' and 'There, there', tucking you in; play with the woollen doll, which we called Winnie, making it dance on the rail of the cot, till your eyes began to close, and I'd kiss you and turn off the light. Do you remember that? Or was it rather the darkness: lying awake and feeling, too, as I shut the door, like an abandoned toy?

Irene would lie awake as well. Her health was weak even before you were old enough to know it. I wouldn't know which one of you to tend first. But she'd nod, beside me, towards the door, reach for the water and the pills and lie back as if she were glad there was a reason why I couldn't give her all my attention. Then I'd scuffle through to you, in my pyjamas and dressing gown, say 'Sshh' and 'It's all right now'; change your clothes. Do you remember those moments, Dorry, in the early hours? Sometimes I'd pick you up and walk you round the room. You were fascinated by the twirled red and blue tassels at the end of my dressing-gown cord. And sometimes I'd forget, and listen out, as I held you, for her breathing and wonder what she was thinking—whether, perhaps, that I'd forsaken her. I'd tiptoe back. How fragile her face was on the pillow.

You thought she made a slave of me.

But she was alone with you all day, with all the chores

to do. She used to push you in the pram down the hill to the shops in Common Road. Do you remember the ration book in her hand and the assistant licking her pencil, taking down the order? Flour, tea, sugar in blue bags. The shop girls fussed over you. When you were older they used to sit you on the counter and give you broken biscuits; though you didn't like that—you were afraid you'd be left in the shop—and once you screamed at the man, smiling, leaning over the bacon-slicer. But she wouldn't have left you. And that grim look in her face, as she wheeled you home; it wasn't what you think. It took all her breath, that push up the hill. And it would have been so much further to push, back from the High Street. I might have sat you on *my* counter, fetched you something from the sweet-rack, shown you off to my customers. But she never did come to the shop: my customers never saw my wife. They had to pump Mrs Cooper for gossip.

She used to buy you instructive toys—do you remember, the coloured bricks, the wooden jigsaw with the picture of farmyard animals?—to keep you occupied. She'd sit in her chair and watch you on the carpet. But you didn't know what to do. You took it all so seriously. You cried when the pieces wouldn't fit, and it became a kind of system, that playing; do it right and she'd kiss you, build the bricks and you'd get your reward. It wasn't her fault. It taxed her,

163

looking after you while she was ill. Don't you remember how relieved she was when I returned in the evenings? I'd walk up from the common with my briefcase and my coat over my arm and something, often, in crackly paper, in my pocket for you. You'd wait for me, your head in the corner of the bay window, pulling the curtain back. She used to come to the door holding you, as if to make sure I would take you from her. Didn't you see how relieved she was, slipping away into the kitchen, when I picked you up? And didn't you see how when I lifted you up in my arms and kissed you, she wouldn't kiss *me*?

Did you judge us, Dorry, even then? If the word love is never spoken, does it mean there isn't any love? If she never kissed me in front of you . . .

But she wasn't that kind of woman. You used to look at that firm, unyielding expression of hers and wonder why I plodded year after year for her at the shop—till you stopped wondering and began to despise me instead. But you never looked closely at that face, into those blue-grey eyes, because if you had you would have seen how much more she knew than you.

Was it her face then? Was that how you first discerned the patterns forming? Her face. Pale, and the smoothness being furrowed and the cheeks beginning to slacken. You had her looks. At the christening they saw that. 'She'll be beautiful too,' murmured Smithy, and Irene looked up. Only the mouth, they said, was like mine, a little loose, a little heavy, as if the things it said would bear a tone of resentment. Was that it? Did you feel that face read your own? And did you feel: whatever I do, she will have predicted it; whatever I do, it will not be my own?

How bright those eyes. And the hair, too, kept its lustre, even when her skin had faded. Your hair was black and glossy, but it never had the blaze of her deep chestnut. Yet you used to toss it from side to side in a way she never did, and you had that lightness and deftness of step as if you'd have liked to dance—if only someone had let you.

Was that how you first saw? Or was it the summer holidays (how quick those years); the long ride in the train, the sea rippling out to the Isle of Wight, the yachts, and the rusty, tarry smells of the pier? We took you up to Waterloo with our suitcases and bags, and little did you know how that journey of ours was already history. That railway line. New houses in Esher and Weybridge, new signs on the stations, and cars, Prefects and Zephyrs, passing down the roads where once the army transports had rumbled. The same and not the same. And that familiar Dorset scenery, green downs and bleached cliffs, unchanged. We might have gone elsewhere, to Wales, to Norfolk, but (since we had to go) she was against anywhere new. Nothing new. Yet (how could you defy her?) everything was eternally new; the old cry of the seagulls, the old tingle of the breeze, the old mystery of the rock-pools—how you loved to squat and explore those delicate little worlds.

Did you sense how she shrank from all that? And did you sense how that scene in which you stood for the first time had already been encountered before and its limits fixed? The sea air was good for her. She used to sit in the deck-chair outside the beach hut, and read the papers. Even on holiday she read the papers. And when she wasn't reading, or leaning back, her face turned from the sun, she'd watch you and me digging holes and making walls to stop the sea, in the same way as she watched you playing on the carpet. She wore a straw sun-hat and a wide, striped cotton frock, and only now and then would she be persuaded—she who should still have been glad to show herself—to change into her swimming costume and tread down to the water. When she did so (did you notice?) it was like a kind of concession: 'Yes, I allow you this—just so much.' And when you watched her closely there was that look of panic in her eyes. Slowly, hesitantly, the three of us—you in the middle—into the waves.

Other people noticed her, other people admired. Though she'd never known how to deal with their glances except by lowering her own eyes. Settling the sunglasses more firmly, pulling the paper more closely round her. People wondered at her, and wondered even more when they saw me beside her, with my lumpish looks, the beginning of a paunch and my limp. You wouldn't have known I was once a mile-runner. The sea air was good for her. She could sit and breathe freely on the beach. But she wouldn't come up, in the evening, for walks on the cliffs. Peveril Point and Durlston Head. Shimmer of the sea; crickets in the long grass; the lighthouse beacon blinking in the dusk. Memories stalked those paths. And she didn't come when I took you, in the bus, to Corfe. We clambered up the ruined castle, and had ice cream and lemonade. Years later you would have visited such a place with studious reverence; devoured the guidebooks; scoured the stones. Ancient monuments; churches; places of historical interest: your eyes hungry for knowledge. But your gaze hadn't acquired that seriousness then (or had it?). Running down the turf slopes, by the frozen tumbles of masonry. It rained. The bus back smelt of wet plastic macs. When we returned she was lying in the bedroom of our holiday flat and I couldn't tell whether she was glad or sorry we'd spent the day without her.

Those holidays. We rented a place where you could only glimpse the sea in the gaps between other houses. We could have afforded more but we'd become thrifty. Gulls perched on the chimney pots opposite. The rooms smelt of bared skin and calamine lotion, and there were old magazines and crime novels, bits of dried seaweed and a torn shrimp-net left by previous tenants. In the night we could hear each other's breathing. And what else, Dorry? You couldn't have told, could you, whether those gasps of hers were gasps of pain or joy? But you slept soundly then, full of air and exercise. Your little body was engrossed in its own adventurousness. You raced over the beach and you weren't afraid (it always surprised me) of the water. Later you became a good swimmer. School swimming galas: winner of the back-stroke, second in the diving. Life-saving. Why did you stop all that? You scurried bravely, as if you had a challenge to make, across the sand and you only checked yourself when you caught her eyes trained upon you. Was it then? When you walked along the top of the breakwater? There were breakwaters at intervals along the beach, high and barnacled, and the uprights of some were only a yard apart and perhaps only nine inches thick. You climbed up on one, where it was low in the sand, above the water-mark, and walked out, not on the horizontal planks, but on the narrow uprights, leaping from one to the next. You knew she was watching you. I saw your head set in defiance, and your legs tremble at the risk (how you needed to run risks) you were taking. But your light limbs carried you through, gingerly, on your toes like a ballerina, over the narrow posts. 'Dorothy!' she yelled, getting up from her chair, taking off her glasses. People looked. The uprights were seven or eight feet high out there and the sand beneath was wet and hard. 'She'll fall,' she said. But you didn't fall, or stop, and only swung yourself down, reluctantly, when the posts became too far apart to attempt. How fragile you seemed walking back across the sand. You saw that look in her eyes, afterwards, as if she wouldn't acknowledge your daring. And you saw that glance she gave me because I'd stood with my mouth open and done nothing myself (I knew you wouldn't fall) to rescue you.

How many years did we go to Dorset? '53, '54, '55. We had a holiday every year, though every year she'd say, putting her hand to her throat, 'Can we afford to leave the shop?' Afford? Later we ventured further afield: Lyme Regis, Padstow, Teignmouth. But we had the car then. The Morris Oxford. We bought it when you were seven or eight; and only for you; so that we could take you out for rides and educational visits. Sunday outings to the country (I did only the papers on Sundays then). Picnics by the Thames and on Box Hill, on which she would come as if under constraint, sitting in the car while we got out the basket and the blanket to spread on the grass. After a while she'd sometimes say, 'No, you go; I'll stay here, I don't mind.' You saw how it hurt me to leave her, how I worried about her all day, so that it was never exactly fun we had by ourselves. And then, one day, she ceased to come out at all; and you spent your weekends reading, timidly studying for exams, and I opened the shop all day Sundays. I only used the car to drive to work (I never did at first—I used to like that walk over the common—but it became hard, lugging my lame leg up the hill). Lyme Regis, Padstow, Teignmouth. They were the only holidays we had. And then you went—you must have been fourteen—on the school trip to Venice, and then again to Greece. History, art; guidebooks from St Mark's and the Parthenon. Neither she nor I had been abroad. Yet we paid for those trips for you. And then you holidayed by yourself (though she said you were too young), with school friends; coming back home and telling us nothing of what you'd done. But by that time she was turned fifty. How quickly. She had to visit the hospital, and the doctor said her heart, too, was weak. And I was fifty-one. And at fifteen there was already a gravity in your face.

Holidays. Holidays.

18

The telephone was ringing on the little shelf next to the doorway into the stock room. Above it, on the wall, was the list of vital telephone numbers (St Helen's Hospital had been crossed out, but it was still the same list) and next to it, fixed with Sellotape, the postcards from Mrs Cooper's more leisured friends. Torquay and San Remo, in predominant blue. 'I'll get it,' said Mrs Cooper, as he began to raise himself from his stool by the fridge. The sun had moved round so that the awning obscured it, but a shaft penetrated inwards from a corner of the window. It fell fully on her face at the phone; but her skin was pale and chill-looking. She stepped back, holding a hand over the mouthpiece, deliberately jostling Sandra at the paper counter—who, in Mrs Cooper's view, was not worthy enough to answer the phone.

'It's Pond Street, Mr Chapman. They say they don't have

the usual orders for Callard's and Fry's. Have you forgotten them' (she hesitated—Mr Chapman never forgot)—'or have you got them here?'

'No, that's fine, Mrs Cooper. I didn't make those orders.'

'Didn't—?' She looked momentarily flummoxed at this unprecedented lapse. 'Didn't— But what shall I—? Here, are you all right, Mr Chapman?'

He was looking straight at her, but as if he didn't see her. His fingers gripped the rim of the fridge.

'Tell them,' he said, as if forcing aside a distraction, 'I'll explain when I bring their money round. And tell them that might be a little later this afternoon.'

She paused, raised a puzzled eyebrow, but turned back to the phone. As she spoke she glanced at him, then at the blue postcards above the shelf.

'Please come in, Mrs Cooper.' He twisted the sign from 'Open' to 'Closed' and bolted the door on the inside, on a damp September evening in 1958. And there she was in a blue twin-set, putting a face to the letter she'd written, sitting behind the counter, brushing imaginary specks from her knee.

'I'm sorry it had to be this late, but I couldn't show you the ropes with customers coming in.'

'Oh, no trouble, Mr Chapman.'

Her hair was fair, still thick, and the beak-like nose and straining throat less prominent amid a general plumpness.

'Now let me show you what's what . . .'

And so he'd explained, extending an outspread hand to the four corners of the shop, with an air, perhaps, of proprietorial pride. For they'd swelled and multiplied, those items to which he gestured. The coloured wrappers had thickened and brightened, like synthetic fruit on the wooden shelves; the trellis-work of racks and cardboard displays flourished. A new till and scales stood on the counter. And, outside, bright new blue paint, a large new name-board and a clutter of signs, some of them lit at night, adhering to or projecting from the walls, made it seem that the treasures within had spilled out onto the pavement.

And yet it wasn't pride, now that he addressed his first ever employee, so much as an urge not to waver from the role expected of him, that made him sweep his hands so grandly.

She followed him, assessing him behind her smile.

'Up till now, Mrs Cooper, I've managed pretty well by myself. But it's my wife. Er, she's not well, she has to visit the hospital, and there may be times when I'll need to be able to leave the shop. This'll mean, of course, that now and then you'll be left in charge yourself.'

'Oh'—a warmer glint came into her eyes—'I'll manage. It's nothing serious, I hope?'

'Asthma. With complications.'

Her gaze drifted over the shelves and the counter with the new till. There were none of the gobbling vulture looks in that rounder profile, and yet there was something unnerving about her desire to please.

He showed her the stock room, his system of stock lists and how to use the till and scales.

She bent closer with little blinks and nods, as if being admitted to intimate secrets.

'Well, if you've nothing further to ask, perhaps I can give you a lift home. I expect you've a husband and family to look after.'

'Family yes, husband no. I've divorced my husband,' she said deliberately.

'Oh,' he said, withdrawing tactfully.

But she went on: 'Yes—some time ago now. I'm left with his kids of course. I call them "his" because I wouldn't own to them myself. Is that your car then?' She nodded towards the Morris, just visible from the Briar Street window.

She brushed more specks from her skirt and looked up, satisfied by the confusion in his face and the expression of sympathy, which she waved aside.

'Not to worry, Mr Chapman. I'll get by.'

She crossed her legs, sitting on the wooden stool. Her nylons made slithering noises.

In the car she motioned to him to pull up at the corner of a road in which lights were already lit in the tunnel-like entrances of a squat block of flats.

'Here'll do, Mr Chapman, thanks very much. I wouldn't take you out of your way. You go on to——?'

'Oh—Leigh Drive.'

'Leigh Drive. Oh yes, that's nice, up there. Well—' she said, struggling to get her knees, her handbag and a laden shopping basket from between the seat and the door frame, 'quarter to nine, Monday morning—I'll be there.' And so she was, on the dot, and always so, faithfully, tirelessly, for sixteen years—he never imagined she would become a permanent fixture—the fair hair growing crisp and grey, horn-rim glasses encircling the eyes, the neck growing gaunter, ever working and straining to lift the bony face, like some creature peering from its cage to see what it was missing.

She stooped at the car door as he leant over to pull it shut and gave a commiserating look: 'I do hope Mrs Chapman gets better, Mr Chapman.'

But Mrs Chapman didn't. No. How many times did he drive to Doctor Field's to collect the prescriptions for isoprenaline, and thence to Knight's or Simpson's to have them made up? There were laurel bushes and a rowan tree by the doctor's front path and when he entered the waiting room the faces looked up, some with recognition, from copies of *Punch* and *Life* that came from his shop. How many times to the allergist for injections? And how many times to the gloomy hallways of the Chest Department at St Helen's, to see Doctor Cunningham? The corridors smelt of carbolic and laundered sheets, and he sat in the outpatients' cafeteria, sipping tea and reading the sombre notices on the wall. 'Give Blood', 'Drink Milk'. She would come out through the swing doors, afterwards, to join him. How sure she looked, how undaunted, appearing behind the glass, not like a sick woman at all. Sitting down at the table, she'd shrug at the inquiring glance he gave her: 'Oh, nothing. They can do nothing—why don't they say so and be done with it?' And gulping the tea he brought her, she'd look at her watch and say, 'Well, let's be off—you better be back to work.' Yet once she said, coming out from her check-up—'He wants a word with you—in his office—I don't know why.'

And she looked at him sharply as he got up, as if he might betray her.

'These tablets and inhalers don't cure a thing—you realise that?'

Doctor Cunningham, tall, smooth-faced, strong-jawed, with the wholesome expression of a young, intelligent schoolmaster or games instructor, leant back, holding a fountain pen.

'They merely alleviate the attacks. I'm afraid we need to know more, Mr Chapman.'

'More?'

There were papers and files scattered over his desk, which he scanned as if about to make a friendly reprimand on a student's report.

'Your wife's condition seems to have worsened steadily since the birth of your daughter—that's to say in the past nine years.'

'Yes.'

'And before that, since, at least, the end of the war, little aggravation. Intermittent, comparatively mild attacks.'

He looked up quickly from his record sheets as if in need of corroboration.

'Yes.'

'And a history of migraine . . . Cast your mind back, Mr Chapman.' He suddenly put down his fountain pen and stroked his chin. 'Would you say there has been— with your wife that's to say—any pattern of emotional distress?'

'Pattern?' He stiffened, remembering her glance.

'Anything perhaps—please be frank—in your own relations with your wife?'

The office was warm, comfortable, with a maroon carpet and a gas fire surrounded by glossy brown tiles; but outside the view of the hospital—tall windows, fire escapes, the black pipes of a boiler house—lay flat and frozen in a dead November light as if projected on a screen.

The close-shaven face smiled sympathetically.

'For instance—do you know much about your wife before she met you? Does she ever speak of that period?'

Over the gas fire was a wooden mantelpiece, and on one corner, just above Doctor Cunningham's head, a silver cup on which he just made out the words '. . . Seven-a-Side Competition 195 . . .'

'No, not a lot.'

'You're sure of that?' The doctor raised his eyes a fraction and glanced at one of his buff files. Then he looked up again and half grinned, as if at his own formality.

'Don't think I'm grilling you, Mr Chapman. These questions do have a point.' He leant forward with his arms on the desk. 'You see, we know very little about asthma, but when there's no definite physical cause there's very often an emotional factor. Your wife's a remarkable woman, Mr Chapman: unusually calm, unusually patient as far as her physical symptoms go; unusually—if you'll forgive me—uncooperative when it comes to investigating a cure. That's why I ask you these questions. They're in your wife's best interest.'

He had picked up his fountain pen and held it horizontally between his hands.

He wanted to say: 'How do you know what is in Irene's best interest?'

'Do think over the things I've asked you, Mr Chapman. And do, please, talk it over with your wife. A lot might depend—I get this impression from her—on the sort of help you're able to give her.' He put down the fountain pen and one of the hands pulled back the cuff from the other to expose a wristwatch. 'Then perhaps we can have another little chat.' He got up. 'You know, there are times when your wife almost seems not to want to get better. We can't have that. I gather you and Doctor Field had some difficulty in persuading her to attend here. But unless we can be clearer about the cause, her condition's unlikely to get any easier.'

The smooth face eyed him as if it might be withholding some vital piece of information—or as if he were.

And had he persuaded her to attend so that other people would determine the pattern, decide her interests? So that she would be cured and possess the thing it already pleased her to renounce? Restored to him: the bargain broken?

And she had given him, in her place, Dorothy.

'Goodbye, Mr Chapman.'

A plume of steam released itself from the boiler house, like a white hole in the flat vista. Outside in the corridor a girl was being pushed along in a wheelchair while a nurse walked beside her reading a clipboard chart.

In the car, looking forward, her handbag on her knees, she said as they drove back:

'Don't talk to the doctor again, Willy.'

No, she did not get better. How many more visits to Doctor Cunningham? Though he never spoke again, true to her command, to that suave-voiced man with his files and sheets of notes. Nor was he asked. She made sure of that. 'They can do nothing, Willy.' Another drug, another test; and each time her looks affirmed in advance what would be the result: no change. In between her attacks her breath wheezed continuously, her voice fluttered and rattled. Bouts of bronchitis. A scarf round her neck even in warm weather. And that face slowly being worn away; the cheeks hollow and drained from sleeplessness, the mouth stretched from the effort of breathing. Only the eyes remained, ashy-blue and steady, as if they watched in some mirror the dismantling of her other features and approved the process. As if, if she could have done so, she would have torn off that thin mask of loveliness at the very beginning. For that was never the real thing.

The attacks were worse at night. They frightened him with their violence. Often they slept with the windows open and the pale green curtains drawn back, but there was never enough air in that room. Was it to be saved she gasped and clawed, or to be left alone? For sometimes she clutched with those flailing hands, sometimes fended. And it was never, it seemed, against the illness she struggled but against something else.

No change. Outside the hospital, through the cafeteria window, there were railings, notices, a row of plane trees, and the dark, glossy statue of some Victorian benefactor. Outpatients, with sticks and thick coats, trailed over the asphalt, and mushroom-coloured ambulances glided in and out of the entrance gates. Any pattern of emotional distress? There was a flower stall beyond the railings on the pavement, and as he drank his tea he watched the woman with a red headscarf and a faded apron pick the bunches of gold and bronze chrysanthemums, daffodils or irises and wrap them, with a twist, in the sheets of paper.

Should he have asked, pressed, more than he did? Gone unannounced, despite her strictures, to Doctor Cunningham? Or confronted Doctor Field, hammered, flailing, on the surgery door on one of those visits when all he did was take the prescription form from the green felt board; clutched the poor man by the collar: 'Doctor, save my wife! What is happening to my wife?' No: that would have alarmed her more than any illness. For didn't he know by now, didn't he understand, the terms of the agreement? He watched the flower lady, from the window, shaking out the wet stems, stripping the surplus leaves with a knife.

19

The new till thumped and rang on the counter, the change tinkled, and Mrs Cooper said, dropping in the coins, putting the pound notes under the clip, as if she herself were the cause of success, 'Busy day, Mr Chapman. How much today?'

Money. It was mounting in the little piles in the till, and on the shelves of the safe in the stock room where he locked it overnight. Twelve, thirteen pounds a day. Prices were up, but people were buying. Bigger orders, new lines; and already, so they said, his paper deliveries were exceeding Henderson's across the common. They smiled when they saw him come in, twice a week, to bank his cash. And at night, after checking the lights, the locks, the burglar alarm, he bore home in his briefcase the figures (Cash, Petty Cash, Shop Takings, Stock Book, Trading Account, Profit and Loss); neat, symmetrical columns, which now and then she would want to see. 'Good, Willy,' she'd approve. The maroon-covered books and the file of accounts would be open on the baize tablecloth. He was a slow calculator—hadn't he always been slow, brainless at school?—and Dorry, whose arithmetic, even then, was deft, might have helped him, sitting by his side, totting the figures. But Irene wouldn't have it. She would not let Dorry even glance at those books. So that when she crept in from her bedroom, where she did her homework, he would only say, with a joking sigh, 'Doing my homework too, Dorry.' But it wasn't a joke; it was more an apology. And he saw the look of criticism in her eyes.

'Good, Willy, good,' as he closed the books. 'Now you rest. I'll make a cup of tea.' And she would raise herself up, with an air of relief and fresh purpose, clatter in the kitchen, as if it were better than any medicine, better than any of Doctor Cunningham's treatments.

Across the road Powell, puffing a little, brought out his crates of oranges and lemons and stacked them on the trestles. Better produce, and more of it. Oranges from Morocco, lemons from Cyprus. Do you remember when you never saw a banana? Longer queues through his shop door. But still he put the best goods on the table outside, polishing the apples on his sleeve, arranging the tomatoes and creamy sticks of celery on the carpets of imitation grass. And still he wore the same grey cardigans over his scars. The home-decorating shop was thriving. In the Calypso coffee bar (for so it had become) surly youths with swept-back hair were sitting at the tables; Mrs Cooper frowned on them and their jukebox music, but the bluff proprietor, pumping the coffee machine, welcomed them paternally. The attendants in Armstrong's garage, in blue overalls with yellow collars, waltzed on the long arms of the petrol pumps. And in Hancock, Joyce and Jones, Hancock was congratulating himself on the surges in the property market. A slight taunt showed under the peppery moustache as he dropped in for his cigars or his evening paper, and said, watching him rattle the pennies in the till, 'Coming on, is it?'; and the same taunt would remain, just visible, as he added, 'Irene any better?' The Sunbeam exchanged for a Wolseley, and the raffishness of bachelordom for the suavities of success. Leather gloves and camel coats. Golf on Sundays with architects and property dealers. Dinner parties at which the lovely Mrs Hancock would shine as hostess. And everyone agreed (the guests would finger their glasses beside importunate or jealous wives) that Helen Hancock was the perfect foil to his success. Old 'Cock had picked a peach.

*

He fitted the bubblegum machine outside the shop: red, white and yellow balls of gum jostling inside the perspex cover with plastic rings and trinkets. And a cigarette vendor, next to the newspaper placards and the oblong board on the abutting wall in Briar Street on which, every week, a man would paste the coming programmes at the Odeon. John Mills and Kenneth More in cheerful re-enactments of the war. History enshrined in make-believe. Like the lurid stories in the boys' comics he sold in the shop: grim-jawed fighter pilots and ogreish Germans. What war? A packet of gum please, and another card in the series 'Great Battles of World War Two'.

He hung the advertisements and the illuminated signs from the facia. 'Craven A', 'Corona', 'Gold Flake', 'Players Please', 'Lyons Maid Sold Here'. Wired them up himself, and scanned the advertisers' catalogues for additions and replacements. New awnings, black and white striped, and neon lighting over the door. And the windows—the windows were his own special concern. He allowed Mrs Cooper to arrange the displays only under the strictest supervision, and most often it was he alone who at slack periods or after evening closing would snake and stalk through the precarious stands, as through tangled foliage, positioning the imitation sweets—plastic chocolates and wooden toffees—the cardboard cutouts, the silver and gold paper, and emerging afterwards on to the pavement to gauge the effect. People complimented him on his windows, their profusion, their colour. 'Highly commended' in the local trade gazette for window dressing. At dusk the corner of Briar Street scintillated like a fairground. And he was silently pleased at the effect of his labours—of something which promised real goods, real riches within, but was itself quite specious. So that he looked forward to those seasons when special occasions allowed him to heighten the trickery. Christmas, Easter. The allure of tinsel and fake snow in the window, the enticements of chocolate boxes and gift-pack cigars. Easter eggs. Fireworks. Useless things.

Fourteen, fifteen pounds a day. He folded the papers with a flick between his thumb and forefingers and cupped his palm for the coins. Up the road they came from the station, with their briefcases and raincoats and work-weary expressions; the same faces stopping by in the evening as stopped by in the morning. 'Evening, Mr Chapman', 'Okay, Mr Chapman?' 'My usual, Mr Chapman.'

And he didn't alter for any of them his shopkeeper's image, his 'much obliged' and 'thanking you'. It was they who bought and he who sold. That was the arrangement. Let them think of him as some cutout figure, popping up like the sums on the till, behind the counter: Mr Chapman, the sweet shop man.

On Saturday mornings the High Street thronged. The same faces, down to the department stores and the new supermarket. Frozen food, electric mixers, long-playing records. Something new, something new in a shiny cover or a crisp cardboard box. And on the way back a call at Chapman's, to pay the papers and buy the weekend's tobacco. A drink in the Prince William. They had the jukebox now, and the television in the corner. Then football, a visit somewhere on Sunday. What randomness. 'Don't overdo it, will you, Mr Chapman?' But why should he mind? He only sold. Ceaselessly he filled his shelves and embellished his windows so their useless bounty might never fail. And when he knew what they whispered (echoes of Mrs Cooper's gossip couldn't escape him)—'He's tied to that shop—Thinks of nothing else—Loves to rake it in'—he didn't mind. Let them whisper. Let them cast him in the miser's role. He wouldn't question it. For did they think it belonged to him, that cutout behind the counter?

He watched himself fold the papers between his thumb and fingers; ring the till, swop pleasantries with customers, weigh up quarter-pounds and half-pounds in the scales; put the money in the safe at night, check the cash float, check the alarms, check the doors. Watched the figures mount in the maroon books. Watched himself drive home at night, briefcase and raincoat on the back seat, left at the traffic lights, up the Common Road, under the red chains of the sodium lamps. Watched himself construct his performance, as she watched herself, in the mirror, slowly being dismantled. Weakening of the lungs; a strain on the heart. That last holiday in Teignmouth—Dorry had found her solution by taking all her books with her to study. Going afterwards to Doctor Field's. 'She no longer has migraines, doctor.' 'That's quite common, Mr Chapman, for a woman, er, at her time of life.' He watched himself at night, listening to her laboured breathing, feeling his body temporarily recede, but seeing its daytime animation capering before him like some jerky phantom. And in the morning as he let Mrs Cooper in, drank the milky tea she brought him and heard her ask, 'Mrs Chapman any better?' he'd watch himself as he said: 'No change.'

20

'Know the latest?'

Smithy, working the pedal rather laboriously, winched him up, swathed in white, on the barber's seat and wiped his comb and scissors. His old face was pale and his eyes yellowish in the mirror, and the fingers tucking the towel in his collar were cold.

'Friend Hancock's branching out.'

There was a smell of cologne and Brilliantine, adverts for razors and Durex. Two young assistants clipped at the other chairs and their faces seemed to be waiting, as Hancock and Joyce had once waited.

'Had it from Schofield, and from the man himself.'

He bent closer to his ear. For Smithy's art was the art of discreetly gathered and exchanged information. Didn't they come to him, all of them, for their fortnightly clip—Simpson, Kelly from the Prince William, Ford the postmaster, Schofield, Hancock? Only old Powell's perpetually cropped hair was a mystery. And if things slipped out when they spoke, couldn't Smithy be trusted, in return, to impart some useful snippet? But always with tact, always with disinterest. For what should Smithy care, piecing together the patterns of the High Street but going home at night to his spinster sister? Besides, he was old: his fingers were cold when they touched your neck.

'He wants to open an office in Lewisham. The idea's to move Joyce out there so he can rule the roost here. Head Office. Joyce won't have any of it, and I don't blame him— they're supposed to be equal partners. They're not exactly friends at the moment—I got that from Schofield. Cocky's looking for a third partner so as to play things off.'

'Lewisham?'

'Empires start somewhere. He's on the make. But he's got wife trouble. Got this from Joyce. She does all right: everything on a plate. Schofield was describing their place. But she's getting tired of being just one of the furnishings. Joyce says she'd do a flit on him if he didn't buy her off.'

'Stories.'

'Who's to say? Schofield says something could happen. She's no longer exactly the belle of Sydenham Hill. We're all getting on, pal.'

The clippers and the scissors snipped in silence. The

barber's pole twirled outside. Then Smithy said, picking up the comb, in a surer, routine voice as if the previous topic had never been raised: 'Business all right?' He nodded. 'Irene?' 'No better.' The fingers gripped his head and tilted it to one side: 'Keep still now. Don't you worry. Those doctors'll come up with something. And Dorothy?'

He put the comb and scissors in his breast pocket and held the wooden-handled mirror up to the back of his neck.

'There. That's you neat and trim for your customers.' He put the mirror back on the hook on the wall. 'I see Mrs Cooper's having a nice little jaw about you to one of them.' He cocked his eye towards the Briar Street window, where, across the wet road, through the gleam and clutter of the window display, Mrs Cooper could be seen, arms folded, talking to a woman in a navy coat.

'Better go and live up to your publicity.'

Smithy took the towel from his collar and removed the sheet, scattering hair clippings to the floor. He got up from his seat. Then Smithy threw the sheet into the bin and, taking a brush from beside the sink, began brushing his jacket, twisting him slowly round on the floor with a slight pressure from his fingers, until he slipped the brush under his arm, put both his bloodless hands on his customer's shoulders, and the two of them stared at their reflections in the mirror.

*

'Know what I heard?'

There were five suits in the wardrobe. Five suits for a man who worked six and a half days out of seven. And he might have done his work in a shirt and a pullover or an old cardigan like Powell. But she insisted, bought him suits for Christmas and birthdays—what else should he need?—chose the material herself. So he hoisted on the red braces, in the dim, early-morning bedroom, tucked in his shirt—his stomach had begun to press against the line of his buttons—and tightened the maroon tie.

'Know what Smithy told me?'

The tray with the tea cups was on the bedside table, next to her medicines and inhaler. The bedside lamp was on and she lay propped up against the pillows. In a little while, when he'd gone, she'd lie back; for often, after a restless night, she would only sleep in the early morning, in between his departure and Dorothy's rising. But that was not before she'd got up, slipped on her dressing gown and breakfasted with him at the kitchen table.

'Hancock's opening a new branch. In Lewisham. He's looking for a third partner.'

'Oh,' she answered, as if she'd already had the information, noted it as she did those predictable columns in the newspapers. But she looked up, suddenly wary, so that he didn't add at first, as Smithy had done, that all was not well between Hancock and Helen. Supposing she took that as a veiled allusion to themselves?

'Empire building,' he said and twanged the red elastic of his braces, like a clown, against his shirt. 'Only a story, I expect.'

Every morning the tea, the hard light of the bedside lamp which showed the lines in her face; the electric fire in winter. Every morning he would dress and go down to prepare the breakfast—the shadowy forms of the garden would stare at him beyond the kitchen window—and he would scarcely need to glance at a clock or his watch to know whether he was on time. Up at five-thirty; out at six-fifteen. Put the cash books in the briefcase; polish shoes; warm the car engine. 'Smithy says Hancock and Helen aren't so hand in glove.' And if he'd faltered once—sat down on the edge of the bed, torn the maroon tie from his neck that he'd tied so diligently—? But such mutinies could never have occurred, for her glance would have caught him before he slipped and fell: 'Play your part.' In the mirror his hair was thinning above the brow, it ran in black streaks over the scalp, and his face had assumed the moulded fleshiness of men—you saw them in the shop, asking for cigarettes, and lingering outside the Prince William—who carry their bodies around like so much ballast.

'Only a story,' he said, twanging his braces like cata-pults—and was that a smile at the corners of her lips?

He took the toast from the grill and the boiled egg from the bubbling pan. She did not eat breakfast, only drank the tea, but the table was laid, the blue and white crockery, the pale blue napkins—even at six in the morning. Darkness pressed against the window pane, where in summer they could see the dewy lawn, the lilac tree, its stem grown thick after twenty-five years. The house was still, save for the tap-tap of his spoon against the egg and the 'heee . . . heee' of her breath, and you would scarcely have known that in the room above Dorothy lay asleep, books on the shelf over the bed where once they had propped the striped wool-len doll and the jigsaws. Every morning as he went down to make the tea he paused to listen at her door—why did he listen?—and sometimes he heard her stir, wakened by his own movements. But stillness usually. Stillness: so that sometimes, far from complaining, he pitied the seven and eight o'clock risers who did not know the early morning calm, before the traffic began, before the world jerked into action. Her breath hissed in the chair opposite his. There were wrinkles in the cleft of her breasts. But she drank her tea deliberately, holding the cup between her hands, dipping her head forward rhythmically to sip; and as she drank she seemed to be saying too: 'Yes, this is the best hour. You will go, to your old place, and return. Dorothy is still in bed. And I can sleep now. The day is poised; for an hour or so there is peace.'

He checked his pocket for the keys, his wallet, picked up his briefcase. She helped him on with his oatmeal scarf. It might have been he who commanded, as he drew the dressing gown about that wheezing throat and said, 'Stay in the warm'; were it not for her answering eyes: 'Go on, go on.' Past the hall mirror, the umbrella stand and out into the dark morning—a frosty ring as his feet struck the front path—where sometimes it seemed he was quite alone in a world which had suspended its activity. Under the amber sodium lamps. And even in the shop, after he had sent off the paper boys (they were a different bunch then but their careless loyalty was the same) there was still a calm. Those minutes before he opened. A few cars in the High Street, footsteps, scuttling on the pavement. Soon they would be coming in their droves, summoned by trains, clocks, streaming to their work, bustling in at the shop door for their daily purchases. And he would be there, bobbing at the counter to receive them. 'Morning, Mr Casey, morning, Mr Saville, Mr King.' All was ready. But he would listen, for a few minutes, to the crinkling of the shelves, the hum and tick of the fridge, and sniff—it was still there but no one but he perhaps could smell it—that faint whiff of coconut he had first sniffed when the shelves were bare and dust lay on the counter and old Jones had stood in his black coat. Stillness. And while he waited, hands resting on the morning's headlines, he laughed inwardly, not the old laugh—a dry laugh, thin like her breath, which didn't change the look on his face. But a laugh.

And that same year, when he was fifty and the shop twenty-five years old, he said to her one night, closing the maroon books—her smile had lit her face then—'Toys, I will sell toys.'

21

Dorothy. Why did you have to come into the shop? To disturb those patterns? To see my look of disguised excitement, faint apology, as I greeted you from behind the counter? To hear the catch in my voice as I said, 'Mrs Cooper, my daughter Dorothy'? You could have got the bus as far as the Common Road, but you got off in the High Street, in your blue uniform and your blue beret, a satchel under your arm, and walked down to the corner of Briar Street. To see me without Irene? To see if I was any different without her?

Half-past four, five o'clock. Under the brightening lights, through the deepening dusk, other children were going home from school, in groups, in reckless gaggles, but you always seemed alone. Even when you came in flanked by your friends—Sally Lyle and Susan Dean—you stood apart, untouched by their boisterousness and their forwardness, watching them giggle at the counter and say, 'Oh,

Mr Chapman!' as I slipped them free chocolates. Though anyone could see, of those three, you were the prettiest, the one who most deserved to be to the fore.

You watched me arrange the toys in the Briar Street window. For they were arriving now, picked from the wholesalers' catalogues, in boxes that rattled and squeaked and threatened to jerk into imitation life. Meccano and Lego, Yogi Bear dolls and model kits of the Lone Ranger. There was a frown on your face as I clambered into the window with them. A man of fifty fussing over toys? But it was my job to sell them. You stood with your arms holding that satchel in front of you and your fingers tapping restlessly on the leather, for you never quite knew what to do with those long, delicate hands. You'd let them fall awkwardly by your side and sometimes one of them would reach up, just like her, to your throat, but you'd remember suddenly and let it drop quickly again. 'Here,' I said, 'put that satchel down, you can help.' And you were in two minds whether you ought to or not. I got out from the box the set of three little clockwork chimpanzees. Each wore a hat like a fez. One had a pipe, another a tambourine, another a pair of bongos, and when you turned the key in their backs their heads swivelled and their arms moved. 'Where should they go?' I said. And you said, hesitating at first, and then with a little sharp decision, 'Why not there?'—and pointed to the display rack over the counter above my head. I hung them there, Dorry (you see, I didn't question, didn't hesitate). And later, when I'd sold three sets of those monkeys and people pointed to the ones above me, I said, 'No, they're not for sale.' 'There,' I said, fixing them, 'like that?' But you looked away.

For you'd finished with your own toys. You thought we'd thrown them out, but I merely put them, to be kept, in the trunk in the spare bedroom. You no longer wanted to play or be thought of as a child. You'd got a place at the High School; you were going to make your mark, and it wasn't games you looked for any more. Was that why you walked uneasily between your breezier friends? Why you buried your face behind books? And why you threw those little fits and sulks at home, picking quarrels over the dinner table—for that was a way of creating a little drama, of making your mark, without ever having to leave familiar ground?

'Doesn't it bother you?'

You raised your head and spoke urgently, so that we stopped and looked at you, our spoons half-way between plate and lips.

'Doesn't it bother you—that there might be a war?'

On the leather footrest by her chair were the papers she'd

been reading. Their headlines said: 'Ships Move Towards Cuba', 'Britain Urges Removal of Missiles'.

You looked at her first and then, when her lips tightened in annoyance, to me, to see if I would move to her defence or yours.

'There won't be a war, nothing will happen,' she said.

'How do you know?'

'I don't. It's what I think.'

She resumed eating. You watched, not eating, your face trembling. I thought: thirteen, and talking of war. And then you flung down your spoon and pushed aside your plate.

'Neither of you care! What do you read the papers for if you don't care what happens? It's not something you can just ignore—'

'No—nor is it something to make a scene over when we're eating. If you want an argument, have it with one of your fancy teachers at school, don't be clever with us at the dinner table!' She began suddenly to gasp for air.

Your cheeks burned. There was that little hard furrow in your brow. You looked at me, to test me.

'Dorry, don't upset your mother,' I said. And I knew that would send you up out of your chair, out of the door (how many times did we hear that door slam behind you after something she'd said or I'd said, or something we hadn't said?), up the stairs, your steps heavy on the landing, into the refuge of your bedroom.

And I knew it would make me come up to you to make my truce.

'Why does she do it?' she said, her gasps subsiding. 'Why does she do it?' She sat with her elbows on the table, her own plate pushed away. She put the napkin which you'd dropped back in its silver ring. 'She'll do something stupid one of these days, don't you think, Willy?' She got up, moved to her seat by the window and looked at the head-lines on the papers. Then she said at last, searching my face: 'All right, go to her.'

There were pictures of Kennedy over your bed. Photographs out of *Time* and *Life* and the *Illustrated London News* which I got from the shop. Kennedy in Vienna. Kennedy beneath the white statue of Lincoln. Other girls pinned up the grinning faces of pop-stars: Billy Fury, Adam Faith; centre-spreads from the fan magazines I sold. Too simple and trivial for you, Dorry?

'She didn't mean to be unkind.'

You lay with your head pressed to the pillow, to hide your tears.

'She's ill, remember.'

But you didn't answer.

Then you turned at last.

'You always take her side.'

'It's not like that. There aren't "sides". It's not a fight.'

'Isn't it?'

You fell back again on the pillow. Your left leg, in a white school sock, swung over the edge of the bed; a silvery down at the knee. How still that room was, how familiar. Yet it would become soon 'your' room exclusively; the room of a young woman, at which I would pause and knock before entering.

I stroked your shoulder.

'Don't make an enemy of her, Dorry.'

You looked at me as if I'd already been defeated.

'What does she want?'

'I think what she wants is peace.'

22

The Saturday crowds in the High Street grew bigger and bigger. They bobbed like figures carried in water past the cluttered port-hole of the shop window. Eighteen, nineteen pounds a day. And was it just my imagination or were there more youngsters among those crowds, with money to spend and little looks, as they walked, of arrogance and temerity? They drew out notes from their pockets to buy clothes that were made solely for them. Blue jeans that hugged their hips; skirts that got shorter and shorter. I saw them look at me across the counter as if I'd never been young. And was there really once a William Chapman, aged eighteen or nineteen, who'd taken the tram every morning to work, dressed in a grey waistcoat and a stiff collar, as if he were already old?

'You've got competition, old man,' said Hancock. There were creases under his eyes and his movements had lost their athlete's jauntiness, but he still wore the air—with that crisp, thick-striped shirt, those long sideburns and the way he lit his cigar, in the shop now, not waiting till he had gone, peeling off the roll of cellophane and crushing it in his hand—of a contestant anxious to prove he can win.

'It's not on my books, but that site opposite Samuel Road—going to be a newsagent's. One of those groups.'

His brown eyes gave a little dart as he crackled the cellophane.

'Thought you should know. Not so hot for the one-man business, is it, these days?'

But as if I cared. Competition? Had I ever competed? The shop was a gift, I'd got it for nothing. Rivals didn't bother me. (Besides, I saw it when it opened that October: a clean, functional establishment; swing glass doors, stainless steel, rubber matting by the entrance, and a staff that changed every six weeks. Magazines spread loosely to look more numerous than they were, a mere sampling of sweets, no toys. And after a year it closed.)

'They're the newcomers,' I said. 'It's me they'll have to compete with.'

'That's the style.' Hancock's eyes narrowed concedingly as if they'd really hoped for some expression of dismay.

'While we're on the subject'—he removed the cigar, still

unlit, from his mouth—'you might have heard already, we're opening this new office in Lewisham. In about a month. Having a little party to celebrate. Just Joyce, Ted Schofield, a few people from the golf club. I'd, er, invite you, old man, but of course, with Irene—' He struck a match. 'How is she?'

'No change really. Helen?'

'Oh fine, fine.' He pulled the match away from the end of his cigar and waved it furiously, flapping his hand long after the flame was out. 'Something Irene might be interested to know, by the by. Been meaning to tell you. I've been seeing a bit of her brother—Paul. Been a bit down on his luck recently. I'm thinking of letting him in on the firm. He needs some sort of break and we need someone new, now we're expanding.'

'We haven't seen Paul for years.'

'Really? Is that so? Well, tell Irene. She'll remember when we used to be great buddies before the war—me, Paul and—'

He held his cigar a few inches from his mouth. 'But I mustn't chatter.' One eye was cocked as if gauging an effect. 'I've got business.'

He rubbed his hands together, puffing blue fumes, and strode to the door. As he opened it he took the cigar from his mouth again, turned and said—was there a sly note in his voice?—'Was that Dorothy I saw popping in here last night? Growing up, isn't she?'

The shoppers swirled along the High Street. I read the headlines in the mornings, under my print-stained fingers: 'Kennedy to Tour Europe', 'Kennedy Acclaimed in Berlin', 'Kennedy Shot Dead'.

What was the point of all that study, Dorry, all those books? Was it to spite me? Because you guessed what my school reports must have said—'Slow', 'Could try harder'—and you saw what a plodding brain I had, leaning over the baize tablecloth, mouthing those figures silently as I checked them with my pencil? Your own reports were so much better, but they weren't unmixed: 'Great promise but not always co-operative in class', 'First-rate work but apt to be moody'. Your form-mistress said: 'She's a very bright girl, but she needs to come out of herself.' Do you remember? It was after the school play—*The Merchant of Venice*—put on with the boys from John Russell. They wanted you to play Portia, the biggest part, but you wouldn't. You played Shylock's daughter. There were traces of stage make-up, incompletely removed, on your face, which made you look younger, not older than you were—and you overheard that remark as you came out from the side door of the hall to where I stood with Mrs Bennet. Parents were waiting, fussily, to collect sons and daughters. You were angry with her for talking about you and ashamed of me because I stood in my grey work suit—I'd come straight from the shop to the play—my raincoat over my clasped hands; and you thought Mrs Bennet, with her spry, cultivated voice, would find me dull and stupid. You stood in the lobby by the coat-rack—I saw you over Mrs Bennet's shoulder—pretending to read the noticeboard, and did not come forward till Mrs Bennet said, sighing commiseratively: 'But she ought to be ambitious. She's got the world ahead of her. Oh—there you are, my dear.'

We walked, the three of us, to the car park. Trees cast long shadows in the light from the hall onto netball markings on the asphalt. Mrs Bennet said: 'Try a bigger part next year, Dorothy,' and patted your shoulder as we said goodbye.

In the car you asked: 'Well, what did you think?' 'Oh I thought you were good.' 'No—the play,' you said. And I muttered something feebly in reply. What did I know about Shakespeare, Dorry? I'd sat in an uncomfortable wooden chair after a hard day at the shop, while on the stage schoolchildren in costume played the parts of grown-ups and spoke lines I did not understand.

*

You were almost sixteen. Little hillocks of breasts had grown under your school pullover, and you were aware beneath your skirt of the contours of your legs. You crossed them carefully and tucked your skirt under your knees. You tried to pretend that you weren't attractive—though, in the play, a schoolboy lover had wooed you with long speeches. But you couldn't do it by covering your knees, or letting your hair fall over your face, or raising arguments with us over the dinner table so as to divert attention. And besides you knew—lingering by the mirror and looking sideways at yourself as if you didn't want to see—that it couldn't be hidden. And you really wanted, didn't you, though the thought of it frightened you, to live up to it?

Down the High Street after school. It wasn't the quickest way home. Was it to receive the darting glances of men leaning from car windows as you crossed at the zebra, looking up, turning their heads as you passed on the pavement, muttering low words? Or of boys your own age sauntering circuitously home, in restless gangs? I saw them meeting girls in Briar Street, next to the cinema adverts. Mrs Cooper tut-tutted and sometimes banged the window to shoo them off. Their breath steamed in the dusk. They wore Parka anoraks. Their hair was longer than the school approved, their trousers tighter; they carried records, with their school books, under their arms—the Rolling Stones and Donovan with textbooks of physics and geography. And it wasn't Shakespeare and poetry they spoke of. Was it that, Dorry? Did you have to run that gauntlet, to test yourself? Though it made your head sit uneasily on your shoulders and you didn't know how to reply with any naturalness to those adventurous looks.

Nothing touches you, you touch nothing. Sixteen, in a blue school beret. You could have kept your poise and learnt the trick of it. You were beautiful and young. Wasn't that something to rejoice over? You could have performed the trick, without fear and without needing to make your mark. For hadn't you once—at the schools swimming gala—stood up, unafraid, high over the swimming pool, over the blue tiles wobbling beneath—that was no adventure, you knew how to keep your balance—and hadn't you plunged, with a perfect arch, and bobbed up again, to take second prize, with a laugh?

Shakespeare, history books, volumes of poetry. Postcards from art galleries—replacing Kennedy—on the wall; and faded ink-splotched school copies of Latin texts, Virgil and the *Metamorphoses*, whose contents I puzzled from the English heading before each extract: 'Narcissus and Echo', 'Diana and Actaeon'. I put the mug of coffee on your desk, knocking first at your door, and treading softly over the carpet. For your head was lowered and you were intent on your reading. Your hair hung forward in the light of the anglepoise lamp and the line of your neck seemed fragile and exposed as you leant. You were doing your project on Keats and over your shoulder I read lines of verse (did you know, Dorry, how I peeped into those books when you weren't there?) which I didn't understand:

Bold lover, never, never canst thou kiss . . .

I put the mug on your desk. You said in a quiet, unsteady voice, 'Oh, thanks,' but you didn't turn and smile at your father.

23

We bought you dresses. She would have said: She doesn't need them, not so many—but she yielded, for my sake. Bright dresses—how they changed, Dorry, as you grew up, from wide skirts to little skimpy things next to nothing— lying over the back of a chair for you to find at Christmas or on birthdays. Dresses to make a young girl feel special, and that cost her father a pretty penny. For we had money. Thirty, forty pounds a day. I worked all day Sundays, and we no longer took holidays. And even without the shop we had money. For she still scanned the closing prices in the paper, made phone calls, and struggled out, in her weak state, to meet agents, and sign cheques for crystal and porcelain. 'They're beautiful,' I said of all those things she bought. But she replied, her tired eyes somehow disinterested: 'They will keep their value.'

Bright dresses—deep red suited you best—that should

have been worn at dances and parties. Weren't there parties to go to? I sometimes saw them, driving home late from the shop, in Mannering Road and Clifford Rise and in Leigh Drive itself: little gaggles, sixteen and seventeen, no older than you, in short skirts and leather jackets, arriving at bay-windowed houses where the parents were out for the evening or away for the weekend, and from which record-players boomed. *'Talkin' 'bout my ge-en-eration . . .'*

But you didn't wear those dresses. You put them on to please me—you came down the stairs and stood like a shy doll in the doorway. And you wore them on the predictable occasions (do you remember, Dorry, those drear Christmases, when we dutifully had the neighbours in for drinks and you and I walked after dinner, not talking, round dark, empty streets, where the decorations in front windows looked like shop-fronts?). But you didn't go out in them, though you liked them and thought you deserved them—I saw that. You hung them up in your wardrobe and preferred your white school blouses and navy skirts or that shapeless brown sweater and slacks.

No parties. No self-conscious but light-headed youths ringing at the front door to take you to dances and cinemas. Were you above that? Was it more daring excitements you wanted? Or had she spoken to you—surely not—told you of wolves that prowl? No time to go out. Books to be read, exams to be worked for, essays to be written.

Yet you knew, nonetheless, John Schofield—Schofield's lanky and precocious son who'd done the lighting at the school play—and you knew more than I did about what was going on up there, among the trees and the old villas and the new estates at Sydenham Hill. You told me it all later—that time, the first time, she was taken to hospital. That was the only time we ever really talked.

Houses through the trees, and lights, illuminating costly furniture, in the houses. That was where your mother's family had a house; and I remember when it was mostly all woods and fields and my father used to walk there on Sundays. They'd built a lot up there: luxury houses for executives, tall, clean-cut flats, but with banks of turf and carefully preserved clumps of trees in the best of taste. The people inside the houses were building too. Hancock was building (you never liked him because of his businessman's swagger—too crude a contrast to me?—but most of all because he winked at you once as you came home from school): new branches in the suburbs; bigger figures on the 'For Sale' signs in his window. And Helen was building. More gadgetry in the kitchen so she could lounge and entertain more. A bigger wardrobe so she could lounge more prettily; richer fare on the sideboard so she could entertain more lavishly. You wouldn't remember her from your christening; her breathy charms and her quick shrill giggle. Hancock had chosen her for her obvious looks and curving figure. For he wanted a wife to prove his merit, a prize on display other men might envy.

Candlelight on the faces of the guests at table and on the bare arms of the hostess serving the meal; jokes about the cost of living, and an atmosphere like that before a race where each contestant smiles sportingly and wills the other to lose. It wasn't enough, that enviable trophy. More business, more houses to sell. More adornments for wife and home so that the prize would prove the achievement. And though he strode over the High Street with that swaggering gait his restless face was never content.

I can see his glinting eye as he offered Paul that partnership. 'I could fix you up here, if you like, old man.' And I can see Paul's stiff features trying not to flinch at the condescension—'I'll think about it.'

Where had Paul been all that time? Seventeen years. Seventeen years since he returned from the war, sold up what was left of the Harrisons' laundry and looked for openings with the money. And it was still a fight, though the war was over, finding the contacts, making one's mark. Those failed schemes in London; a partnership, at last, in a textile business in Leeds. Irene told me all about it, Dorry.

Paul wrote to her. But she never replied, and she never—this was the gist of the story—lent him a penny. And when the business folded in Leeds (and his marriage with it) Paul had no one to turn to but an estate agent friend in London. 'Great buddies before the war.' But Irene never went into that. She never did say much about the time before we met.

Soft lights and expensive furniture, in the house where the two friends struck their terms, made their bargain. What did each stand to gain? Paul: a job at the expense of pride? Hancock: the satisfaction of the upper hand? 'Take your time, old man—don't let me force you.'

But something else was at stake in that plush house. What did Helen hope to gain; a dozen years their younger, getting up from the table, moving perhaps, so they could both watch her, over the noiseless carpet, to look out of the window at the stillness of houses, trees? A little adventure?

Was it true, Dorry, that Hancock beat her—when it was all over and she came back to him—so she couldn't show her face?

How did you know all that? Coming home from school on the bus with John Schofield, who was bookish enough for you not to be troubled by his company. Making fun (that was the fashion among free-thinking teenagers) of your affluent parents. But even Schofield, who gossiped so readily with Smithy, wouldn't have told his own son so much. Paul himself then? Your own uncle. When was it? Those evenings when you said you were rehearsing the school play? Going to Paul's flat in Camberwell? Did his face still have a trace of those keen looks he wore at my wedding? Did he see Irene in you? Did he welcome you, Dorry? Because he had questions to ask, things to tell; and because you reminded him of a time when the picture was still complete? Under the apple tree, in a black peaked cap. The fair flanked by the strong.

You should have been at rehearsals. You hardly went out otherwise. Mrs Bennet wanted you to play a bigger part. But was it better than drama—all those things he had to tell you?

A little adventure. It didn't last long. Helen came back and Hancock beat her. The bruises healed but something else didn't. She had to go for visits to a hospital. She returns there even now on occasion. She still serves the guests at Sydenham Hill; but her giggly laugh has snapped and the faces round the table are fewer now, they say. Hancock doesn't allow his guests too much laughter. He wears a fixed face like a statue's—even when he comes in here for cigars—as if he wants to be regarded as beyond reproach. And when I ask, 'How's Helen?' he answers, 'How's Dorothy?'

Soft lights over the table. The captured moment.

Why did I wince, Dorry, why did it shock me so, that evening after dinner? You didn't go straight to your room, and your little head was flushed with anticipation and daring. You made an enemy of Irene that evening. No, it wasn't what happened with Paul and the Hancocks. She even said of that, with a sort of strange approval: 'Well—there's justice there.' It was that note of adventure in your voice.

You made an enemy of her. But not of me. So why did I wince, as if I were being accused myself, why did I find myself playing the distressed father?—when you placed one hand on the table, drew up your head and blurted out those words as if they were the caption to some vivid and indelible photograph: 'Something has happened. Mrs Hancock's left Mr Hancock. She's gone off with Uncle Paul. I know it's happened because Uncle Paul told me it would.'

Dorry. You'll come. You'll come back.

THREE

24

The sun blazed in the High Street, but it had lost its morning freshness, and inside the shop, despite the electric fan
and the door opened to the street, the air was close and
heavy. It made Mrs Cooper itch and prickle beneath her
nylon shop coat and grow irritable, so that she glanced
more accusingly at Sandra and muttered when the girl got
in her way or took her time at the till: 'Confound you!'
She wiped her glasses. Flies buzzed round the shelves; the
counter was sticky; the coins and notes customers handed
her were hot and damp with sweat. These things gave her a
feeling of distaste—which was quite unlike the feeling she
had had as she left home at seven, patting her hair, the dew
still bright on the patch of grass by the entrance to the flats,
and the word 'Holiday' ringing in her mind as something
to put before Mr Chapman.

'Confound you!'

'Temper!' said Sandra.

The clock over the door showed ten to one. Sandra went to lunch first, from one to two. Mrs Cooper's own lunch break was officially one-thirty to two-thirty, but in practice she usually took less. Loyalty to Mr Chapman—and unwillingness to leave him alone for long with Sandra—made her scurry back from her sallies to the supermarket as early as two. Sometimes she took no lunch break at all, merely sat for a while in the stock room. Mr Chapman never took a break—despite her warnings. Just sat on his stool with a cup of coffee and a sandwich—a cheese sandwich—which he would put down, circular bites out of it, whenever a customer needed serving. Since his wife's death she herself had begun to cut his sandwich ('Cottage cheese only, Mrs Cooper—doctor's orders') or fetch him things from the baker's. That was a valued privilege. And yet she wished, rather, he'd take a proper lunch. Go over, perhaps, to the Prince William, and leave her solely in charge. Hadn't he said, on that wet evening sixteen years ago, that there'd be times when she'd have to mind the shop herself? And yet it seemed that, except for those visits to the hospital, which were over now, he'd never yet trusted her to be alone regularly at the counter.

Fridays had their consolations, it was true. She and Sandra took their lunch as usual, but at two-thirty Mr Chapman would leave, taking in his briefcase some packages from the safe in the stock room, and drive over to Pond Street. There were the two to be paid over there—Bryant and Miss Fox—and the odd order to discuss. He would be gone perhaps three quarters of an hour, and she would relish that time as an opportunity to hold sway over Sandra.

She took her eyes from the clock. Five to one. Sandra fidgeted by the till. Oh yes, *she*'d be ready to dash off on the stroke. Flitting down the High Street, ready to fritter away her pay packet. She thought of setting the girl some task that would cut into her lunch time.

'Sandra,' she said commandingly, 'before you go to lunch—'

But then Mr Chapman surprised her.

'That's all right, Mrs Cooper. I'd like you to go to lunch first today.'

'I beg your pardon?'

'If that's all right.' Mr Chapman edged forward from the refrigerator. 'Sandra was late. I think you should go first, for a change. Let her cope with the lunchtime rush.'

She stiffened.

Change? She always went to lunch second; the pattern had never changed.

'But I always—' she began. But Mr Chapman's glassy look made her falter.

'Today,' he said, in oddly final tones, 'is different.'

It must be because he wanted to be alone with the girl. He wanted her to go so they could talk about her behind her back.

She raised her neck and swallowed the little upsurge in her throat.

'Besides,' Mr Chapman stared more waterily, 'in this heat—I expect you're ready for a breather.'

Breather indeed!

'I've my shopping to do,' she said, rebutting the suggestion she had time to relax.

She looked at Sandra as if it was she who had directly contrived all this. And Sandra, seeing Mrs Cooper for once genuinely at bay, gave a look of out-and-out ferocity.

'Good, then,' Mr Chapman said. 'You go off till two, and, Sandra, you take from two to three.' (Mrs Cooper's eyebrows shot up at the whole hour he would be alone with Sandra.) 'I'll go to Pond Street when you come back. It'll mean of course, Mrs Cooper,' Mr Chapman paused and his eyes seemed to take on a distinctly tender gaze, 'that you'll be alone in the shop while I'm gone. But,' he paused again, 'perhaps it's time you were used to managing by yourself.'

Mrs Cooper sniffed at the attempt at appeasement.

But then—what did he mean?—'time you were used to managing by yourself '? Her feelings rose at the sudden prospect of him yielding at last to her much-repeated advice—taking care of his weary body in those plump armchairs at Leigh Drive—dozing under a sunshade in the garden (with a fold-up garden table and an iced drink)—where she would at last join him, but only after first staunchly conducting the day's business at the shop. Eventually they'd sell the shop. They wouldn't need it anyway, with all that money (she'd find out how much it really was) *Mrs* Chapman had left. They'd simply stop work. And they'd take, at last, that holiday. That long, long holiday . . .

But it didn't alter the fact that there was something between him and that girl.

'Well—' She drew a breath. 'One o'clock it is, then. You won't mind if I rest my legs a while in the stock room?'

Mr Chapman nodded, turning to a customer.

She went into the stock room, filled a tumbler of water at the sink and pulled one of the battered easy chairs as far back as possible, opposite the doorway into the shop, so that she sat, like a hidden observer, spying on the others through the veil of the plastic strips. The strips fluttered now and then in the breeze from the electric fan. She couldn't see Mr Chapman, only occasionally his left shoulder, but Sandra rocked on her stool before her, got up, moved to and fro along the counter and sometimes glanced sharply in at her as at an animal in a cage.

Well, she wouldn't budge until she absolutely had to. She'd stay here and watch them as long as she could. Spend her whole lunch hour here if need be. She strained her ears for words, but caught nothing. She looked around at the cluttered stock room—the piles of cardboard boxes, the door to the lavatory, the sink and mirror in the far corner with the collection of brooms, brushes and floorcloths heaped beside it, the thumbed and tattered lists on the wall, the murky skylight above with its rust-streaked glass, masking even now the brilliant sunshine—and felt something of the prisoner's desolation. She sniffed. He never bothered about the stock room, let it get into the filthiest state. It was almost as if he relished the difference between its shabbiness and the brilliance of the shop itself. Once a fortnight she tidied it—though he never asked—swept the dust and scraps of paper from the floor, cleaned the sink and lavatory, made it as spotless as possible. But he never thanked her.

She looked at Sandra's back on the stool and her tumble of glossy hair, through the plastic strips. She wasn't deceived.

From her inner recess the shop, even the street beyond with its dazzle of traffic, seemed momentarily fanciful and intangible—a surface you could stick your hand through.

How hot it was! Her neck itched. Her skin crawled and pricked. The heat made her feel soiled, abused. Going to lunch first! Upsetting the pattern!

Lunchtime customers were crowding the counter, but, between their shoulders, she just glimpsed, out there in the street, the door of Hancock and Joyce open and Mr Hancock step out into the sunlight. Would he come to the shop first, across the road? No: along the pavement, past Powell's, and straight—she knew without having to keep sight of him—to the Prince William. A stiff, upright figure as he strode. But she wasn't deceived. Everyone knew: that wife of his. She was funny in the head. They'd put her away once. Eight years ago she'd run off with some other man. And someone had told her once, on good authority, that that other man was none other than Mr Chapman's brother-in-law.

All deceit and running away. She watched the hot faces at the counter. Look at Dorothy, *his* daughter, running away like that. Some man, a university lecturer—he'd said that much. And look at her own wretched desertion, twenty-seven years ago. It was a sultry, heavy afternoon— the kids, at least, were asleep—and she'd known he wasn't coming back. He was all fixed up with that bag of tricks in Birmingham. Letter on the bedside table. She'd sat un-moving on the sofa in that room left untidy by the boys.

Cushions on the floor; toys. And even later, when the boys had grown and she moved to the new flat, even now, she hadn't shaken off from herself that sense of the world receding and that room fixing round her, with the upset toys, still and frozen. Then she'd got up and pursed her lips and begun to clear the mess. And she hadn't stopped since.

Through the doorway in front of her Mr Chapman appeared, edging towards the till—how laboriously he moved sometimes—and as he did so he seemed to lean over deliberately towards the girl.

The plastic strips shimmered for a moment, like striped deckchairs on a hot beach, like coloured sunshades . . .

Twenty past by the clock. Her shopping had to be done. At least *she* had no illusions. Let him have his little fancy and let them talk about her while she was gone. She could still act, she could still have her scene. She'd get her own back on that little bag of tricks.

She put the empty tumbler back above the sink and drew out her handbag from the shopping basket propped against the wall. Eyeing herself in the mirror, she powdered her nose, spread the collar of her blouse a little more flatly over her shoulders and sprayed a jet of sandalwood under her chin. She entered the shop with a sudden flinging back of the plastic strips and paused for a moment, taking breath, levelling a glance at Sandra, in the doorway.

'Off to the shops. Anything I can get you, Mr Chapman?'

'Er, no thanks, Mrs Cooper.'

She brushed past the girl and the man—sixty years old!—and out into the hot envelope of the street.

Mr Chapman watched her turn right under the awning and pass by the window. How old is that woman? he thought.

25

1969. You were twenty that June. A student at London University. No longer a girl. Your smooth swaying stride and your softened woman's figure—in blue jeans and a purple coloured top, now you were going to university— should have proclaimed it. Save for that uncertain way you held your head, as if you were surprised to find, so soon, you'd grown up.

You had left school for the last time. Out of the gates, with the others, scuffling homewards, onto the noisy bus, through the High Street, warily, in your uniform; for the last time. 'O'-levels, 'A'-levels, your essay on Keats which won the school prize: a place at university. Did you step away from it all, as you stepped out of your uniform, as if a new life beckoned?

Blue jeans and a purple corduroy jacket; hair long and straight and unstyled. Alone in that room the other side of

London, with a gas-ring, your books and your independ-ence. Don't think I wasn't proud of you, Dorry. My own daughter at university. But why didn't you seem glad, even at your own success? And why did it seem to me (other youngsters, whom I winked at, over the counter, wore those bright, flamboyant clothes because it was fun) that you wore your student's outfit as if it were only another uniform?

Who was happier, Dorry, you or I, when we were twenty?

You even came back to us that summer—tired of that gloomy bedsitter where no one had forced you to go. You caught the train up to your lectures in the morning, and did not return, often, till late, very late. Irene would look at you when you were late as if testing you for something.

But they found you a new room, the next autumn, in one of the halls of residence. Small and neat. There was an anglepoise lamp; a pin-up board; a bed which folded back against the wall; and scarcely enough room on the formica shelves for all your books. But you would be looked after there. There was central heating and a launderette and they would clean your room for you and give you meals in the dining hall; and it was for you they'd built those new clean-lined buildings (there were still piles of scaffolding and sand beneath your window), employing the best architects to draw the plans. See how far the milk and orange juice had gone.

And you wouldn't be lonely, for in that neat residence

hall, like a luxurious barracks, there were fifty other girls like you, each with a room like yours with a number on the door and a slot for a name-card. I saw them, and felt embarrassed, as I helped you carry in your cases and bags. They giggled or gave little aloof, intense glances. Doors were half opened and record-players competed. As we passed along the corridor I glimpsed them, sitting on beds and floors, looking serious, cradling thick coffee mugs, demonstratively smoking cigarettes.

New, clean-lined buildings; purple bricks, glass, and wooden slats; newly sown grass outside your room in which rows of saplings had been planted. I felt old and out of place as I left and walked round the grass to the car; so that I was relieved by the gardener, with raw-looking hands, tying up the saplings, who nodded as I passed.

You stayed there two years—oh they moved you in your third year to another building, a bigger room, but it still had a number and a name-card. You came home in the holidays and sometimes you phoned and sometimes wrote. But it seemed as if you could never tell us clearly what you were doing or what was happening. 'I'm working hard,' you said. 'My tutor says I could get a First.' As if all that time you spent, until the beginning of that last year, were spent in waiting, waiting.

*

'Ingratitude,' we said, like an excuse.

'Don't you miss her, Mr Chapman?' Mrs Cooper asked, stirring the morning tea.

'She's only the other side of London.'

'And she's grown up now of course, isn't she? Old enough to lead her own life.'

Her eyes had swivelled behind the spectacles, looking for reactions.

'What is it she's studying exactly? English? I mean, what's it for?'

'Oh—not like this'—he glanced at the newspapers. 'Literature. Poetry.'

'Oh.'

The gaudy colours of the toy display in the Briar Street window were reflected in the lenses of her glasses. Her sleeve brushed the magazine counter from which young faces grinned and pouted: *Honey, Nineteen, Disc, Melody Maker*. She looked grave, unmoved, amid all the dazzle.

And yet, he knew—in eleven years he'd had time to discover it—that beneath her toil and tenacity, Mrs Cooper nursed dreams of her own.

1969. The kids were coming out of school, barging down the pavement as if the world was theirs. And stepping out, at the kerbside, from a pearl-grey Rover and having to pick his way through them, was Hancock. He walked briskly and purposefully—as well he might. For those house prices were rising, faster and faster. There would be a real boom soon: thousands added in a matter of months. He would flatter himself he'd foreseen it and watch the fees flow in (as he himself, behind his counter, watched the money fill the till—four hundred, five hundred pounds a week).

But there was a stiffness now and an aloofness in Hancock's bearing as he stepped, scarcely seeing them, through those waves of school children. No swagger in those long legs; no roguishness in that once sprightly face. As if all that had stopped, years ago.

Was it the stiffness of discretion—or of age?

26

Clomp, clomp. What was that? Smithy's young assistant Keith, hastening into the shop in his new leather boots and flared trousers, and standing for a moment, open-mouthed, in the middle of the floor, not seeing him as he crouched, replacing stock behind the counter—while the little spasm in Mrs Cooper's throat—he saw it even from where he stooped—rose in sudden alarm.

'Mr Chapman!'

For all his twenty-one years, the smart clothes, the medallion round his neck, Keith looked for a moment like a helpless schoolboy come to seek the master's aid.

'It's Mr Smithy, Mr Chapman. I don't think he's breathing.'

Wail of the ambulance up the High Street and the flash of its blue light as it passed the Prince William and Powell's and the Diana and drew up beyond the

235

entrance to Briar Street. It parked close to Smithy's door. The ambulance men made an attempt at concealment, opening the rear doors ready. But people had stopped to watch—Mrs Cooper watched through the window full of toys—and they had time to see that the body on the stretcher as it was carried out was entirely draped by the red blanket.

'Through here, Mr Chapman. Look.'

And there, in the little back room of the barber shop, was Smithy, in the easy chair, his head to one side, the glass of water that he was going to drink smashed on the floor. 'Don't touch anything,' he said. 'Nothing must be touched.' Although why he said it, he didn't know. Nor why Keith and Sullivan, Smithy's other assistant, bowed, ditheringly, to his command, put the 'Closed' sign on the door when he told them, sent away the single customer still lingering, half-shorn, in the shop, let him deal himself with the ambulance men.

November 16th, 1969. The figures on the pavement who had stopped to look moved on and the traffic in the High Street seemed to resume a halted progress like a film jerking back into life. In the shops they returned to business, to sudden energetic talk, activity. But they had seen: old Powell behind his racks of fruit, Hancock behind his photographs of property, and the proprietor of the Diana pushing aside the plastic menu placard hanging in the window. And they'd known. It was Smithy.

'Did it go all right?' she asked as he appeared at the door in his coat and his black tie. He shrugged.

She returned to her seat, under the standard lamp, and seemed just a little perplexed when he did not sit down immediately after entering from the hall, but stood looking out of the window at the lilac tree.

'Grace all right?'

'She's not taking it badly. She's going to her cousin's.'

That afternoon at the crematorium he'd stood with the little group of mourners and helped Smithy's sister in and out of the car and apologised because Irene was too ill to come. And Grace had said, 'Look after that wife of yours'; and he'd said with a wan smile, 'Oh, it's she who looks after me.'

She watched him sit down and not volunteer further comment.

'Shall I tell you something?' she said. 'I once went into Smithy's shop. It was in the war when I was in London with Father. I went to see the shop was all right; and then Smithy gave me a cup of tea, in his back room.'

'You went into our shop?' he said.

'Yes.' Her face was hollow and thin, but the gaze was

firm, as if she'd known at the time she would store up those past moments to recall them now.

'That was nearly thirty years ago,' he said.

It wouldn't last. Outside the hospital the flower lady trimmed and cut her bunches of flowers. Doctor Marsh replaced Doctor Cunningham on her appointment card, but Doctor Marsh could do no more than Doctor Cunningham, save to send her to Doctor Fletcher at St Thomas's. But that was not for the asthma; that was for her heart.

'Brrring! Brrring!' The telephone rang on the shelf next to the cigarette racks and Mrs Cooper answered. Over a year since Smithy's death; and Sullivan had taken over the barber shop and the red-and-white pole no longer twisted over the corner of Briar Street—'The wrong image for today,' Sullivan said.

'It's Mrs Pritchard.'

Mrs Cooper held out the receiver, and as he took it, placed it to his ear, and watched the expression of peculiar anticipation on Mrs Cooper's face, it seemed to him he had already heard the terse message, had already thrown his coat on and was driving, dry-mouthed, to the hospital; had enacted that scene, many times, before, though he never believed it was real—so that the thin, frightened voice of Mrs Pritchard (the woman they'd hired to do the house-work) sounded like some voice from inside him:

'It's Mrs Chapman. They've taken her to the hospital.'

27

How strangely untroubled you looked, appearing there at the swing door which the nurse, raising a finger and pointing, opened for you. You had come at once, taking a taxi at each end, so that it seemed you arrived only minutes after I phoned. You wore a long, dark red dress under your coat, and black boots, and you walked with a sure and steady stride, so that I thought: Yes, *she* too seemed to look her best in times of trouble—against the dark green blackout curtain; walking down a corridor in that same hospital, where her father died.

We hugged. Your cheek was cold from the wintry air outside but your breath was warm. We had never embraced like that before. You squeezed my wrist, and went to speak, purposefully, to the sister, and you didn't seem the same girl as I'd left in that neat room with its number and its slot for a name-card.

'Listen, Dad, it wasn't a severe attack. She'll be all right. The same as they told you. She's been sedated. There's nothing we can do here. Let's go home.'

How untroubled you looked. You sat me by the fire, made tea and cooked a supper which I didn't want, but which you made me eat. I ate slowly, in silence. And then we talked. That was the only time we ever really talked. I told you about old Harrison. Why did I dwell on old Harrison? He lay in a coma in that same hospital in 1945, while outside they danced and sang and celebrated victory with bonfires. And you told me—that was the time you chose to tell—about Hancock and those meetings with Paul. I never knew you knew so much about her family. And you spoke with a commiserative and tentative look, as if you were telling me something that ought to be kept from me.

For there was one thing you didn't tell me that night, wasn't there? Though I knew. Don't ask me how. Call it a father's instinct. You sat in the armchair opposite, leaning forward, your face like a torch in my eyes, and now and then your hand pulled smooth that red dress over your knees. But that movement wasn't like it used to be. There was something new in your voice and in your eye, and I knew: it had happened at last; you were no longer waiting, waiting. When, Dorry? It must have been sometime that term. Where? In that neat room with its number on the door and its rows of books?

'So Grandfather gave her the money?'

'Yes.'

'But why her, why not Uncle Paul or Grandmother?'

'Because he wanted, I think, to be forgiven.'

'For what?'

'I don't know. He always made demands of her. They never got on.'

'And that money bought the shop?'

'No—this was after the war. We bought the shop in '37. She had some money when we married.'

'And Grandfather's money?'

'Hers. None of it went into the shop. I think she felt it wasn't to be touched. She made sure it kept its value. Her investments—and all these things.'

You looked around pensively at the crystal and the china behind the glass in the cabinet. You seemed glad to be alone with me.

'But after Grandfather's death you needn't have kept on the shop.'

'No—but we did.'

'And then she never saw her family again, did she, after the war? I mean, Uncle Paul and Grandmother—?'

So many questions, Dorry, about the past—when you

had stepped so boldly into the present. I paused, peered into my cup of tea.

'But how are you doing now? Things okay?'

You lowered your eyes. You didn't want to answer questions either.

'Oh—I've started the special paper for Part Two.'

'What's that, then?'

'The English Romantic Poets.'

The mantelpiece clock chimed one in the morning. Late enough. But I didn't want to go up to lie alone without her, and to think of her lying alone. Or to leave you.

I said, 'I'll phone the hospital.'

'No—it's all right. They've got our number. If there's any need they'll phone you.' You pressed me back into the armchair.

'Don't worry, Dad, she'll be all right.'

'All right *now* maybe.'

You sighed reproachfully, at those despairing words.

I said, 'You will forgive her, won't you? You won't be hard on her?' You glanced up again questioningly. 'I know it seems she's always been against you.'

'Oh—that was only really since that business with Uncle Paul . . .'

'No, but before, before. She always . . . she always found it hard to be—to give certain things.'

'Things?'

'You know what I mean. You know.'

You frowned.

But I saw you knew.

'What I want to say is that she was always like that. It was the same for me too.'

'Even when you got married?'

'Yes, I suppose even then.'

'So you knew what you were doing?' You looked at me like a woman who means to get her way.

'No, Dorry. No, I never did.'

I put my head in my hand and looked up through my fingers at your eyes.

'Forgive me too.'

28

Sandra rocked gently on her stool. The lunchtime rush of customers had slackened and the clock was nearing two. She wasn't bothered by Mr Chapman's switching of the lunch breaks—she had none of Mrs Cooper's mania for routine. After Mrs Cooper had left she'd sighed, puffing out her cheeks and said, 'She's a fusser, ain't she?'—but he hadn't taken up the point. And now he was looking at her again from his stool by the fridge—oh not in a way she was used to (the way old men looked at her on buses and trains), but almost disappointedly, regretfully, as if he expected her to be something she wasn't.

'And what will you be doing this weekend, Sandra?' he suddenly said.

'Oh—might go down the coast, Sunday. Or up the swimming pool.'

Her shoe slipped from her foot beneath the counter onto

the floor, but she made no effort to retrieve it. She ran her toe over the wooden panel on the inside of the counter. Her legs were sticky where they crossed. Her cheek rested on her palm which was sticky too. Still he looked. She kept her eyes to the front of the shop where, beyond the window, the sunlight flashed on car windows and, to the right, on the empty beer glasses on the low wall outside the Prince William. 'Well, sorry,' she said to herself, recrossing her legs and wondering simultaneously what she *would* do at the weekend, 'Whatever it is, I'm not it.' And she turned at last to Mr Chapman, whose heavy, purplish face seemed suddenly quite forlorn, like some stone figure that has inexplicably melted and lost its shape.

'Well, there is no use disguising the fact,' she said, easing herself into her seat and pursing her lips.

She had come home that morning after two weeks in hospital; he'd left Mrs Cooper in charge of the shop. Somehow he hoped a new woman might have returned to him, but he saw by that flatness of the lips, it was not so.

'A heart condition is a heart condition,' she continued.

It was almost Christmas, and cold. Outside, the garden looked damp and raw. She asked for a blanket and he got her one—the large red and brown blanket which they'd used as a picnic rug in the days of their Sunday drives. She asked for her handbag and her medicines and he put them on the trolley beside her chair, along with the inhaler, the papers, and the antique collectors' journals which she still liked to scour, sending off for catalogues. She looked very weak. But only once, as he tucked the blanket round her and felt for a moment like a father putting a child to bed, had her expression admitted this weakness. And then it was in the form of resentment, annoyance. Her mouth twisted curiously as he leant over her.

He stayed at home with her all that day. She spoke briefly about what the doctors said. There was a risk: no exertion; precautions must be taken. And he talked about the shop. He didn't anticipate such large Christmas sales this year— but he'd said the same the year before.

Then he was going to ask: 'Should we be thinking about selling the shop?'

But that evening she said, as if to forestall him, 'I think we should get another shop.' And in the New Year they bought Pond Street.

29

'I'll be off to Pond Street, then, Mrs Cooper.'

He stood in the doorway, parting the plastic strips, having exchanged his shop coat for his jacket, rinsed his hands and face, and put the wage packets from the safe—they were made up differently this week—in his briefcase.

Mrs Cooper had returned, puffing, from her shopping, with an air of accusation, as if she were about to discover some scandal. Sandra had slipped out, to her own lunch, pressing a new stick of chewing gum into her mouth, and as she passed Mrs Cooper in front of the counter the two women had glowered icily at each other.

'Have you eaten?' Mrs Cooper asked him, and without waiting for a response she turned to rummage in her shopping bag. 'I got a sandwich from the snack bar—chicken, you can eat that. And there's some apples from Powell's.'

'That's kind of you.' He pushed the bags to one side. 'Later, eh?'

Magnanimously, she waved aside the coins he held out to her.

'Don't be silly. You'll be back within the hour, then? Before *she* comes back.'

'No, Mrs Cooper. I imagine I'll be quite a while. I thought I'd walk.'

'Walk!'

Mrs Cooper stared wildly.

'It's the other side of the common! You've never walked to Pond Street before, you've always driven.' The lump rose and quaked in her throat. 'Mr Chapman, be sensible! In this heat—with your leg—and when the doctor keeps telling you not to overdo it. You might—' her voice suddenly lost all subtlety—'What on earth do you want to walk for?!'

He'd predicted all this. It was almost amusing to watch it occurring just as he expected.

'I have my reasons, Mrs Cooper. It *is*'—he nodded to the doorway—'a fine day.'

He stooped to shut the catch on his briefcase and do up the straps.

She looked unbelievingly at him.

'You're a fool,' she said with sudden involuntary force. Then seemed dazed by her own words.

He raised his head.

'That's as may be,' he said calmly.

He did up the second strap on the briefcase and straightened his jacket. She stood aside, stunned, as he lifted up the flap in the counter and nodded as he said, 'Look after things, won't you?

'Bye now.'

'Bye.' She couldn't say anything else.

The toy monkeys shook over the counter as he shut the shop door. She watched him turn right, then cross the road and stand poised for a while on the traffic island.

Why had she said those words to him? A sudden panic seized her.

But she'd meant them.

He stepped onto the opposite kerb. There was only the dull ache in his chest. Black trickles of melted tar gleamed in the gutter, and the cars as they gusted by seemed to raise a hotter, not a cooler draught. He walked through the thick shadows of the trees on the paving stones, as if entering some long-rehearsed scene. And as he walked they noticed him: Hobbes; Simpson, behind his cool green and blue chemist's bottles; the secretary in Hancock's, sitting back now from her typewriter while the boss was at lunch. And they wondered, what was he doing, Mr Chapman, who was only ever to be seen in his shop or driving to and from it, and who never walked anywhere—except to the bank?

Simpson's, Hancock's, the Diana. On the corner, under the faded, dark green awning, the wasps buzzed over Powell's strawberries and plums. And there, in the shady recess of the shop, as if he really had nothing to do with the sun and the bright fruit on his stalls, in his grey, eternal cardigan which seemed to match his bloodless skin and ashen hair, old Powell himself, raising a hand, half surprised, as he passed. He would never know if it was true: that scar that was supposed to cover half his body.

Traffic filtered out of Allandale Road. A bus, a delivery van. And there, on the opposite corner, outside the Prince William, like holiday-makers, they sat and sprawled, shirts unbuttoned, glasses shining, with ten more minutes of drinking to go.

He turned into Allandale Road. As he did so, Hancock emerged, on the opposite side, from the back entrance to the saloon, squaring his shoulders, raising his head but blinking in the brightness. And blinking too, as he crossed the road, at the sight of the sweet shop owner on the pavement with his briefcase.

The same and not the same. I once joked about the Prince William, Dorry. I said to Irene: 'The Prince Willy—they named it after me.'

That was one evening before the war, when I was still preparing the shop for opening, and I asked her to meet me, at six, in the Prince William. There was a beer garden then, grass and wooden tables and cherry trees—where Armstrong's garage is now—and there was a big wooden pub sign hanging at the front: Prince William himself in a bronze breastplate, sash and wig, and a smoky background suggestive of battles and storms. That was the only time the High Street regulars saw Irene. They looked at her, over their drinks, and perhaps they confided to each other later, already spreading my legend: 'That woman with that new feller, Chapman, in the pub last night. You'll never believe it—his wife.'

I told her to meet me after work and to wear the blue and white dress she wore on our honeymoon, because I wanted just one perfect evening. She came. She wore the dress. She looked like someone acting under instructions. She sipped the Pimms I bought her; she smiled across the wooden table, and even laughed at my joke, because she knew this was expected of her and it wouldn't happen again and I must have one perfect picture . . .

I still keep that picture, Dorry. A mental photograph. Though the beer garden's gone, Prince William in his breastplate's gone . . . and she's gone.

We walked back over the grass of the common, under

the trees. How green this part of London always was. And up in the bedroom, behind the green curtains, the scent of Pimms and lemon on her lips . . . I let you touch me but I'm not touched, I let you take me but I'm not possessed, I let you . . .

That was in '38. Two weeks later I slipped off a ladder and damaged my back. And a year after that—that was after the shop opened and Mother and Father died—the war broke out. But I didn't fight. I wasn't fit for active service. I only learnt to count, to number, not to touch.

30

'Something up with the car?'

He gripped the briefcase more tightly, as if Hancock, stepping over onto his side, might have been about to snatch it.

'No. No. I thought I'd walk. For a change.'

'Sure you're up to it, old man?'

Hancock's breath smelt of drink. The face was bleary-eyed, brick red. Five years ago the voice might have held a taunt (you—with your limp and weak chest—walk to Pond Street!), but now it seemed almost to waver with sympathy.

'Pay-day at Pond Street?'

'Yes.'

They stared inertly at each other as if looking into mirrors. Save for Hancock's visits to the shop, they scarcely met, and now that they came face to face in the street it was as if something needed explaining.

'I—er—was going to pop in on my way back.'

'That's all right. Mrs Cooper's there.'

'Of course. Look—are you sure you should be walking over there?'

'Sure enough.'

Hancock shuffled awkwardly.

'Well—mind how you go.' He held out a hand indecisively. It was as if he were about to offer support—or needed to be steadied himself. But he changed the gesture in mid-course and pointed to the briefcase.

'Hang on to the goods,' he said drily.

Down Allandale Road. Past Armstrong's garage. Armstrong's pump attendants, who no longer were issued with blue and yellow overalls, lounging in the heat in faded singlets and jeans. Up above, the garish blue canopy with the company insignia and a sign saying 'Quadruple Stamps'—as if to make up for the hard prices on the petrol pumps. Those Arabs had driven a tough bargain. But on the forecourt there were great glistening black patches. See, it still gets spilt, precious stuff.

Across Allandale Road. Shade on this side. Breathing hard already. Pain in the chest just nudging. He would have to gauge it carefully; rest now and then.

A few shops to left and right. An electrician's, an

Asian food shop, a betting shop; and then the rows of tall, bay-fronted Victorian houses, with basements and steps up to the door, converted into offices and dental surgeries, or knocked down to make way for new blocks. Builders' merchant's; a car showroom; the squat, oblong office of a firm that made light bulbs. Dairy on the left opposite Finch Street (horses once, snorting and clopping; troughs outside, yellowish at the rim). Baptist church, zebra crossing, then more shops. Follow the road where it descends and curves to the left, and you get to where Mrs Cooper lives.

He turned right, out of the shade, into Finch Street, carrying the pain in his chest as if it were something he could retain or release at will. Finch Street was a cul-de-sac. Like the other streets to the right off Allandale Road it ended in railings and the footpath which skirted the common.

I told her, Dorry. That winter she came out of hospital and we bought Pond Street. She would have found out anyway. She had a way of knowing things, of sensing them before I even guessed them, so that what she didn't know you felt compelled to tell her. 'I think Dorry's got a boyfriend,' I said. 'At last,' I added, as though to pass it lightly off. She was sitting in her chair where she always sat now, that Angora shawl round her shoulders, pink with a grey-blue weave in it. She didn't answer at first, as if she were waiting to hear something else.

'Who?' she said quietly.

But I didn't know who. I didn't say it was only a father's guess. I knew nothing precise. You came home that Christmas and you said nothing, but you knew she knew, and you looked at me accusingly. She studied you, as if you might be marked, changed. You found it hard to meet her eyes.

And as though to overcome all that, you said blandly and indifferently one weekend in February: 'Oh, I've met a man at college. A history graduate. We've been going out some time.' As if you were afraid to make your voice sound glad.

'Oh, that's nice. Isn't that nice, Willy? We must meet him sometime.'

You looked at her as if she were mocking you, calling the bluff of your own casualness. As if you'd expected anger, alarm.

'You must bring him down here, Dorry.'

'Maybe.' You shrugged. 'All right.'

And so you brought him, a fortnight later. To outface her challenge and to call her bluff in return? Or do I misjudge you, Dorry? Did you come simply to oblige an ailing mother and a fond father?

Were you still, then, the good, the loyal daughter?

31

The tea things were laid on the trolley and on the mahogany cake stand. Salmon and egg and cress sandwiches, which she wasn't allowed to eat; a cake, a Dundee. Mrs Pritchard had come specially to clean and help in the kitchen and I'd asked Mrs Cooper ('That's all right,' she said, 'I'll manage') to stand in at the shop. We hadn't had a visitor in that house for so long. She put on a cream silk blouse, unworn for years. The sleeves seemed filled only with air. But she covered them with her shawl and sat in her chair, waiting. We heard the car pull up outside. I watched from the window. A blue Mini.

You had a bunch of flowers in your hand which you gave to him as he finished locking the car door. You whispered something as you came up the path. He buttoned his jacket. You straightened your dress. A performance.

'This is Michael. Michael, Mother and Father.'

He was tall, keen-eyed; a large, strong hand held out for mine. His robust, intelligent good looks made me think of Doctor Cunningham, so that I shrank a little, as I did under those cool questions at the hospital, having expected someone somehow less imposing. He spoke deftly and fluently, crossing his long legs on the sofa and clasping his knee, and I felt my own voice falter when I offered: 'History. Now I've always been fascinated by history.' And I felt forlorn as you looked at me reproachfully, then turned your head in embarrassment at the conversation that failed to follow. In the silences, he gazed round, curiously, at the porcelain in the cabinet and the vases on the mantelpiece. His eyes would fix on Irene, then look quickly away. And I noticed, more than once, he gave the same look to you.

Your face reddened. With shame, with anger? I watched the colour deepen, the more the cups chinked, the more she wheezed in her armchair, plucked at her shawl and now and then coughed into her serviette, patting her throat and saying, 'Oh I'm very sorry, please do forgive me, please'— and I watched it flare up as if some draught had fanned it when she brushed crumbs from her blouse and announced:

'Well, Michael, it's so nice to see you. You know, Dorothy doesn't tell us much about you. She keeps her secrets. So you're working for a doctorate. We must think of your futures, mustn't we?' She lifted her cup. 'What exactly are your arrangements?'

I didn't know she would have said that. Believe me, I had nothing to do with those words; and even I sat, with my slice of Dundee cake poised, in surprise, before my lips. Should I have intervened, put down my plate, and said, like a discreet husband, 'Now really dear,' and laughed? Made it clear it was only a game of bluff? But I wasn't clear if it was only a game. Games turn into fights.

'Well, when you say arrangements, Mrs Chapman'— fusion and hostility suddenly upset the deftness—'I'm not sure that I—we—that's to say it doesn't—it's a question of—what exactly do you mean by "arrangements"?'

And I watched Irene, in her chair, almost imperceptibly, draw in her feet.

Later, as you washed up the things together, dutifully, in the kitchen, I overheard snatches of your talk: 'That was fun, wasn't it? . . . I told you, didn't I? . . . *He* doesn't say much, does he? . . . Oh, you were lucky he took time off from his precious shop to see us—he'll be straight off again after this . . . this bloody china . . . so we know what to do now, don't we, Mike? Don't we? . . .'

'Bye.'

'Goodbye.'

She didn't come to the door. She had her excuse. She sat hunched with her shawl in the armchair.

'Glad to have met you.'

I stood in the porch like some helpless mediator. I waved. The car lights winked, moving off down Leigh Drive. That was the only time I saw him, and the last time I saw you, without its being—what shall I say?—under conditions of truce.

He reached the end of Finch Street and passed beyond the gap in the railings.

Mrs Bennet said the world was ahead of you. Twenty-two that summer and your final exams to sit for. A First—as Mrs Bennet might have predicted. But no celebrations or congratulatory gifts and kisses. I only said to Mrs Cooper, who didn't understand, 'She got a First.' 'It's the best you can get,' I explained. 'It means she's got her degree.' And I told Hancock, when he asked. 'Always was a clever girl,' he said. But I moderated my pride, in each case, for fear of the question that would follow—'What will she do now?' You'd phoned up to tell us your result, almost disdainfully ('Oh that's wonderful news, Dorry, that's wonderful'). And later you announced that you'd made up your mind to try for a Ph.D. Then nothing. Not even a word to say you'd be home for the summer. You had to vacate your college room at the end of the term but we could guess, surely enough, where you'd be living. Only a brief letter at the end of July, which said, 'I'm taking a holiday. I'm going to Greece next month with Michael.' 'He'll pay for her I suppose,' was all she said, as if she were washing her hands of something. But I sent you a cheque, secretly, and wrote on the back of it: 'For your holiday—enjoy yourselves.' You didn't return it. And four or five weeks later we got the postcard—a blue sea, white houses, a beach—marked somewhere in Crete; and on the back, signed only by you, was the message: 'Enjoying ourselves.'

When I saw you next, that September, you still had traces of a sun-tan, but you didn't want to discuss your holiday, and I felt jealous and thought of our meagre fort-nights in Dorset.

She was in hospital again then—nothing bad; tests, observation. I hadn't asked you to come. But did you time that visit carefully, knowing she wouldn't be there? We didn't do much talking. You had your large suitcase with you and you said you had to pick up some things. Books, papers, your tape-recorder. Yet most of those things had gone already. So why were you turning out drawers, taking things we could have kept for you, your perfume bottles from the bathroom, the Devon pottery that you bought in

Teignmouth? You didn't go to visit her at the hospital, and I never told her you were at home. 'How's Michael?' I asked you. 'Oh he's fine, fine.' But you didn't say, 'How's Mother?'

And after that, letters, about once a month, which said little. Irene never read them, though she recognised them from the envelope. She left them to me as if they weren't hers to touch. She seemed to be renouncing all contact with things. I opened them in the evening, and took them to the shop the next morning, tucked in my breast pocket (like this letter now), and I kept them, first in a cash tin in the safe, then in another tin—an old Oxo tin—which I have at home.

February, March, April '73. Was it only last year? 'How is she?' was all Irene said after she knew I'd had a letter. 'All right,' I'd say and she'd turn and look away. 'How is she?' But that was more than you ever asked of her. Though she was dwindling, Dorry, in that armchair.

Another spell in hospital, that April. When I went to see her she was wired up and connected to some machine. Little wires from her neck, from her chest, a tube in her arm and nose. And she looked up oddly from beneath all that clutter, like a child who has put on a disguise or hidden behind something but easily been discovered. When she came home she said, 'I'm going to have Barrett round. I want things to be settled.' Barrett was her solicitor, Dorry.

And all this time I was working, harder than ever, in the shop. Though the face I saw in the mirror seemed to have become suddenly the face of an ageing, over-worked, livid-cheeked, corpulent man, a man who needed to ease off, take more recreation, retire. And already in my left side, though I scarcely noticed it till later, was that little pain, with its name like a rare butterfly's.

April, May, June, '73. Then we got your letter, in July. It was the first one I showed her, though I was afraid—no stress, no excitement.

'What will they do?' She looked up blankly. 'What will they live on? She won't have any money.' Though it wasn't the money that troubled her. She raised her face and said— she who'd always seemed able to predict things—'What now? What happens now?' Though behind those words there was something else, a cry, far off, as if sounding over waves—which I knew then I'd never stopped hearing.

I believe she would have seen Barrett again. She would have changed it, Dorry. If there'd been time.

Dear Mother and Father,

I'm giving up my course here. I can always finish the thesis later. Michael's been offered a research post at Bristol and there's a chance of a lecturership. I'm going with him to live with him.

32

The common littered with people. Couples fondling each other on the grass. Prams. Kids. Plastic balls. A commotion and a frenzied splashing down at the paddling pool. He made his way along the asphalt path, screwing up his eyes against the sun. He patted momentarily his breast pocket.

You can see it all from here, Dorry. The world ahead of you. Down there on the right, the stretch of the High Street where it flanks the common. Traffic lights beyond. Then the railway bridge: green sign with a white arrow pointing to the station. Domed roof of the Town Hall, gabled roof of Gibbs' department store. There are the shops, straight ahead, on Common Road, where she used to get all her things; Mason's the butcher's, Cullen's, Henderson's. Beyond them—you could have seen the clock tower once, over the rooftops—the school where my parents toiled to send me. And, far-distant, half-left, poking up from the shoulder of the hill, the grey, ill-proportioned spire of St Stephen's.

I met her here those first times, Dorry; here on the common. She looked as though she were lingering on some errand. And up there, at St Stephen's, you were christened, and your grandfather, whom you never saw, was buried, near the plaque to his already dead son. We never moved out of these narrow bounds. Born here, schooled here, worked here. And even when I met her I stood here on the common and thought: enough, now everything is in its place, and I in mine.

Spire of St Stephen's, domed roof of the Town Hall, grey paths across the green common; trams passing. The sun was warm on our necks as we leant on the railings. But I never believed you could have the real thing.

She would have acted, Dorry; would have seen Barrett. There was that last week. She would have said, 'Willy—'

July, '73. Up the Common Road, past Mason's and Cullen's, past the evening plane trees, my briefcase, with the books, on the back seat. She was waiting for me to come. I used to let myself in, so as not to disturb her. How many times had I done these things? Past the clock and the mirror in the hall. It must have been between the time Mrs

Pritchard left and I shut the shop. Her head was on one side. The cap still on her tube of pills: she hadn't reached for them. Her lips were blue and cold and had a sickly smell when I bent to touch them.

He always claimed he'd seen her. That morning. Though they didn't believe him, Stephen and Bob. Don't believe what old Phil tells you. He didn't tell Mr Chapman. It was an honour to do the round Mr Chapman's house was on. Leigh Drive: number thirty-three. There was dew on the garden and sparrows chirping. She must have heard him put the papers through—always three or four dailies at thirty-three. For he saw her at the front window as he propped his bike on the opposite kerb. It was the only time he'd seen her. And she stood there for a moment, behind the window, pulling back the lace curtain—did she want to call him, to say something?—like someone trapped in a glass case.

Up that slide, Dorry—there where the kids are playing. When she said, 'Why don't you?' I did, I obeyed. I clambered up that slide and slid down.

Mrs Cooper wiped her glasses. There hadn't been a customer for nearly a quarter of an hour. Three o'clock. The mid-afternoon lull. She sat by the till. Her glasses were misty. Where was he? Halfway up the Common Road? In Russell Street? Gasping, straining his poor heart. Mr Chapman—she'd do anything, anything. She rested her elbow on the counter and propped her cheek in her palm. No customers; the shop to herself. She rocked gently back and forth on two legs of her stool, crossing her legs one over the other—a slither of nylon—and feeling her shoe on her right foot, under the counter, hang just by the toes.

Sandra stood before the mirror in the changing cubicle. It was hot and oppressive down here in the basement of the shop. The electric lights, the music, the blow-ups of Mick Jagger and Paul Newman on the walls, put there to make it seem they were watching you undress. Two rows of cubicles with flimsy curtains. Though the thing was, of course, not to draw the curtains. She stood in her bra and briefs looking at herself. Yes, she was all right in the right places. She didn't need a bra—she had a good mind to take it off and go back to the shop with only her T-shirt on, just to see that old bag's eyes pop. She'd tried on the red dress. Yes, it looked great on her. She would buy it, with Mr Chapman's money. But she paused, irresolutely, before the mirror. Just for a moment, it was as though some other person looked back at her, unreachable behind the glass.

*

Children's playground. Grey spire of St Stephen's. Dome of the Town Hall. Everything in its place. He put his left thumb in his breast pocket and touched the letter.

'You will see in the end.'

Yes, well all right. Even though she never changed the will, most of that money should have been yours. I didn't need it. But—don't you see? I kept it because it was all I had that was hers. It was her price, my dues from the bargain. And I would only have kept it—not touched it. So that in the end, anyway—

And supposing I'd given you the money—with indecent promptness, after the funeral? 'Here—it's mine, but I don't want it.' You'd have gone off with it, for good—to him in Bristol. Don't you see? I kept that money to keep you too.

So I wrote you that letter in August. She'd been dead only three weeks.

Dear Dorothy,

You know that Mother made clear in her will that no money of hers should be passed on by me to you, except through a will of my own. You know my feelings about it. You know had she ever discussed it I would have persuaded her against it. But out of respect for her wishes—out of respect

for your dead mother—I think we must do what
she wanted.

Where did I find those sanctimonious words? I should have
added: 'Out of respect for her wishes you ought to stay with
me, be with me.' You were her gift. And you wrote back—
that was only a month after we cremated her—'What about
the respect due to me?'

I waited for you to come. All through last winter.
I thought: if you come back, what does the money
matter? But only your demanding letters came. Were we
really at war?

I waited through Christmas. I did all those things I'd
done before—got up at five-fifteen, made my breakfast,
sat at the table at night with my books on the green baize
cloth—automatically and mechanically, as if she were still
there. I touched nothing. The furniture, the china, her
chair by the window. I said to Mrs Pritchard: Nothing
must be changed. The same and not the same. And in the
shop I felt my face, over the counter, go hard like a shell. I
thought, this is what happens: you harden, you set in your
mould. I worked on like a machine, counting the weekly
takings I no longer needed. Though that was a winter of
sudden thrift: power-cuts; no oil, no lights in the shop
windows, a three-day week. And I saw on Hancock's face

as he came in for cigars a stony look like my own: it's all over, that mad boom, now we can count the cost.

The cost? I had these pains in my side. I knew it was my heart. I went to Doctor Field's. And then to the hospital, where they tested me and cardiographed me and entered little notes in files. How fragile we are. Doctor Field explained and prescribed tablets. They're the same ones as my wife took, I said, and he said, 'Yes.' Then he told me: 'And you must take the pressure off. Perhaps it's time you were thinking of giving up that shop of yours.'

Mrs Cooper said, 'Well he's right too. You could give it up now. Take a complete rest. I'd manage for you.' She had the air of a hired nurse who has earned a share in her patient's decisions. Along the High Street she was broadcasting, with her own embellishments, my story—our story, Dorry. 'Went off and left him, she did. Only turned up for the funeral. Went off with some student—and him with a heart condition. Little bitch.' Though I knew what she was thinking: 'Poor, poor Mr Chapman—the old tight-wad.' 'Come, come and spend Christmas with me,' she said. 'You can't spend it all on your own.' And I knew I had to watch out.

I waited, Dorry. The money was only a token. I never meant us to fight.

33

He reached the Common Road, under the shade of the plane trees. The pain in his chest was like a tight breast-plate. He paused for a moment by one of the peeling tree trunks, gathering his breath; removed his jacket and hooked it over his right shoulder. A 'Mr Whippy' van, pink and cream, with a jangling loudspeaker that played 'Greensleeves', had drawn up on the pavement. Hands reaching. Good weather for business.

He crossed over the road, breathing deeply, waiting for the gaps in the traffic, then turned up Russell Street.

I used to walk along this same road, Russell Street, on my way to school, with a briefcase in my hand then. For Mum and Dad said, now you've got to the grammar school you must have a briefcase, not a satchel like the ordinary kids. I used to get the tram from where we lived, which was not far from where Mrs Cooper's flat is, down Allandale Road, then walk over the common. At four o'clock back again, less briskly, by the same route; though not before taking the detour, with the others, down Pond Street—to Mr Vincent's shop.

If someone had said then: One day you will own that shop; one day you will walk along Russell Street with your briefcase containing wage-packets and order forms, I wouldn't have been surprised. If someone had said, There, where you walk across the common, you will meet your future wife, there she will decide to marry you, I would have replied, All right, so be it. I didn't believe, despite being at grammar school, that the future belonged to me. I thought: things would come to you anyway, and when they did they would already be turned into history.

Shady on this side of Russell Street. Gaunt Edwardian houses offsetting the new estate on the other side. Then the turning-off which, if you follow it, curves up past the old people's home to St Stephen's church. Then the brick wall—there are slogans on it in chalk and aerosol spray—'Russell Bootboys', 'Judy Freeman fucks coons'; ambitiously sketched bits of anatomy—which someone has tried to remove. Then the railings, the double row of chestnuts, their outer branches jutting over the railings and the pavement. Pause here. Breathe. The shade under chestnut trees is always dense and cool. They are one of the first trees to sprout in spring and to shed in the autumn. That was something I learnt at school, Dorry, by not paying attention; by looking from the window.

School gates open, splitting the wrought-iron motto in two. *Virtus et Fortitudo.* Asphalt area beneath the blocks of classrooms—silent now. To the right of the gates, beyond the trunks of the chestnuts, in a square plot bordered with marigolds, the memorial.

Perhaps I knew him then, perhaps I was already his memory, this old, breathless figure, the same and not the same as me, with a briefcase, walking now down Russell Street. Perhaps I knew Mr Vincent's shop would become Mr Chapman's; perhaps I knew when I walked home over the common that I was crossing the path I would one day take home to my wife. Life was set out like a map. Like the waxy, pastel-coloured maps that hung, that afternoon, in the History Room. 'Europe after the Seven Years War'; 'The World—Present Day'. The history master was explaining about Henry VIII. From that second-floor room you could see, if you looked one way, the playing fields with the white goal posts, and, the other way, the asphalt, the chestnut trees, the gates leading out into Russell Street. It was an icy afternoon in March but the sun was bright. Shrill cries were coming from the playing fields. History. The master said I didn't have the right attitude. 'Does not concentrate; poor essays' ('Henry VIII dissolved the monasteries because he'd have done so anyway'). Even that afternoon he tried to recall me to the present (in a history lesson, Dorry!) with his sharp 'Are you with us, Chapman? Not paying attention again!' But I put my head to the window and the view like a map, and I saw.

That was the day before the school sports. I was the favourite for the mile. I'd won it the year before and equalled the school record, and I was seldom beaten in house matches. I was sixteen, not athletic-looking, but I had strong legs and stamina. I was hopeless at schoolwork but I had this one talent for distance running. I'd win again they said—and even the history master had to concede (the class laughed) as he caught me gazing out of the window—'All right, Chapman, you'll have your moment tomorrow, but would you mind telling us now why Thomas Cromwell was executed?'

He moved on past the school gates, put the briefcase down, paused again, held his left side, waited.

34

'Right, let's be having you!'

The voice of Mr Hill, the games master—veteran of Great War drill halls and still apt to let his sergeant's voice rap and chafe them as if they were troops departing for the front—rang out over the track. His black starter's pistol lay on the grass and he strode now up and down in front of them, his stopwatch dangling from his neck, calling out their names, which he knew perfectly well, and ticking them off on his list, as if, at this moment of action, it were all the more necessary to keep precise records.

'Right, up to the line when I tell you.'

In front of them the black cinder track, already churned and pitted by the afternoon's events, stretched away to the finishing line and the judge's table, then curved to the left. The mile; the culminating event of the day. Ahead, beyond the hawthorn hedge and the cricket sight-screens, the playing fields. On the inside, the high jump and long jump pits; on the outside, the spectators. Boys in blue uniforms; exhorting parents. To the left, across the track, the elm trees and wooden fence marking the school boundary. Tops of the houses in Woodruff Road beyond; the spire of St Stephen's.

A fresh wind stirred the branches of the elm trees and the sun sailed out and then was shuttered again behind swift clouds. The day was bright, but colder than one expected for late March, and the watching parents stamped their feet and rubbed gloved hands, partly from chilliness and partly to prove their heartiness as spectators.

'He's the one to watch.'

Thompson was speaking to him as they waited, jogging and limbering behind the starting line. He was nodding towards a tall, muscular boy, built like a sprinter rather than a distance runner, with dark hair and clean features, whose face, at that moment, looked tense and severe.

'He's won the 440. If he wins this he'll get the *Victor Ludorum*, as well as the Mile Cup.'

'If we let him win.'

He smiled; and for the first time heard his voice sound as if he were playing a part.

Thompson grinned. Thompson was captain of his house, a senior prefect and one of the honoured of the school. He would stand by the track one day, vigorously shouting on his own son.

'You'll let me take up the running at first as usual?' he said, deferring graciously. The parting in his sandy hair was clean and straight, even now at the end of a day's athletics.

'Why? Won't you try yourself? This isn't a house match.'

Thompson shook his head protestingly. His duties were to his house, the school, to fair play and credit where due. There was nothing he wouldn't sacrifice for these things.

'No. It's your race.'

They paced to and fro, loosening their limbs, waiting for the judge's signal and Mr Hill's command. They wore white shorts and singlets and, since they were finalists in a major event, had black numbers on white cards fixed to their backs. He watched them flexing and drawing breath. There were signs of strain, of apprehension on the waiting faces, mixed with odd looks of pride and earnestness, as if they were thinking, only this moment matters, only the race counts. They paused, communing with themselves, summoning their strength, glancing down at their bodies and up again, as if looking into mirrors.

And he felt none of this—not any more. He stood on the grass at the track-side, bending and stretching his legs mechanically, as if he, the favourite, were not really a participant, as if the race about to be run were already decided. For wasn't it? He looked beyond Thompson at the dark-haired boy, whose face with its clean, grave expression suddenly turned with a look of hostility.

'Take your marks!'

Mr Hill's voice rasped and the crowd at the track-side quietened distinctly, like a theatre audience when the lights go down. He took his place on the line, between Thompson and Cox. He was expected to win. From out of the crowd he heard his own name, carried shrilly on the wind: 'Chapmaaan ...' He had won the 880, beating that same dark-haired boy into third place, and he was famous in the school, if for nothing else, for the mile. 'Chapmaan ...' He was expected to win, but the crowd would like a battle. People liked battles.

'Wait for it then.'

Mr Hill walked pompously across in front of them, inspecting the ranks, waving his pistol in his right hand as if about to carry out an execution.

Black cinders, with the white lanes marked ahead. March, 1931. Four-thirty, by the school clock tower. Most of them would be leaving that summer.

The sun came out from behind a cloud, shining into their faces, gilding their expectant brows and jutting chins, making tiny specks in the cinders sparkle in front of them.

Now!

A mile. Five and a third laps of the black track. Plenty of time. Time to think as well as act; time to watch as well as take part. That was the beauty of distance running. A send-off cheer from the crowd; the blur of faces by the finishing line; and by the time they had rounded the first bend a pace and a pattern had emerged. The dark-haired boy, wearing number three, in the lead: to be expected. Holloway chasing him, then Thompson, making his sacrifice; then Peters, Cox, with his number card already coming loose, and himself, without having consciously planned it, tucked in in mid-field. Hawthorn hedge on the right; sound of breathing and scuffed cinders; and their own shadows, in the sun, suddenly swinging round from behind them and appearing on their left.

To be expected—number three in front. Valiantly to the fore. A fierce pace. Never mind. Stick to the mid-field. Settle back, watch.

Boundary fence and Woodruff Road on the right.

Shouts of the crowd sounding thin over this side of the track. Round the bend towards the starting line. This is the point at which you realise what it entails, running a mile. Legs already tired, breath short; and over four laps to go. Never mind. The end of the second lap's worse. Third and fourth laps hardest of all. But somewhere in the middle you find a second strength. The pains in the calves, the ache in the chest are only signs that the body is working. A machine.

He felt it now, thudding beneath him like a motor, bearing him up as if he were being carried by something that wasn't part of him.

Keep your eye on the landmarks as you round the bends: St Stephen's spire, into the back straight; the clock tower, into the home straight. That's the trick of it. 'Not paying attention again, Chapman!' But, didn't he see, that was precisely what he *was* doing? Looking at things that were fixed while you moved yourself. That was how you endured.

They came out of the back straight and round the bend towards the third lap. The number three had a good three yards' lead and had only slackened pace slightly. Holloway followed, shoulders rolling a little. Thompson clung gamely onto Holloway—he had enough perhaps for another lap. Cox had edged forward into fourth place and Peters slipped back; so that in the front running there were three distinct divisions, about nine yards spanning them all. The sun shone again as they entered the home straight and he saw Peters dropping back, red-faced and curly-headed, at his right shoulder, screwing up his eyes exasperatedly.

Past the winning post, round the first bend, the shadows on the grass swivelling round mockingly in front of them. Barely half the race run, but already—you can sense it—they are getting lost in their struggles. A grimness setting in. They don't notice the wails of the crowd or the encouragement of the figures clustered round the winning post and the judge's desk—sports masters, house monitors in blazers and flannels, Mr Hill, bending over the track, waving what seems a threatening fist as they approach; the clock tower, the spire. Don't they see, the secret is not to think of the race? But they notice only the endless dark circuit of the track. A grimness. The crowd senses it. The cheering changes tone. They like a battle.

Winning post for the third time. He ought to move up now, not let the gap open. Cox was in second place; Holloway struggling; Thompson falling back, spent at last. Peters had pressed ahead again, and he could hear a determined breathing—it was Price perhaps, or Skinner—close behind him. Move up now. It was expected.

'Chapmaaan ...'

He pressed his toes down harder and stretched his pace. The machine adjusts: the power is there. He moved up past Peters and alongside Thompson who turned, as he passed, a haggard, sweaty face, proud of having done his bit, performed his duty, and fell back. Then he settled in behind Holloway.

A surge of noise from the crowd. The back straight. Holloway was a heavy lumberer; stamina, but no finish.

Cox would try, and Peters, behind, might have something left. But his eyes were on the black number three, holding its position perhaps four yards ahead.

How brave, how solitary. The eternal athlete, the eternal champion, running into his future.

He picked up the briefcase and walked on slowly past the war memorial.

Into the top bend. The sun was out, tinselling the grass, shining on the straining bodies in front of him. He looked at the black numbers on the white singlets, 3, 4, 8, all careering on, and suddenly felt that he wanted to laugh.

He kicked his legs into another spurt, passed Holloway and moved beside Cox as they entered the home straight. The crowd yelled—the last lap about to begin—wrapping them in a tunnel of fervour. They love this. This is the stuff of which stories are told. He could hear them saying, when the race was over: 'The way Chapman moved up', 'The way Cox fought back'; spreading the legend. And they themselves, the competitors, in the changing room afterwards, flushed with the drama: heroes.

He overtook Cox, who held on, gasping, behind him. Past the jumping pits. Past the trestle table, set back from the track—next to the loudspeaker apparatus and the judge's desk—on which were laid out the trophies. Cups, shields, glinting in the sun. A glimpse of the prizes to be won. Then the bell, at the finishing line, ferociously clanged; Mr Hill's bugle of a mouth; a confusion of yelled names. Chapman had poised himself. To be expected. Keep up the performance.

The hawthorn hedge; back of the sight-screens. For the last time. The figure two yards in front had given a backward glance as they left the bell behind, and the face, appearing for an instant over the shoulder, was taut with determination. He looked at the tensed torso—the shoulders, still steady, the sleek black hair. How innocent it seemed. A better body than his, the kind of body that would wear well and look good in photographs and always seem in its prime. Whereas his own body (they laughed at him in class) had a sort of unyouthful clownishness about it. The sun went in. He drew closer to the unyielding leader. He winced suddenly. Then he was past. Only the black track ahead: fence, spire of St Stephen's.

What had he done? Excitement in the crowd. He had passed the leader on the bottom bend with still most of the lap to go—not, as usual, on the last bend. Begun his final spurt early. That was unexpected.

He ran down the back straight. He thought: why was Thomas Cromwell executed?

Round the top bend. Pain in the chest. To be expected. The crowd in uproar. They saw he hadn't shaken off his rival: the former leader was catching up again. He knew it.

School clock tower. The minute hand had moved only that little. The race is decided. It's over as soon as it starts. They think it's a battle but it's only a performance. They think it's action but it's only a pattern. You move and keep your eyes on what is fixed. And if you win it blinds you. You think, 'This moment is mine.' It's yours, like the silver cup they give you with your name on it ('Mile Champion, 1931'), but you forget it's only a performance, and it's the moment that captures you. Down the straight. The last time. If you win, you lose. The crowd is screaming. There will be the victory ceremony, the trophies, proud smiles, grandiloquent words on the loudspeaker. *Virtus et Fortitudo*. After the excitement, the crowd will go away, light cigarettes, buy evening papers.

The dark-haired boy was perhaps only a yard behind. Hold him off a little longer. But let him have his moment. Let him think it's the real thing.

The jumping pits, the trophy stand. For the last time. The tape stretched out ahead. Heads arching in over the finishing line. A photographer for the school magazine, with a boater, squatting on the track beyond the tape.

The dark-haired boy's name was Harrison. Jack Harrison.

285

He had a younger brother who was captain of cricket. He would be leaving in the summer. His parents were there, among the crowd, smartly dressed in tweeds, the father imposing, the mother pale-skinned, chestnut-haired. And *she* might have been there, the sister, Irene.

They would be shouting now, the mother and father, the father bellowing himself hoarse (would he remember him later—'Chapman'?) as they urged their son to take the lead once more. There would be cries of delight as they watched him breast the finishing tape; frenzied clapping and self-important smiles as they watched him walk up to take the 440 Trophy, the Mile Cup, the *Victor Ludorum*. The father would light a cigar. Honour to the family. Rejoicing in the home that night.

There he was, at his shoulder, in the outer lane. Brow wet, chin jutting. He could force him back, if he wanted to, run faster. The power was there. Thirty yards to go. Neck and neck. Sun in their eyes. Twenty, fifteen.

All right. Now.

35

You were standing in the hallway with the front door open. I had seen the car parked outside as I drove up Leigh Drive. The blue Mini—his Mini; the boot open and already packed with boxes, clothes on hangers, polythene bags, jumble. You didn't know I was there. You must have been upstairs when I pulled up on the drive. And you weren't expecting me. It was only five on a sunny evening in May. You didn't know I had this pain in my chest, attacks of breathlessness, and that that afternoon I'd shut the shop early. Otherwise, you chose your moment well.

I got out of the car, walked over to the Mini, then in at the front gate. There were tulips out by the front path. You were standing at the foot of the stairs, sideways on, adjusting your grip on a loaded cardboard box. It was one of the cardboard boxes in which goods used to arrive at the shop. You raised it up from beneath with your knee. You hadn't seen me and weren't expecting me. When people aren't expecting to be seen they look their truest. How innocent you looked. You were wearing jeans and a white blouse, and the way you shifted the box with your leg was so determined, so absorbed. Then, as you turned, you looked up and saw me. Your eyes hardened, as if a childish prank had turned suddenly into a crime. But before that they flickered: a moment of fear, of precariousness, as if, if I'd made a sudden move, you might have toppled.

'Father.'

'Dorry.'

My eyes took their photograph of that moment. Your face framed in the doorway; half turned; your profile caught in the mirror behind. You looked trapped. In the box you were carrying I saw the edge of the little wooden chest—polished walnut with a brass catch—in which Irene had kept her jewels. You didn't have a key. You must have known where I put them—in the drawer of the bureau.

'Dorry, what are you doing?'

You clung to the cardboard box as if I'd have wrenched it from you.

'I'm taking the last of my things.'

'Those are her things.'

'*Were.* They're mine now.'

I stood on the porch steps, my keys in my hand. You

had occupied the house and were forbidding me entrance. There was a pain in my chest like a metal bar, which you weren't aware of. We stood like that, for what seemed an infinity. I thought: I can see what ought to happen, what should happen; but it won't, it will turn the other way. If you hadn't been holding that box I would have stepped forward to embrace you.

'Dorry, let's talk.'

'No. Not now.'

Your voice was exasperated rather than defiant. I noticed another cardboard box at the foot of the stairs with one of her fur stoles inside, just visible beneath a sheet of brown paper. I remembered when she bought it.

'Dorry, we ought to talk. We can settle this.'

You shook your head. The box was getting heavy in your hands, but you clung to it like a defence.

'Will you let me take this to the car?'

There were a score of phrases ready to hand—'Now listen here, my girl . . . You've no right . . . Take those things back this minute'—but I said nothing. I thought: I'm not going to fight; if there is no fight then no one wins.

I said, 'Dorry, what are you doing?'

The weight of the box was beginning to threaten your pose. You raised it again with your knee. There was a moment when it seemed your act of daring might end in comic catastrophe—necklaces strewn over the stairs, emeralds and pearls over the hall carpet. But you steadied yourself, propping the box against the stair-post.

I stepped inside. 'Why didn't you tell me you were coming?'

A stupid question, I know. But it made it seem as if I'd half expected you; that the fact that you were looting the house wasn't important.

'Oh don't worry—I would have left you a note!'

Your brow knotted. If I had fought you it would have been so much easier, wouldn't it?

'Dorry, I had no idea—'

'Well you've caught me in the act, haven't you? I thought you'd be at your shop.' You hissed the last word.

'I shut the shop early today. I'm not so well, you know, Dorry: I have to take things easier—'

'Well if it's all such a strain why don't you shut that bloody shop for good! Give it up for good!' Your fingers clawed at the box. Then you added suddenly: 'You can now, can't you? She's been dead nine months, you know!'

That was your victory cry. You stepped forward, hugging the box, as if you knew you could step through me. I didn't prevent you. On the wall behind you was your photograph—you in her arms, with me looking on, at your christening. I held my side. I said, 'Look, I'm not

290

well. I've got to sit down. Come to me—when you've finished.'

But I didn't go to sit down at once. I leant against the stair-post like some dumb, helpless statue, while you passed to and fro, ignoring me, taking away her things like trophies. I thought: she gave you to me in place of what she couldn't give herself; now you are taking from me what had been hers. Through the open door, I watched you lay her furs on the back seat of the car, carefully, lovingly—a way you never treated her.

When you passed me for the fourth time I said, 'I'll be in there,' and tottered into the living room. I sat in the armchair, facing the windows, with my back straight, my knees square in front of me and my arms on the armrests as if I were made of bronze. The garden was in shade but there was sun on the lilac tree. I said to myself: I will give you the money. And when I give you the money I will give up the shop. But first you must come to me one last time.

Upstairs you were opening and closing drawers. I thought, Mrs Pritchard will learn of it, Mrs Cooper will get wind of it. I would have to perform for her benefit, invent another legend: 'You see, that's what daughters do, Mrs Cooper, that's the thanks you get for all your trouble.' I heard you pass in the hall. You said nothing, not even 'Goodbye'.

36

Bryant and Miss Fox looked up over the counter, amazed, as if they hadn't expected to see him; then they looked doubly shocked, seeing the state he was in—gasping, sweat pouring off him.

'Didn't you come in the car?' Bryant asked.

He leant on the counter.

'I walked. It's all right.'

'Quick, Susan—a chair for Mr Chapman.'

Miss Fox opened the flap in the counter, brought out a wooden, round-backed chair, and he sat down in it, like an honoured customer.

'And a glass of water, if you wouldn't mind,' he said.

He reached for the bottle of pills in his pocket.

'Why on earth did you walk?' said Bryant, almost scoldingly. 'In this weather. You shouldn't.'

'It's all right. I know what I'm doing. Be fine in a moment.'

Bryant was bald on top but with sleek growths of pale hair at the back and sides; he wore thick glasses over brown, needly eyes. Miss Fox, just turned twenty, was plump and brisk.

'There,' he said, having dissolved the tablet under his tongue and drained the tumblerful of water.

They both still looked at him as if he were some escaped convict.

Normally on Fridays he got to Pond Street at a quarter to three. It was half-past three now. Not such a great difference. But they seemed to sense everything had changed.

'Well—what's new?'

Bryant tried to appear unperplexed. He rubbed his chin uneasily. 'Oh—average week. Ice cream and soft drinks up, of course, with the weather. Sure you're okay?'

He felt weak, despite the effects of the pill, but he said, 'Yes, yes.'

'Think it will last?'

He looked up, momentarily puzzled.

'The weather.'

'Oh—the forecast was good this morning.'

Bryant ran his palm over his bald crown.

'As long as it lasts for the weekend,' said Miss Fox.

'Going away somewhere?'

'Broadstairs. With my sister.'

'That's nice.'

A customer entered and Bryant said in a self-conscious, impatient voice, 'Susan, see to this gentleman, will you?'

Bryant leant forward towards him, while Miss Fox moved down the counter. Bryant liked to display his authority and to indicate to Miss Fox that he had a special, confidential relationship with Mr Chapman which allowed him to delegate tasks. It was all quite transparent. He was hoping soon the shop would be his. He was waiting for Mr Chapman to pass it on. He even hoped that the Briar Street shop, Mrs Cooper's claims notwithstanding, might one day be his.

'About those copies of the orders which I phoned about. There was only one, Jackson's—and he came yesterday. Have you got the others?'

'No.' He patted the briefcase. 'There's some receipts, some wholesalers' lists—and, the usual. I didn't make out those orders.'

'But—' Bryant looked confused—'we're getting rather low on some lines.'

'Never mind. You'll see,' he said calmly.

Bryant frowned, scratched his cheek, seemed to be about to ask something, but then smoothed his expression. He resented his employer's insistence on doing so much of the paperwork himself; and the fact that that paperwork was now becoming lax and haphazard seemed further proof that the boss should step down.

Miss Fox moved up the counter, having served the customer.

'Broadstairs?' resumed Mr Chapman, undoing the straps of his briefcase.

'Yes—my sister and her husband have a holiday flat down there.'

'Holidays, eh?'

The girl smiled. She had a sober, rather flat face which rippled now and then with girlishness. He half suspected that Bryant and Miss Fox didn't get on.

'Parents going down too?'

'Yes—maybe.'

'Good.' He fished in his briefcase. 'Well I'd better do what I came to do.'

The pain in his chest had subsided and he breathed more easily. Bryant and the girl still looked perturbed, but they seemed more reassured when he produced the familiar buff envelopes. Well, they would be surprised again. Out of common propriety they wouldn't open their packets and count their money now. They would see the usual figure on the advice slip inside the opaque envelope windows. Perhaps later, after he'd gone, they would check their money separately and not dare to tell the other their discovery, in case of jealousies, recriminations. But they would know. One hundred for Miss Fox. Five hundred for Bryant.

Paid.

Sandra walked into the shop, the new dress, in a smart pink and brown carrier bag, in her hand. She was late, but she didn't care. Mr Chapman wasn't back yet. Only the old cow, alone at the counter. She swung the carrier bag casually and met Mrs Cooper's eyes.

'You're not going to walk back again?' said Bryant belligerently. Then, placatingly, 'Here, let me run you back in my car.'

'It's all right,' he said, 'I know what I'm doing.' And then, reshouldering his jacket and eyeing his watch, 'You'll be getting the rush from the school any minute.'

'Get the bus back along the High Street,' Miss Fox urged, looking confused.

'Yes, maybe. You enjoy that weekend now. So long.'

He took a last, curious glance around the shop. He'd never told them, Bryant or Miss Fox, that once he'd come here on the way home after school, for comics and liquorice sticks. Vincent was a fat, round-faced, jovial man—like some figure in a pack of 'Happy Families'. Now his own name was over the door.

He stepped out and up towards the school, not down towards the High Street; and was aware of their eyes, inside, watching him helplessly, as if, as he left, he had turned the key in the door.

'And what's this, then?' said Mrs Cooper. Her hand was on the edge of the carrier bag, into which she had peered beadily, spotting the red dress.

Down Russell Street. Steadily. The body is a machine. The sun fell on his back, sending a shadow out in front of him which gave his blunt and portly frame an air of sprightly elongation. Behind him they were coming out of school. Out through the mottoed iron gates. Blazers slung over shoulders, sleeves rolled; loose, restless limbs. They carried books and bags carelessly and had their uniforms adapted so as to keep in the fashion: wide-bottomed trousers—once it was tapered legs and sharp-toed shoes—and platform heels. They scuffed along by the railings, under the chestnut trees, loosening the blue and cream striped tie he had once worn. White shirts and blue blazers under dappled leaves. He let them pass him as if he were being overtaken in a race.

'Nothing better to squander your money on?' said Mrs Cooper.

'Can spend it how I like, can't I?' said Sandra. She bent over the fridge, took out a can of Coca-Cola, pulled off the ring-tab and, as Mrs Cooper's lips drew tighter, said coolly, 'It's all right, I'll ring it up.'

'Nothing but spend!' Mrs Cooper said. She'd put a hand inside the carrier bag and was feeling the slippery material.

'As a matter of fact,' Sandra added, 'I wasn't really spending anything. More of a present.' She tilted her head aloofly. 'Mr Chapman gave me an extra twenty-five quid this morning. He said to buy a new dress with it.'

She swallowed a gulp of Coke.

'What did you say?!' Mrs Cooper's face was pale and contorted as if she were about to scream. 'What?!' She clutched the carrier bag and looked suddenly, with widening eyes, at the front of Sandra's T-shirt as if she'd spotted the signal to attack.

Not now, not now. Wait, watch. Look at what's fixed.

He was leaning with one hand on the railings beside the children's playground. Someone said, 'You all right?' and held out a hand, and he said, 'Yes,' though it was difficult to speak. The common was as crowded as when he'd passed in the opposite direction. Children on the swings in the playground and under the willow beside the paddling pool. Schoolkids going home. Boys from John Russell meeting girls from Allandale and St Clare's and sprawling on the grass. But none of this belonged to him. He felt cold in the sunlight.

Not now. Breathe. Spire of St Stephen's, dome of the Town Hall. Look at these things. I was an athlete once.

The grass beside the playground was worn and thin. He lowered his head to stop the giddiness. Against the foot of the railings litter had blown and wedged itself. Cigarette packets, newspapers, sweet wrappers.

Dorry, I sent you the £15,000. You'll come.

37

They watched him cross by the traffic island and then disappear for a moment as he stepped onto the near pavement. It was almost four-thirty. He was walking in a shuffling, unsteady fashion, his sleeves rolled, his jacket draped loosely over one shoulder.

Mrs Cooper gripped the edge of the counter. All things being normal, she would have been ready now, as he staggered in through the door, with her 'I told you so' and her 'What did you expect?', ready with her taunts and then, sitting him down, fussing round him, with her undiminished devotion. But something had happened. She had torn apart the red dress. She had pulled and Sandra had pulled; and she had felt suddenly, in pulling, that it wasn't a dress at all but Mr Chapman she was pulling, back and forth, in the most shameless way; and when it had ripped suddenly down the seam it was as though Mr Chapman had come apart, in the same flimsy fashion, and that was all there was left of him.

'He never bought you this,' she said.

''Ere, give it 'ere!'

'Little liar! Little bitch!'

Then Sandra had said those words, and her eyes had stung with tears.

All things being normal, she might even have experienced a feeling of relief, of inexplicable pride, watching his lumbering frame returning across the High Street, still breathing, still living, the fool, like some winner at the finishing line. But all that had changed. She clung to the counter, to its worn wooden surface. How well she knew, after sixteen years, every lump, crack and ridge on that counter.

Sandra sat erectly on her stool. The dress lay, almost torn in two, in the crumpled bag at her feet. But it was worth it. What did it matter, a new dress, a bit of flimsy colour? It was worth it to be able to say at last: 'You'll never have him.'

He walked in at the door. It seemed for a moment that he might have blundered mistakenly into some shop that was no longer his own—or that he might see, behind the counter, some grotesque replica of himself confronting him. He had to concentrate, not only to recover his breath, but to overcome the sense of strangeness. Then he saw that something had happened. They were standing looking at him with the distinct stillness of people after there has been action.

'Mr Chapman—you look dreadful.'

Mrs Cooper spoke. Expected words. But she uttered them in a peculiar way, with neither anxiety nor reproof, as if she were merely mouthing a part.

'I'll be all right in a minute—' he wheezed. 'Must admit—overdone it a bit.'

He lurched towards the counter. The little still tableau seemed suddenly to start into life again, as if by clockwork. Sandra, who was by the flap, lifted it for him but said nothing. He noticed that she wasn't wearing a bra.

'Be with you in a moment—just get my breath back.'

He put a hand out to part the veil of plastic strips.

Mrs Cooper, like some attentive valet, followed him mechanically into the stock room. He stood for a moment by the cardboard boxes, clutching the briefcase.

'Here, let me. You sit down,' Mrs Cooper said. The same old predictable phrases, but they no longer had that wheedling, abrasive tone. They were spoken almost with meekness.

She took the briefcase and put it in its regular place, on top of the safe. Then she hung his jacket on the wooden hanger on the peg by the sink. She filled a glass of water from the tap. She seemed to be going through these simple motions in order to hide something.

'Pill?'

'Breast pocket,' he said, not thinking—and then remembered, and looked on aghast. Standing by the sink, Mrs Cooper reached inside the pocket and pulled out, with the little phial of pills, the folded piece of light blue notepaper. At any other time obsequiousness would not have prevented her, even in his presence, from opening it and quickly scanning the contents. But now she simply glanced at it incuriously without unfolding it and put it back where it had come from.

She undid the bottle and tipped out a pill onto her left palm.

'There.'

She held out the glass in her right hand and the pill in her left, as if offering food to some unfriendly animal.

'Thanks.'

'What a thing to do,' she said as he took the pill. 'What did you do that for?'—but still in that subdued, unscolding tone. And she added softly, before turning and walking back into the shop:

'You know, she won't come back.'

*

He sat for several minutes in the stock room, digesting Mrs Cooper's words. They were the first words of hers in sixteen years that had actually penetrated him, pierced him with a sense that she was tuned to his secretest thoughts. But what struck him most was the manner in which they were said— as if their force applied to her; as if she herself were deserted, abandoned, and no longer pretended.

He swallowed the pill. You were supposed to melt them in the mouth, not swallow them, but it didn't matter.

What had happened in his absence? He looked through the plastic strips to where Mrs Cooper and Sandra were dealing with a flurry of customers. They looked unnaturally busy, ignoring each other's presence, like people who know they have done wrong.

He drained his glass of water and, after rinsing his face and arms at the sink, shuffled, still breathless, back into the shop.

'Everything—er—all right?' he asked, standing by the plastic strips.

'Yes—yes,' Mrs Cooper replied.

Sandra said nothing and scarcely turned. Why had she taken off her bra? It made her look vulnerable rather than provocative. There was a bag by her feet, a chocolate and pink carrier bag torn at the handle. As his eyes moved to it Mrs Cooper looked up helplessly. Then he understood. The whole history of the afternoon became clear to him: Sandra had bought the dress. It was in the carrier bag. Mrs Cooper had discovered, misinterpreted. There had been a fight.

Suddenly he wanted to laugh. Did Mrs Cooper see—looking at him imploringly, as if he were about to punish her—that he really wanted to laugh?

'Mrs Cooper, Sandra,' he announced. 'I'm going to shut the shop.'

They looked up, lips parted.

'I'm going to shut the shop at half-past five. You can leave early.'

And not come back, thought Sandra.

He no longer wants us, thought Mrs Cooper.

The clock over the door stood at ten-past five.

'I'm none too well, you can see that—I'm closing early.'

They didn't protest.

'Sandra, before you go, would you mind doing the awning?'

He took up his position at the counter. The evening rush had begun, and he started to flick the evening papers off the pile, fold them and hold them out, his hand cupped for the coins.

'Much obliged. Thanking you.'

You had to perform to the last. Even with a pain like an iron bolt in your chest.

He watched Sandra outside on the pavement, struggling with the High Street awning. Her body was unavoidably on show as she reached with the pole, but—unlike Phil, displaying his strength in the morning—she seemed suddenly unnerved by the fact. When two youths, passing by, feinted a grab at her, she rounded on them almost menacingly.

She re-entered the shop, slid the pole into its resting place and then stood, rubbing her palms on her skirt.

'Is it all right then—if I go?'

The clock showed only twenty past—but it made no difference.

'Yes, of course.'

No snapped interjection came from Mrs Cooper.

Sandra lifted the flap in the counter and passed into the stock room. She returned with her shoulder bag and then, hesitating momentarily and lowering her eyes, stooped to pick up the tattered carrier bag. She lifted it, crumpling the paper tight and held it protectively over her bra-less breasts.

Mrs Cooper's hands scurried extra quickly over the piles of papers.

'Right, then—'

'Okay, Sandra. Have a good weekend.'

'Oh—yeh.' And she turned to the door.

After she'd left, he couldn't resist asking Mrs Cooper,

'What was in that bag?' And Mrs Cooper said, without meeting his eyes, 'Oh, nothing important, I shouldn't think.'

They worked on in silence at the counter. He waited for her to say, true to form: 'If you want to go home, Mr Chapman, it's all right, I don't mind, I'll stay and close up.' But she didn't. When half-past came he said, 'Off you go, then,' and she took off her shop coat and gathered her things without a murmur.

'Tomorrow, then, Mr Chapman.'

'Yes. Tomorrow.'

Somehow it seemed they both knew they were pretending.

She walked briskly to the door and only then did she pause.

'Goodbye, then.'

'Goodbye, Janet.'

He had called her Janet.

38

Half-past five. It seemed as if he were making his escape. He had always known it would be like this. Tomorrow they would discover the fraud, the deception: the costume discarded, the things left untouched so as to make it seem nothing had changed.

He watched Mrs Cooper lug her shopping bag across Briar Street and pass out of sight round the corner where Smithy's pole had twirled. Then he lifted up the flap in the counter. There was a timely gap in the succession of customers. The pain in his chest gave little evil prods. He moved to the door, twisted round the plastic sign to 'Closed', released the latch and slipped across the two bolts at the top and bottom.

There. It was done.

He moved back to the counter. Now the 'Closed' sign was up and the door locked it seemed he was somehow shut off from the flow of the High Street. The noise of the homeward traffic, thickening on the near side of the road, seemed muted, and the cars and pedestrians passing by the window might have been moving in some vast sun-barred aquarium.

He sat down on his stool. No need to hurry. Half-past five. They would be coming home now, in their hordes; work over, pleasure in store. Down at the station the trains would unload from Cannon Street and London Bridge; hot and crumpled commuters, sweaty and fidgety from the stifling carriages, but freed, at last. Across the road the Prince William would open its cool saloons to receive them. The landlord would be blessing the sunshine. Thirsty weather: good weather for trade. And along the High Street the shops which kept the normal hours would be closing. Business done: life begins. Simpson would count his cash. Powell would take in his trestles. In his wood-panelled office, behind the shading blinds and with the electric fan whirring on the filing cabinet, Hancock would lock away papers, give a terse goodnight to his departing staff, and even though it was a warm, careless evening in June, would make sure his jacket was buttoned, his tie in place, his shoulders straight before leaving.

He looked round at the crowded shelves of the shop. The cellophane wrappers crinkled, as ever, as under some invisible, covetous touch, and the toys dangling and perched in the Briar Street window seemed to jostle visibly, as if the plastic dolls, action-men and model knights in armour, whose promise was to be like the real thing, were actually about to come to life. He felt like a conjuror, amid his tricks, for whom, alone, there is no illusion.

He opened the till drawer. Everything must be done as normal. He pulled back the spring-clip over the five-pound notes and started to count.

At Briar Street they would expect to call, as usual, walking up from the station, for their little trifles of tobacco and newsprint. But they would find the shop closed. Chapman—who never closed; who was always open, Sundays too, raking in the cash, which he never had time to spend; who was always there with your cigarettes or paper, as late as seven in the evening. They would rattle, annoyed, at the door and rap on the glass; and peering in they would see him, sitting in his usual place, still and unperturbed, like the statue of someone who had once been a shopkeeper. See—there was someone already, and another, looking at the 'Closed' sign as if it did not mean what it said and staring in, hand held over eyes, as into the cage of some unobliging pet. He raised a hand and moved it slowly in a lazy, indifferent wave. They would gather perhaps at the corner; try to force the door. And perhaps he should let them. Fling back the bolts. Let them swarm in to plunder and grab. Gorge themselves on sweets and ice creams, fight over the boxes of Havanas. And he would sit motionless in the midst of the looting, as if, after they had emptied the shelves, they would set to work to dismantle his effigy.

He lifted himself from the stool onto his feet. The pain seemed to rock inside him like a weight that would overturn him. He steadied. Not now. But he wouldn't take a pill. People were stopping now and then at the door and trying the handle but he took no notice of them. He started to count the one-pound notes, then the coins. Everything must be done as usual; everything must look the same. He carried the money in the little pink and blue bank bags and placed them inside the green cash tin inside the safe. Then he made a note of the figure inside the maroon cash book. These were actions he had carried out so many times that he could do them almost without thinking; and yet, this time, they seemed like unique operations, as if he hadn't counted up and closed numberless times before. He shut the cash book. £92. Twenty years ago you would have been glad to take ten. He put the cash book in his briefcase and locked the safe. He had got the safe in '49. There were scratch marks on its door and the black paint on the handle was worn away to the metal from years of opening and shutting. He went back into the shop; switched off the electric fan, checked the fridge, set the time switch for the display lights, put his hand down to the lever beneath the telephone which activated the burglar alarm—but then withdrew it. It didn't matter now—they could break in and steal. The shop door was already fastened. He would leave by the rear door in the stock room. It led to a narrow passage which turned at a right angle into Briar Street. For some time he had meant to fit a better lock on it. But today it could be left unlocked. Once outside he could even throw away the keys. Toss them out into the swirl of the High Street.

Someone else was rattling at the door, looking in and making pleading, desperate gestures. He took no notice. He looked at the counter and the shelves. Then he turned his back on the shop and passed through the plastic strips. Best to go by the back. Actors slip out by back exits, leaving their roles on the stage. He moved to the wash basin to rinse his hands and comb his hair. He expected to see for a moment, in the mirror, the face of a young man, unchanged, with a thirties stiff collar and a waistcoat.

He put on his jacket, took up his briefcase and then opened the rear door. He walked along the passageway, where, here and there, tufts of grass and dandelions grew in the cracks in the concrete, then out, across the wide pavement, by the cinema adverts, to the car.

The car was drawn up, half on the pavement, pointing

away from the High Street. Normally he drove down Briar Street, avoiding the awkward U-turn out into the main road. But it didn't matter now. Normally he didn't shut at half-past five; normally he didn't walk to Pond Street. A sudden exhilaration came over him. He took a packet of cigars from under the dashboard and lit one. The doctor had warned. Then he swung out, in a break in the traffic, into Briar Street and out into the queue of cars in the High Street.

He did not look back. Not at the front window, with his name, in blue and gold, emblazoned above; nor at the door, at which they were still tapping and rattling perhaps, trying to discern him within. No, there was no longer a sweet shop owner.

The sun shone from the direction of the town hall, dazzling on car bonnets and in the glass frontages where Simpson's and Hobbes' had already shut shop. Only the Diana was open, dilatorily serving out limp salads and milkshakes, the manager chasing flies behind the counter. The traffic moved slowly, in two lanes, down towards Allandale Road and the traffic lights by the common. Always congested at this time; both directions. Drivers were propped on elbows against open windows, holding up idle arms and drumming irritably with their fingers on car roofs. A motorcyclist revved impatiently. And on the pavement the pedestrians walked with that peculiar agitation of people travelling home from work on a Friday evening. Why did they look so intent, so vexed, when, up above, the lime trees shone, green-gold, in the sun?

His foot rocked on the pedals as he crept forward in the line of cars. They were drinking in the Prince William as he passed. Through the open saloon doors he was half prepared to glimpse the big, ornate French windows, the beer garden.

Past the Prince William. Past the Council buildings where once the baths had been where Dorry swam. He placed his left hand on his chest as he drew up again for the lights, and blew the blue cigar smoke, painfully pleasant, out of his mouth. Common on the left, criss-crossed with paths.

What was the name of that thesis you were writing, Dorry? 'Romantic Poetry and the Sense of History'? And now you are living with a historian. What do you learn from history, Dorry? Was it history that made you come and plunder your father's house? Or the opposite? Did you want to escape history, to put it all behind you—me; her, those twenty-odd years in that house? To have your moment, your victory at last, with one wild gesture? But—don't you see?—it's the moment (framed in the doorway with your heavy box of loot) that captures you.

And have you escaped history, down there in Bristol? Found new life? Encumbered with all those things of hers, encumbered with the money I sent you (that money, which was only converted history). Don't you see, you're no freer than before, no freer than I am? And the only thing that can dissolve history now is if, by a miracle, you come.

39

He turned into Leigh Drive. He had put on the car radio. The weatherman was saying, in apologetic tones, that rain was expected for the morning. But along the curving pavements, the sycamores and rowan trees were stirring blithely in the deepening sun. Earlier homecomers were already out, in shaded front gardens, watering flowers and trimming edges. Mr Norris, in number twenty-eight, knobbly-kneed in long khaki shorts, like a dauntless colonial. Mr Dixon, in number thirty, with a pair of shears.

He drove onto the crazy paving of the garage drive and stopped. The neighbours, with their clippers and hoses, would look up, seeing the cream-coloured Hillman, and think, 'He's early'; and then continue their tasks. 'Don't blame him, on an evening like this.' They would see his usual stout figure stepping from the car; but they wouldn't see the pain swelling inside his ribs. Mr Dixon waved. He got out, the engine running, to unlock the garage. The metal handles were hot to touch and as he pulled open the heavy doors he had to gauge the effort carefully. Not now. He returned to the car, drove it into the garage, emerged again with his briefcase, and shut, laboriously, the two doors. Then he walked along the path by the bay window and the hydrangeas to the front door.

Outside, all was clear, obvious. Inside he seemed to enter a submerged, aqueous world in which the past was embedded like sunken treasure. He'd drawn all the curtains in the morning to keep the house cool; and he moved now, slowly, like a diver with heavy boots, through a shady, flickering world, shot with eddies and swirls of light, where the sun found its way through chinks or penetrated dimly, as into the hollows of a wreck, through the rippled curtains. He hung his jacket over the post at the foot of the stairs and put his briefcase in the usual place beside the umbrella stand. The ticking barometer-clock, the photographs on the wall loomed through the ooze, and as he opened the door into the living room, the polished cabinets, one for china, one for glass, the green baize on the oval table, the spiralling stem of the standard lamp swam into view, as if he were really discovering, let down in his diving suit, a world left long ago, miraculously preserved. 'See, things remain.'

He crossed to the French windows and drew back the

beige curtains, so that the murky relics inside were suddenly raised once more into the fresh, familiar light of the present. Should he redraw them? Was it more fitting to return to the veiled museum-world? But he kept them open. The lilac was half within the shadow of the house, but its upper leaves, where the mauve cones had already bloomed and died, fluttered in the sunshine. He opened the quarter lights of the window so that the sound of lawn-mowers, clippers, a smell of cut grass trickled in on the breeze.

She could never get enough air. Or was it that air assailed her?

He turned round again to face the room. The clock on the mantelpiece showed half-past six. Its hands might have stopped for ever at that position, like a clock rescued from some catastrophe, recording the exact moment of disaster. But not yet, not yet.

Normally, when he returned from the shop he would change his clothes, eat the meal that Mrs Pritchard left, prepared but uncooked, in the kitchen, wash up, sit at the table and make up his books—or, on an evening like this, potter gently in the garden. But there was no need of those things now. He had been lifted clear, it seemed, of that frame of routine that had been built around him, able to see it at last like some visitor from outside. So that his feet led him to wander now, with the immunity of a ghost, round this deserted monument of a house.

He climbed the stairs. Each step cost an effort. Yet he could almost encourage the pain now. He passed into the bedroom, gloomy behind the drawn curtains; into Dorry's room—lingering several minutes; into the spare bedroom with its long, quilt-covered trunk. He ran his eyes diligently over objects, like a curator making a final tour before the gallery is locked.

It is all here, Dorry. Locked in little mementos, fixed in little tokens of the past. As if its only purpose were to be saved for this final glance.

He opened the heavy lid of the trunk. This required concentration. His hands reached down to a red tin box, hidden beneath other boxes full of objects wrapped in tissue paper and old newspaper.

You never delved this far when you came. Did I prevent you? These are the letters she wrote to me when I was a Quartermaster's clerk in Hampshire and she worked at the Food Office. How good we always were at minding the store. How well we've kept everything. Up till now.

His eyes studied the worn envelopes, with the addresses crossed out, several times, for re-use, and the red stamps with the head of George VI. But he didn't open the folded notepaper.

Sometimes, in museums, Dorry, you think what you see isn't real. And these (he took another batch of envelopes from the tin box), these are all your letters from college—when you would write just to me and not to her.

The china shepherd and shepherdess on the dressing table still anticipated their embrace. He wasn't aware how many times he slipped from one room to another, inspecting their silent contents. Was it to make sure all was complete, secure? To summon life from those unmoving objects? To laugh at their fraudulence? Perhaps he was already sitting, motionless himself, in the armchair where he'd decided he would sit, and it was only some shadow of himself, touching but not touching these frozen items of stock, who drifted now—out of his daughter's room—onto the landing at the top of the stairs.

I don't believe in ghosts, Dorry. But sometimes, alone in this house, I've thought she's watching me, her moist eyes stalking me still, ensuring that I keep all just as it was. Perhaps she's watching me now. Is her face set, Dorry, in that old tenacity? Or smiling? Or torn with remorse? And what does she want now, watching over me? Is she saying: Forget her, Willy? Or is she hoping, too—you will come?

He grasped the bannister to descend. His head swam, looking down. Don't fall. He came down, gingerly at first, then more rapidly. No more precautions. He picked up his jacket from the stair-post. He moved across the hall, not looking at the photographs on the wall. The needle in the barometer pointed to 'Change'.

In the living room he eyed the clock as if there were some deadline.

Twenty past seven. You wouldn't come till after my normal time for getting in.

The shadow had crept further up the lilac tree. Bryant would have closed, an hour ago, at Pond Street. Miss Fox would be on her way to Broadstairs. Sandra would be home—trying on again that new dress? Mrs Cooper would have opened her pay packet at last, and discovered, beside her normal wage, the five hundred pounds.

He moved to the armchair by the standard lamp, turning it to face the window, and sat down. Though he sat, the pain didn't diminish. Her shawl was draped where it had always been, over the headrest. He held his jacket in his lap. When she died she was waiting for me to come.

He looked out at the lilac and the sun-flecked garden.

I always liked gardening, Dorry. If I hadn't been a shopkeeper I'd have been a gardener. Arranging the flower beds was like arranging the sweets in the shop window. I never knew if she liked gardens too. She wouldn't come outside, because of her asthma. Though she used to sit watching me intently, from the window, mowing the grass, tending the flowers. But perhaps she preferred all those lifeless, lasting things: cut glass, willow-pattern plates, vases with pictures of flowers, not real flowers, on them. And she left them to me, as you can't leave real flowers, as her memorial.

The clock chimed half-past seven. The pain rose in his chest so that his face, always so wooden, so expressionless, might have been convulsed and torn.

Memorials. They don't matter. They don't belong to us. They are only things we leave behind so we can vanish safely. Disguises to set us free. That's why I built my own memorial so compliantly—the one she allotted me, down there in the High Street. A memorial of trifles, useless things. And what will you do with my memorial, Dorry?

Something caught in his throat like a stuck laugh. Not yet.

Spit on my memorial, Dorry, sell it up, forget it. That's what memorials are for. You might have had the real thing. You got the money. And you didn't have to extort it, for it would have been yours, anyway, in the end. That money was always meant to be passed on. It was never hers; it was only the token of something. She used it to buy useless bits of glass and china. And do you know where it really came from? It belonged to her uncles, your great-uncles; three of them. They were knocked down like pins in the First War, and now they have their own, bronze memorial, outside the town hall. That was long before I met her. She never talked about the past, but she told me about that money, in one of those letters, up there in the Oxo tin in the trunk. It never belonged to her. It belonged to the bronze soldiers. And what will you buy with it, Dorry? History?

He gripped the armrests. Metal pain was filling his limbs and welding him to the chair. Was all this happening in an instant or was it the effect of years, an age? Be still, look at the things that are fixed. Sunlight cascaded over the lilac and the flower beds. The garden beckoned, as things do which cannot be touched. She will not come. She will come. He clutched the jacket with the letter in it. Today is your birthday. The lilac swayed. Tomorrow rain would fall on it—the weatherman had said on the radio—patter through the dawn light onto the leaves. There would be a victory, but not his. She would come: he would be a cold statue. Can you capture the moment without it capturing you? His chest was transfixed. You stood on the edge of the diving board. It seemed you might be poised there for ever. He couldn't move. He was a powerless skittle towards which was hurtling an invisible ball. Not yet. You stood on your toes, raised your arms. She will not come. The lilac shimmered. The garden framed in the window was like a photograph.

All right. All right—now.